EVERYMAN'S   LIBRARY

EVERYMAN,
I WILL GO WITH THEE,
AND BE THY GUIDE,
IN THY MOST NEED
TO GO BY THY SIDE

IVAN TURGENEV

Fathers and Children

Translated from the Russian by Avril Pyman
with an Introduction by John Bayley

EVERYMAN'S LIBRARY

17

This book is one of 250 volumes in Everyman's Library
which have been distributed to 4500 state schools
throughout the United Kingdom.
The project has been supported by a grant of £4 million
from the Millennium Commission.

First included in Everyman's Library, 1921
This translation first published in Everyman's Library, 1962
Introduction, Bibliography and Chronology © David Campbell
Publishers Ltd., 1991
Typography by Peter B. Willberg

ISBN 1-85715-017-1

A CIP catalogue record for this book is available from the
British Library

Published by Everyman Publishers plc,
Gloucester Mansions, 140A Shaftesbury Avenue,
London WC2H 8HD

Distributed by Random House (UK) Ltd.,
20 Vauxhall Bridge Road, London SW1V 2SA

FATHERS AND
CHILDREN

———

C O N T E N T S

———

FATHERS AND CHILDREN

INTRODUCTION

With every book he wrote Turgenev used to complain that it made him new enemies and stirred up afresh the irritation or anger of old ones. He wanted to please everybody, and, as often happens to gentle good-natured people who try to do that, ended up as the object of universal censure, patronage or contempt. He never grasped the important truth in life that people respect a man for being nasty, for disagreeing violently with them, for denouncing their views. Bitter adversaries get on much better with each other than with the man who makes efforts to placate both sides.

But perhaps they don't see so clearly – see either the world or themselves – as the apparently helpless man in the middle can do. Turgenev was fascinated by men of wrath, as he once called them, even by such extreme specimens of the type as the two ardent and abusive young critics and reformers, Dobrolyubov and Chernyshevsky, whom he used privately to refer to as 'the snake and the rattlesnake'. Their personalities and extreme views appalled him, but he felt they were probably right in some way, for he could always see every side of the question. Not only the radical ideologues but the great giants of literature – Tolstoy and Dostoevsky – could never refrain from patronizing Turgenev, and on occasion expressing open contempt for him and for his books. The young Tolstoy was bitingly sarcastic about the already well-known and distinguished novelist, ten years older than himself, who had shown him every kindness and helped him with advice about publication. 'There goes our great writer,' he commented, 'waggling his democratic haunches.' It was a remark that contrived to be personally, even sexually, disagreeable, as well as suggesting that Turgenev's well-publicized liberal attitudes were a sham put on to win him the approval of his readers, and that of the intellectual classes. Dostoevsky put a particularly venomous and one-sided portrait of Turgenev into his great novel *Demons*, which came out ten years after *Fathers and Children*, and was in part inspired by it and by the idea of two contrasting

generations, their views and outlook. This is a point I shall
return to later.

Whatever criticisms Turgenev attracted during his lifetime,
however, there can be no doubt that the best of his novels
have stood the test of time as well as those of the two giants,
Tolstoy and Dostoevsky. Indeed there is a curious relief in
turning to *Fathers and Children*, *A Nest of Gentlefolk*, or *A Sportsman's Notebook*, after *Anna Karenina* or *The Brothers Karamazov*.
We seem to be in a more precise, a more familiar, a more
regarded world, a world of home and every day, in which the
smaller human needs and feelings can declare themselves and
reveal their own kinds of individual interest. When Turgenev
was young one of his greatest friends was the critic and writer
Vissarion Belinsky, a supreme hero of the old Russian liberal
mythology, who died young from neglected tuberculosis and
from persecution by the authorities. Turgenev never ceased to
revere him and his memory, but he was honest enough to
admit that conversation with a hero of such integrity and such
implacably strong views could become rather a strain. 'After
two or three hours I used to weaken ... I wanted to rest ... I
began to think of a walk, of dinner.' The human need for a
walk and for dinner always gets its due in Turgenev's novels:
we always feel a sense of the minor realities of life, heightened
in themselves by his friendly style, and by his gift for leading
emotion and conviction – love, hatred and sorrow – as it were
into the ordinariness of life and then out again. To put it
perhaps naively: his world seems more 'real' every time we
re-read him; and this is one of the rarest things one can say
about any novelist. No wonder D. S. Mirsky, who wrote the
best and most discerning history of Russian literature, speaks
of *Fathers and Children* as 'one of the greatest novels of the
nineteenth century'.

Like one of his own characters Turgenev became a writer
not by any measured exertion of the will but out of a mixture
of frustration, curiosity and timidity. He used his own timidity
more effectively than other writers have used moral courage.
He began by being frightened of his mother, and through his
fear learning how to placate and control her. She must have
been a terrifying woman, a strong-minded widow with a large

and rich estate and hundreds of serfs, whom she capriciously ill-treated, as she did the son she adored. As a young man Turgenev studied philosophy at the University of St Petersburg, and decided to pursue the subject in Berlin, then the major seat of European learning. A characteristic event occurred on his way there, when the steamer on which he was travelling down the Baltic caught fire. Turgenev is said to have lost his head completely and run around among the passengers demanding to be rescued. Everyone was astonished at the sight of this tall, commanding Russian – he had a magnificent physique – behaving in such an odd way, for the fire was a small thing and soon put out. The malice of friends and enemies kept the tale alive for the rest of Turgenev's life, and he was shamed by it; but arguably it shows his personality in its most sympathetic light. For he himself had the gift of sympathy, in its most spontaneous form: sympathy for himself and for others. He knew what it was like to be weak and afraid, and he never blames or despises weakness.

His residence in Germany turned Turgenev into an ardent admirer of Europe ('I flung myself head foremost into that German ocean required to purify and regenerate me ... and when I emerged I found myself a *Westernizer*, and so I have always remained'); and this did not endear him to that always considerable body of his countrymen who maintained the patriotic conviction that Russians do things differently, and that all things Russian are best. In the first instance Turgenev was totally repelled, and out of the personal experience that breeds conviction, by the brutal despotism of Russian institutions, and of the ruling class of landowners as represented by his own mother. Tolstoy and Dostoevsky can be sentimental about Russia in their own ways, praising a *byt*, or way of life, just because it is Russian. Turgenev never does that. His first original work, the book in which he found his own manner and his own style of writing, is *A Sportsman's Notebook*, a collection of impressions and anecdotes that came from his experience of the countryside. What continues to strike the reader most forcibly about it is the contrast between a wonderfully delicate lyrical sense of nature, the seasons, kinds of weather, times of day and night, and the harsh, dark, unrelenting cruelty of the human scene portrayed in it, a contrast all the more effective because only implied: the author draws no attention to it.

Letting the facts speak for themselves is by far the most effective form of propaganda, and *A Sportsman's Notebook* had a considerable impact on the comparatively small number of people who constituted Russian society and public opinion; even, it is said, on the Tsar himself. Turgenev was thirty-four when the book appeared, far from being a youthful prodigy; and his life for the previous ten years had been wholly taken up with a love affair – if love affair can indeed be said to be the right expression – which was to determine the pattern of his existence until he died. Out hunting near St Petersburg on his twenty-fifth birthday, he had been introduced to the husband of a young Spanish singer, Pauline Garcia-Viardot, and a few days later he met the lady herself, beside the theatre at which she was performing. It was a *coup de foudre*. Pauline had many admirers, and a husband who was tolerably *complaisant*. She added Turgenev to her train, and for many years he followed her tours across Europe and stayed as a friend at the château at Courtavenel, the Viardot family home not far from Rouen.

Turgenev's mother, who had planned for her son a career in the Russian imperial service, was enraged by his liaison and by his wish to remain in Europe and become a writer. She never forgave him, and they were still estranged when she died, terrorizing her serfs and her household to the last. But her son inherited the big estate and its assets, and his financial position which up till then had been precarious – he had been compelled to borrow at high interest against his expectations – changed overnight. He loved returning to Russia and the Russian countryside; but the management of the property was a continual worry to him, the more so because of his liberal feelings and his sensitivity towards the opinions of his friends. Moreover, a seamstress employed by his mother had borne him a daughter, and he became very concerned about the child's future, finally persuading Pauline Viardot to bring her up with her own family. Turgenev adored her, but she became a source of deep anxiety to him in his later life, when he had to mortgage his property to rescue her and her improvident husband from debt.

But worry and deprivation were always to be Turgenev's familiar companions. He continued to bring out novels with success – *Rudin* in 1856, *A Nest of Gentlefolk* a couple of years later, *On the Eve* (the eve of reform and the Emancipation of the serfs) in 1860 – but he was always to be haunted by a sense of failure in the private as in the public sphere. He adored the young but felt an ever increasing sense of isolation from them, an impression of elegy and farewell which especially touching, and haunting, towards the end of *Fathers and Children*, when the old couple are mourning the loss of their son Bazarov. There is no doubt too that Turgenev himself is closely identified with the Kirsanov brothers: one a widower, who grieves for his lost happiness and youth; and the other an embittered and also pathetic dandy, whose heart is in the right place, but who can feel nothing but bewilderment at the attitudes of the young, and estrangement from their mode of life.

In practice, of course, Turgenev was far more adaptable than his characters. Not only did he continue to write novels like *Smoke* (1867) and *The Torrents of Spring* (1872), both of which have a strong political flavour and a sharply satirical awareness of the form and fashion of the times, but he remained in close touch with events in Russia and with the climate of opinion there, contriving to make himself a *bête noire* to the Tsar and his advisers while at the same time incurring the scorn, or the more or less tolerant contempt, of the younger generation of nihilists and anarchists. Turgenev's later years were not happy but they were certainly active: unlike his friend and fellow writer Flaubert he never became a hermit or retired into his own creative shell. He continued to travel, to frequent the literary and political salons of Paris, Germany and – when he could manage it – St Petersburg, and to produce stories and sketches which at their best – such as 'King Lear of the Steppes' (1870) – stand comparison with the work of his earlier years. He even gave an address on the occasion of the unveiling of the Pushkin memorial in Moscow, in the summer of 1880, when his fellow speaker was none other than Dostoevsky. It was typical that Dostoevsky's fiery oration, praising Pushkin as a Russian saviour and example to all European literature, won boundless applause from an enthusiastic Russian audience, while Turgenev's more temperate and thoughtful lecture, delivered from a genuinely European angle, was more coldly received. Turgenev was accustomed to taking second place, and he did it with a good grace though no doubt with inner chagrin. It may have consoled him that he was far more famous in Europe, above all in France and England, than either of the great Russian novelists who were his contemporaries.

In the last years of his life Turgenev suffered from a painful disease, diagnosed as cancer of the spine; he died in Paris in September 1883. The French writers Ernest Renan and Edmond About, who had been his friends, gave memorial addresses at a little ceremony at the Gare de l'Est, after which Turgenev's body was taken back to St Petersburg and buried, as he had always wished, in a cemetery near the grave of the great hero and friend of his youth, the critic Vissarion Belinsky. In his *discours* Renan had emphasized the supreme humanity of his friend, removed from all fanaticism and desire to preach (in his *Vie de Jésus* Renan had presented a wholly 'human' image of Christ) and had also dwelt on Turgenev's rare ability – doubly rare in an age of doctrinaire convictions and assertions of all sorts – to enter into the other person's point of view, to identify as much with the men whose vision bothered and distressed him, as with those with whom he felt in instinctive sympathy.

Turgenev's whole life and art amounted to a refusal to be apocalyptic; and in the age which produced Proudhon and Marx and Zola, to say nothing of Tolstoy and Dostoevsky, that was itself a most unusual attitude for a writer and an ideological figure. He was especially impatient with those prophets of doom and despair who, while urging the need for a total clean sweep in Russia, to be replaced by some millennial vision of social justice, were at the same time wholly contemptuous about Europe and its capitalist civilization. Turgenev liked to point out that this desire and conviction of doom, proclaimed at times even by the civilized and rational émigré

Herzen, was nothing more than what Isaiah Berlin has called 'the dramatization of private despair'. He was equally incredulous at Dostoevsky's apocalyptic optimism, his vision of a redeemed, orthodox Holy Russia leading the European peoples back to Christ, a scenario pleasing to the Tsar and his entourage, who patronized Dostoevsky in the last years of his life. Russians can hardly do without a religious vision of some kind: the one that beguiled Herzen, and many another intellectual, was of the Russian peasant himself, whose faith and simplicity made him the ultimate potential saviour of society. Turgenev was not going to fall for that one. He had known the peasants when he was young, and he shared fully in their historic woes; he and they had been in alliance against the tyranny of his terrifying mother. Even Tolstoy, and Turgenev's own friend, Flaubert, inclined to think in their different ways that the peasant was *dans le vrai*, on the side of God and His representative on earth. Turgenev knew them at first hand, and knew the truth, as he put it, of the old proverb, that 'God himself cannot get the better of the Russian peasant'. Indeed Turgenev saw God and god substitutes as the Russian intellectuals' refuge and luxury. Although he could be both mystical and sentimental in his own way, as in his later writings such as 'Clara Milich' (1883), and 'The Song of Triumphant Love' (1881), there is no real evidence that Turgenev believed in God at all, or had ever done so. He preferred to believe in human love, in the beneficence of Nature herself, and in the possibility of individual human happiness.

For the striking thing about Turgenev's best work, and *Fathers and Children* in particular, is what Wordsworth called 'the deep power of joy'. Henry James, who came to know him well in Paris, and who admired him very much, said that Turgenev's masterpieces – he singles out 'The Singers' and 'Bezhin Meadow' from *A Sportsman's Notebook* – were absolutely original and his own, like those of no other writer. The tribute is all the more remarkable in that James could only read them in French, the language into which they were first translated; and these particular stories represent the best examples of Turgenev's peculiar mastery of a Russian style – precise, rich and delicate, poetical in the best sense – which can have no adequate equivalent in another language. Fortunately it is still true, and particularly true of *Fathers and Children*, that Turgenev's wonderful mastery of detail, his descriptive power which is urbane, easy, but never facile, does come across in a foreign language; and perhaps particularly well in English, a language which Turgenev read and admired, although he spoke it badly.

He was in every sense a good European, fluent in French, German and Spanish (the native language of his life-long friend and mistress) and wholly at home in European civilization and in any continental setting. Indeed the worldly ease with which he behaved, and the comfort and opulence in which he lived in Baden-Baden after he became rich, excited the envy and disapproval of many Russians and inflamed their xenophobic tendencies. No one more so than Dostoevsky, who visited Turgenev when he came to Baden on one of his gambling sprees, and deeply resented the polite but somewhat distant treatment he received. No emotional embraces and endless confabulations *à la russe*. Dostoevsky revenged himself by portraying Turgenev as Karmazinov in *Demons*, an exquisite and fastidious expatriate author whose sense of style was a byword in European literary circles, and who excelled especially in the description of delicate botanical details, always knowing the name of some obscure little flower and finding the right word for the exact shade of its sepals. Dostoevsky's treatment is devastatingly funny but totally unfair, and it wounded Turgenev deeply.

But everything wounded him: he was the most vulnerable of men, and was always grateful, pathetically grateful, for kind words or warm praise from a fellow countryman, or from a disinterested foreigner. When he was given an honorary doctorate by the University of Oxford, four years before his death, he was touchingly delighted to be described by the Public Orator as 'a champion of freedom'. And indeed the words were true, probably truer than the Oxford professor realized. For it is not always the most obvious propaganda in the literary world which has the most influence, or makes the most converts. Shelley's almost juvenile poem *Queen Mab*, full of fantasy and self-indulgent poetic fun, had the most electrifying effect on Chartists and those who toiled for workers' rights in nineteenth-century industrial England, and retained an extraordinary prestige and popularity over many years. Turgenev's books, particularly *A Sportsman's Notebook*, had a great effect on opinion among the reading public in Russia, and even influenced the politicians and the members of the Tsarist establishment who finally brought about the Emancipation of the serfs. In his 1970 Romanes Lecture on 'Turgenev and the Liberal Predicament' Isaiah Berlin recorded that 'a hunted member of a terrorist organization, in a tribute illegally published on the day of Turgenev's funeral, wrote, "A gentleman by birth, an aristocrat by upbringing and character, a gradualist by conviction, Turgenev, perhaps without knowing it himself ... sympathized with and even served the Russian revolution." The special police precautions at Turgenev's funeral were clearly not wholly superfluous.'

*

And so we come to Bazarov, the young 'hero' of *Fathers and Children*. How was he to be regarded, and how did Turgenev himself regard him? In some degree he is, so to speak, a 'realistic' figure, based on young men whom Turgenev had encountered, on a doctor met in a train, on his own old friend Belinsky, and the rebarbative Dobrolyubov, who used to treat Turgenev as Barazov treated the Kirsanov brothers. ('Do not let us go on talking to each other, Ivan Sergeyevich,' he remarked on one occasion to Turgenev. 'It bores me.') Bazarov has nothing to say to the talkative Russian liberals who wanted endlessly to discuss politics and progress and what was to be done. For Bazarov and the nihilists the only thing that mattered was to destroy existing structures. Anything else is 'not our business'.

Turgenev's friend, the reactionary editor Katkov, observed not without malice that Turgenev was afraid of the character he had created. The radicals accused him bitterly of drawing a caricature. As usual, Turgenev could please neither side. But now that history has stilled all the lively polemic and the quarrelling, what really remains to be said and thought about Bazarov? I would say that he was only still alive, as a character, in relation to the other characters, who lead a more, as it were, Turgenevan existence. By himself he is merely a lay figure, with certain rather artificial modes of behaviour invented for him by the author. He dissects frogs, is offhand with the gentry; the children feel at home with him; and so forth. But in himself he never comes alive, or shows signs of being anything other than a portent and a symbol. It is when he is seen with his old mother and father, with the Kirsanovs, Fenechka and the young Arkady, that he has the effect of stimulating in them the life of their own in which Turgenev is truly interested, and which he is so good at bringing out. Otherwise it might be said that he is actively unfair to Bazarov. He never lets him do anything 'positive' (although Lenin's commissar for education, Lunacharsky, described him as the first 'positive' hero in Russian literature); he is made to fall in love in order to show that he is only human like everyone else; and he is killed off rather arbitrarily when the author has no further use for him. As the human centre of the novel he is far from satisfactory.

But that hardly matters. What remains significant is the idea of the younger generation, the 'new men'. *Fathers and Children* is one of the first novels, if not *the* first, to form its structural dynamic on the now familiar idea of a new kind of hero who intrigues, alarms, repels, even disgusts or frightens the reader. The young men who appear in novels in our own time, from Kingsley Amis's *Lucky Jim* onward, show how the pattern has developed. Every novelist in the realist tradition would like to invent such a significant character if he could. And oddly enough Turgenev, for all his love of old-fashioned ways and the countryside and changeless emotions of love, tenderness and sorrow, had a decided flair in this direction. No character in Tolstoy, or even in Dostoevsky, was fastened on by the reading public and the critics as being a type and portent of the times in the way that Turgenev's were. Early in his career he had written *The Diary of a Superfluous Man* (1850), and the phrase at once acquired fame and currency throughout Russian intellectual circles as descriptive of a certain type who could not fit in anywhere, who had no role to play in the stagnant, backward and repressive society of Russia. Although he had something in common with Evgeny Onegin, the hero of Pushkin's novel in verse, and with Lermontov's Pechorin in *A Hero of Our Time*, Turgenev's sensitively feeble character received more immediate notoriety as a label term.

He was based on the author himself of course. And this is really the trouble with Bazarov, who was emphatically not based on his author. However much sympathy he may feel for the idea of this new and alarming breed of young person, Turgenev has nothing in common with him, cannot identify and feel the same sort of empathy that he does with his other characters – the Kirsanovs, Arkady and Fenechka, Bazarov's old parents, even Madame Odintsova and her young sister Katya. Arkady, that basically conservative young man of the past, who like his author is fascinated by Bazarov and thinks that he too will be a nihilist and a radical, will soon revert to type, be happily married to Katya, and will end up by implication breeding a new generation of worthy Russian gentry not so different from himself. As an early example of what might be called the 'generation novel' *Fathers and Children* certainly favours the status quo as opposed to the new and threatening world that is nonetheless coming. And because he cannot identify with Bazarov, however much he may be fascinated by him, Turgenev is far from being a Lucky Jim of his time. His position is not that of the anarch or Lord of Misrule who animates the fiction and takes gleeful pleasure in the disturbances caused by his hero. Covertly he is in sympathy with the anti-Bazarovs, and that was not lost on either faction in Russia who received the novel and whose attention made it famous.

Nor was it lost on Dostoevsky. The great strength of his novel *Demons*, in relation to *Fathers and Children*, lies in what the Russian critic Bakhtin called its 'polyphonic' structure. Like a tumult of voices in endless debate, and of personalities driven by furies into incessant action, the competitive clamour in Dostoevsky's novel wholly overrides the question of the author's own views and intentions. The chief 'demon', young Pyotr Verkhovensky, is an altogether more sinister and dynamic figure than Bazarov, and his father is a pitiless sketch of the wholly ineffectual but self-important (and also sweet-natured) Russian liberal of the 1860s. Beside the competing clamour of new voices in *Demons* – atheists, communists, mystics and Slavophiles – the quiet and meditative mode of *Fathers and Children* might have begun to seem old-fashioned, but in fact that was not the case: the status of Bazarov as a social and a Russian portent, and the debate about what he represented and what were Turgenev's intentions about him, remained as lively as ever. The authority of Dostoevsky was like that of the prophet in the whirlwind or the voice through the cloud: its sheer scale and energy overawed his readers. But the debate that Turgenev had initiated depended on personal factors and on the ambiguity of the author's personal attitude, and that continued to intrigue his readers and stimulate a continuing debate.

Probably it does so no longer. But if the specific social and political interest of *Fathers and Children* has now diminished, that makes the enduring virtues and qualities of the novel shine out more clearly. For it is first and foremost an extremely moving story, and seems effortlessly so: moving in regard to an unchanging world of family affection, love, sorrow and bereavement. Moving, and also joyful. Neither the outline of its plot nor its social significance means as much as the remarkable skill and delicacy with which Turgenev conveys *feeling*: the affection of the brothers for each other, of Fenechka for her baby, of Bazarov's old parents for their brilliant young son. The natural, almost inevitable way in which Arkady and Katya fall in love is equally moving and equally uninsistent; and even Bazarov, as we see and infer, is not only genuinely fond of Arkady but has the same unreflecting capacity for loving and giving which is invisibly celebrated throughout the novel.

Turgenev understood and almost worshipped this kind of affection. A picture of him as a child shows a solemn large-eyed little face and an expression that seems to be longing for love and reassurance. He did not get it; indeed he was starved of parental and family love, and obtained it only through kind-natured nannies and servants; but he never ceased in his adult life to value it before everything. His whole style and being can express it, at their best, without emphasis or display. But it seems to me that a distinction needs to be made here. He understood loving because of his continued anxiety that it had been denied him; because of the anxiety in his relations with Pauline and with his daughter. But there is another sense in which Turgenev, like a French novelist and author – Stendhal or Flaubert for instance – showed an obsessive and as it were professional interest in the nature and degree of love's experiences, what the business was all about. And here he is not so good. His much praised *nouvelle*, *First Love* seems to me to have something faintly suspect about it; a hint of the formulaic, of authorial intention to convey the plangent and 'desolating' truth that one can only love once, and that love, like Eve's apple, is bound to have a worm at the core. The young hero of *First Love* adores an older girl whom he subsequently finds to be his father's mistress. Such a discovery is like many of Turgenev's own, about his own family; and – more important still – it reveals his anxious obsession with whether he himself could ever be lovable. Masochism and adoration had to be a sort of substitute for deeper and more confident affections. When his adored teases him by saying if he loves her he will jump off the wall he is sitting on, the hero of *First Love* finds himself flying through the air, without apparent will or decision; and he hurts himself severely.

But that involuntariness does give a clue to Turgenev's unique success as a novelist of the feelings. Love in *Fathers and Children* does seem involuntary; a helpless groundswell of human vulnerability against which the convictions and self-presentation of human beings appears ultimately trivial and unimportant. Its superiority over most of Turgenev's other fictions, even *A Nest of Gentlefolk* and *First Love*, appears to me to lie in the wholly involuntary manner in which its true subject has been realized and has come into being. Turgenev may have thought he was imagining and creating a man of the future, but in a surer and more compelling way he was reaffirming, and making into art, the values of the past. Although he got on so well in the West; although his books were admired, and he himself became the friend and confrère of the French artists, his was at bottom a very different sort of genius, less abstract and less intellectual, and indeed, in a paradoxical way, more primitive. A primitive strength does lurk behind the Gallic smoothness of his style, and his general 'ideas' – about the frustration and sadness of existence and the disillusionment of the heart, ideas which may well have been derived from Flaubert's conversation and novels – are less important in his best work than what has to be termed his instinctual Russian soul.

We divine this often in the literalness of his manner, a literalness often like that of Tolstoy at his best. Tolstoy, rather surprisingly, had a great admiration for Trollope, and there is a good deal of the 'family' novel of Trollope in *Fathers and Children*: an unpretending penetration about human relationships, as well as a tendency to make what might be called a natural soap opera out of certain aspects of the plot. The end of *Fathers and Children* is tidied up and put away as in the Victorian novel, and Trollope, above all, knew how to arrange such things. Madame Odintsova, never a very convincing character, is married off suitably to a similarly cold fish. She has had her operatic and dramatic moment at the dying Bazarov's bedside; and her function has been to tame him, to appoint an appropriate end in terms of art and fiction for his threatening and destabilizing natural existence. Dostoevsky's 'devil of the future' could never be snuffed out like that. Turgenev does indeed handle the love affair rather gingerly, though in a practised sort of way. An Angry Young Man would take a more spirited and a more brutal line with Madame Odintsova, might unsettle her more, and might have compelled her at least into an affair with him. But Turgenev is an expert at handling the proprieties; and besides he may subconsciously have wanted to show Bazarov in love to be just as ineffectual as the other men in his novels, who have temperaments more like their author's.

At the same time Bazarov is effective enough at the Kirsanovs' place, if only because he makes Fenechka fond of him, and the maid Dunyasha mad about him, and through his attentions to Fenechka provokes Pavel Petrovich into fighting a duel with him. Turgenev rarely if ever gives his own commentary; but his most subtle art is devoted to exhibiting his characters in relation to each other, and in their effects on each other. This is also where his humour comes in. Children and peasants naturally like Bazarov, and get on with him; but an engagingly comic passage shows that Bazarov's contempt for the peasants is fully reciprocated. They play up to him but really know he belongs to the class that doesn't understand anything. In his eyes they are hopelessly ignorant and backward, but 'he had no suspicion that in their eyes even he was something in the nature of a buffoon'. For different reasons the old butler at the Kirsanovs' feels the same instinctive hostility towards Bazarov that is felt by Pavel Petrovich Kirsanov.

But how well Turgenev writes of ordinary everyday things! How inconspicuously and yet in what a masterly way he fills in the time and the details, the passage of monotonous or disorderly minutes which those who are telling a story by novel are instinctively afraid of, and which no nineteeth-century novelist – certainly none in France or England – could manage as well as he. The first two pages of *Fathers and Children* will show what I have in mind; and the death scene of Bazarov, the end of which it is difficult to read without tears, is enhanced by the way in which his parents' grief is reported by an old servant. The father's anger and the mother's anguish make them fall prone together, and as Anfisushka relates it, 'they drooped their poor heads like little lambs at midday'. Bazarov has died not from a disappointment in love but through the stupidity of blind chance.

Virginia Woolf, who greatly admired Turgenev, may well have that scene unconsciously in mind when she described the heroine's death at the end of her own first novel, *The Voyage Out*. And she gets the awkward moments and reflections, the vividness and banality of existence, into the art of her fiction in a way that Turgenev himself would have recognized and admired. Though herself no hand at love scenes – and the tender moments between Katya and Arkady are some of the best in Turgenev – she would have noticed with deep approval the kind of touch he is so good at: Katya's hands are beautiful but *large*, which somehow adds to the touchingness and also to the reality of the moment when Arkady seizes them in his own, and 'catching his breath with ecstasy, pressed them to his heart'. The scene is neither sentimental nor deliberately incongruous, but just true to life; and that is what Turgenev at his very best always is.

John Bayley

SELECT BIBLIOGRAPHY

───────

Compared with Dickens or James, there is comparatively little on Turgenev in English.

AVRAHM YARMOLINSKY, *Turgenev, The Man, His Art and Age*, Orion Press, New York, 1959/Deutsch, 1960 (orginally published New York, 1926) is the standard critical biography: thorough, informative and easy to read, if not especially inspired.

RICHARD FREEBORN, *Turgenev: The Novelists's Novelist*, Oxford University Press, 1960, is an excellent critical study of the novels, including a bibliography of commentaries in English, Russian, German and French.

D. S. MIRSKY, *A History of Russian Literature*, Routledge, 1927, 1949, is a brilliant comparative study.

HARRY HIRSHKOWITZ, *Democratic Ideas In Turgenev's Novels*, AMS Press, New York, 1932, focuses on the political context of the novels, especially *Fathers and Children*.

HENRY JAMES's essays on Turgenev, scattered through various collections of his reviews and critical writing, are still well worth reading as the work of a major novelist who took Turgenev's example to heart.

CHRONOLOGY

DATE	AUTHOR'S LIFE	LITERARY CONTEXT
1818	Born in Oryol, Russia. Childhood spent on family estate at Spasskoye.	Scott: *The Heart of Midlothian*. Austen: *Persuasion*; *Northanger Abbey*. Karamzin: *History of the Russian State* (12 vols, to 1829).
1819		George Eliot born. Byron: *Don Juan* (to 1824). Schopenhauer: *The World as Will and Idea*.
1820		Pushkin: *Ruslan and Lyudmilla*.
1821		Dostoevsky and Flaubert born.
1822–4		Griboedov writes *Woe from Wit*.
1825		Pushkin writes *Boris Godunov*.
1827–34	Attends school and university in Moscow.	
1828		Tolstoy born. Mickiewicz: *Konrad Wallenrod*.
1829		Balzac: *Les Chouans* – first volume of *La Comédie humaine*. Lermontov starts work on *The Demon* (to 1841).
1830		Pushkin writes *The Tales of Belkin*. Stendhal: *Le Rouge et le Noir*.
1831		
1832		Death of Scott and Goethe.
1833		First complete edition of Pushkin's *Evgeny Onegin* published.
1834–7	Attends St Petersburg university.	
1834	*Steno* (a poetic drama).	Belinsky: *Literary Reveries*. Pushkin: *The Queen of Spades*.
1835		Gogol: *Mirgorod*; *Arabesques*.
1836		Gogol: *The Government Inspector*. Pushkin: *The Captain's Daughter*. Chaadaev's first *Philosophical Letter* describes Russia as 'a gap in the intellectual order of things', with no past, present or future.

Congress of Aix-la-Chapelle.

Decembrist Revolt crushed. Nicholas I succeeds Alexander I.
Nicholas develops system of autocratic government based upon militarism and bureaucracy. Especially notorious was the Third Section, under Count Alexander Benckendorf, which acted as the Tsar's main weapon against subversion and revolution and as the principal agency for controlling the behaviour of his subjects.

July revolution in France. Accession of Louis Philippe.

Suppression of Polish uprising.
First Reform Act in Britain.
Abolition of slavery within the British Empire.

FATHERS AND CHILDREN

DATE	AUTHOR'S LIFE	LITERARY CONTEXT
1837		Death of Pushkin in duel. Dickens: *The Pickwick Papers*.
1838–41	Studies at Berlin University. Meets Bakunin, Stankevich and Granovsky, Russian liberal and radical political thinkers.	
1839		Stendhal: *La Chartreuse de Parme*.
1840		Lermontov: *A Hero of Our Time*; *The Novice*. Mérimée: 'Colomba'.
1841	Returns to St Petersburg. Takes the side of the Westernizers in Slavophile v Westernizer debate, while remaining on friendly terms with many conservative Slavophiles, including the Aksakov brothers.	Death of Lermontov in duel. Dickens: *The Old Curiosity Shop*.
1842	Birth of illegitimate daughter by seamstress at Spasskoye.	Gogol: *Dead Souls*; 'The Overcoat'.
1843	*Parasha* – first of his works to attract attention. Meets the critic Belinsky, and Mme Pauline Viardot, with whom he falls in love. Works briefly as a civil servant.	Carlyle: *Past and Present*. Birth of Henry James.
1844		Dickens: *Martin Chuzzlewit*.
1845	Resolves to devote himself full-time to literature.	Mérimée: 'Carmen'.
1847	Follows Pauline Viardot and her husband to Paris. First visit to England.	Thackeray: *Vanity Fair* (to 1848). Balzac: *Le Cousin Pons*. Goncharov: *An Ordinary Story*. Herzen: *Who is to Blame?* Herzen leaves Russia.
1847–50	Lives in France. Most of the stories which later comprised *A Sportsman's Notebook* published in *The Contemporary*.	
1848	Witnesses February revolution in Paris.	George Sand: *La Petite Fadette*. Thackeray: *Pendennis* (to 1850). Death of Belinsky.
1849	*The Bachelor* performed (the only one of his plays of this period not to fall foul of the censor).	Dostoevsky arrested as member of socialist Petrashevsky circle. Sentenced to death and reprieved.

CHRONOLOGY

HISTORICAL EVENTS

Accession of Queen Victoria. First railway line opens in Russia – from St Petersburg to Tsarkoe Selo.

1840s and '50s: Slavophile v Westernizer debate amongst Russian intellectuals. Westernizers advocate progress by assimilating European rationalism and civic freedom. Slavophiles assert spiritual and moral superiority of Russia to the West and argue that future development should be based upon the traditions of the Orthodox Church and the peasant commune or *mir*.
Ban on sale of individual peasants.
Peel becomes British Prime Minister (to 1846).

Nicholas I visits England.

European revolutions. Tsar's manifesto calls upon Russians to arouse themselves for 'faith, Tsar and country'. Russian army occupies Moldavia and Wallachia. In France, abdication of Louis Philippe and constitution of Second Republic. *Communist Manifesto* published. Pan-Slav congress in Prague. Russian armies join those of the Habsburgs in suppressing nationalist rebellion in Hungary under Kossuth.

FATHERS AND CHILDREN

DATE	AUTHOR'S LIFE	LITERARY CONTEXT
1850	Inherits Spasskoye from his mother. *Diary of a Superfluous Man*. Finishes *A Month in the Country*.	First collected edition of Fet's poems published. Tennyson: *In Memoriam*. Browning: *Men and Women*. Dickens: *David Copperfield*. Herzen: *From the Other Shore*. Death of Balzac.
1851		Melville: *Moby-Dick*.
1852	*A Sportsman's Notebook* published in volume form. Confined to Spasskoye under police surveillance after publishing a eulogistic obituary of Gogol (to 1853).	Death of Gogol. Tolstoy: *Childhood*. Harriet Beecher Stowe: *Uncle Tom's Cabin*.
1854		George Sand: *Histoire de ma vie*. First collected edition of Tyutchev's poems published.
1855		Trollope: *The Warden*. Tolstoy: *Sevastapol Sketches* (to 1856).
1856–63	Returns to France, dividing his time between Paris and the Viardots' estate at Courtavenel.	
1856	*Rudin*.	Aksakov: *A Family Chronicle*. Tolstoy: 'A Landlord's Morning'.
1857		Flaubert: *Madame Bovary*. Herzen's radical journal *The Bell* published in London (to 1867). Conrad born.
1858	'Asya'.	Pisemsky: *A Thousand Souls*. Aksakov: *Years of Childhood*.
1859	*A Nest of Gentlefolk*.	Goncharov: *Oblomov*. Ostrovsky: *The Storm*. Tennyson: *Idylls of the King*. George Eliot: *Adam Bede*. Darwin: *The Origin of Species*.
1860	*On the Eve. First Love*.	George Eliot: *The Mill on the Floss*. Chekhov born.
1861	Working on *Fathers and Children* (largely written on the Isle of Wight, where well-off Russians often went for sea-bathing).	Dostoevsky: *The House of the Dead*. Herzen publishes *My Past and Thoughts* (to 1867). Dickens: *Great Expectations*.

CHRONOLOGY

HISTORICAL EVENTS

Great Exhibition in London. Opening of St Petersburg to Moscow railway. Re-establishment of absolutism in Austria and Prussia. Louis Napoleon proclaimed Emperor of France.

Outbreak of Crimean War.

Death of Nicholas I. Accession of Alexander II. Palmerston becomes British Prime Minister (to 1858; and 1859–65).

End of Crimean War. By the terms of the Treaty of Paris, Russia forced to withdraw from the mouth of the Danube, to cease to protect the Orthodox under Turkish rule and to give up her fleet and fortresses on the Black Sea. Indian Mutiny: siege and relief of Lucknow.

Committees set up to prepare the gentry for the emancipation of the serfs from private ownership. Russian colonial expansion in South-East Asia. Russian conquest of the Caucasus completed: surrender of Shamil.

Garibaldi and 'The Thousand' conquer Sicily. Port of Vladivostock founded to serve Russia's recent annexations from China. Emancipation of the serfs (February), the climax of the Tsar's programme of reform. While his achievement had great moral and symbolic significance, many peasants felt themselves cheated by the terms of the complex emancipation statute. Outbreak of American Civil War. Lincoln becomes President of USA. Victor Emmanuel first King of Italy.

DATE	AUTHOR'S LIFE	LITERARY CONTEXT
1862	*Fathers and Children.* Quarrels with Tolstoy during a hunting breakfast in the house of the poet Fet. In spite of this, Turgenev took an active part in getting Tolstoy translated into French, and did much for his reputation in the West.	Hugo: *Les Misérables.* Flaubert: *Salammbô.* Chernyshevsky imprisoned and exiled to Siberia (to 1883).
1863	Meets Flaubert in Paris. Settles in Baden with the Viardots (to 1871).	Chernyshevsky: *What is to be Done?* Tolstoy: *The Cossacks.* Nekrasov: *Red-Nosed Frost.* Death of Thackeray.
1864	Charged with aiding London expatriate group headed by Herzen. Cleared by senatorial committee in St Petersburg. Beginning of long breach with Herzen.	Dostoevsky: *Notes from Underground.* Nekrasov: *Who Can Be Happy and Free in Russia?* (to 1876). Trollope: *Can You Forgive Her?* (to 1865).
1865		Tolstoy: *War and Peace* (to 1869). Leskov: 'Lady Macbeth of the Mtensk District'. Dickens: *Our Mutual Friend.* Swinburne: *Atalanta in Calydon.*
1866		Dostoevsky: *Crime and Punishment.*
1867	*Smoke.*	Marx: *Das Kapital*, vol. 1. Zola: *Thérèse Raquin.* Trollope: *The Last Chronicle of Barset.*
1868		Dostoevsky: *The Idiot.* Browning: *The Ring and the Book.* Lavrov: *Historical Letters.*
1869		Flaubert: *L'Education sentimentale.* Goncharov: *The Precipice.*
1870	'King Lear of the Steppes'. Lives briefly in London.	Death of Herzen and Dickens. D. G. Rossetti: *Poems.*
1871	Settles in Paris with the Viardots.	Dostoevsky: *Demons* (to 1872). George Eliot: *Middlemarch* (to 1872). Zola publishes the *Rougon-Macquart* series of novels (to 1893).

CHRONOLOGY

Bismarck becomes chief minister of Prussia. Financial reform in Russia; a ministry of finance and a state bank created.

1860s and '70s: 'Nihilism' – rationalist philosophy sceptical of all forms of established authority – becomes widespread amongst young radical intellectuals in Russia.

Polish rebellion. Poland incorporated in Russian Empire.

The first International formed in London. Establishment of the Zemstva, organs of rural self-government and a significant liberal influence in Tsarist Russia. Reform of the judiciary; trial by jury instituted and a Russian bar established.

Slavery formally abolished in USA. Russian colonial expansion in Central Asia (to 1881).

Dmitri Karakozov, a young nobleman, tries to assassinate the Tsar; he attributes his action to the influence of the radical journal, *The Contemporary*, which is suppressed by the government.

Second Pan-Slav congress in Moscow. Sale of Alaska to USA. Second Reform Act in Britain.

Gladstone becomes British Prime Minister (to 1874).

Suez Canal opens.

Lenin born. Franco-Prussian War. End of Second Empire and foundation of Third Republic in France.

Paris Commune set up and suppressed. Fall of Paris ends war. Wilhelm I of Prussia proclaimed Emperor of a united Germany.

DATE	AUTHOR'S LIFE	LITERARY CONTEXT
1872	*Spring Torrents.*	Leskov: *Cathedral Folk.*
1873		
1875	Meets Henry James in Paris.	Tolstoy: *Anna Karenina* (to 1878). Saltykov-Shchedrin: *The Golovlyovs* (to 1880).
1876		George Eliot: *Daniel Deronda.* Henry James: *Roderick Hudson.* Twain: *Tom Sawyer.* Death of George Sand.
1877	*Virgin Soil.*	Zola: *L'Assommoir.* Flaubert: *Trois Contes.*
1878	Makes up quarrel with Tolstoy and visits him at Yasnaya Polyana.	Hardy: *The Return of the Native.* James: *Daisy Miller.*
1879	Receives honorary DCL at Oxford for 'advancing the liberation of the Russian serfs'.	Tolstoy: *A Confession* (to 1882). Ibsen: *A Doll's House.* Dostoevsky: *The Brothers Karamazov* (to 1880).
1880		Chekhov publishes first stories in *The Dragonfly.* Death of Flaubert and George Eliot. Bely and Blok born.
1881	'The Song of Triumphant Love'.	James: *The Portrait of a Lady.* Ibsen: *Ghosts.* Death of Dostoevsky.
1882	'Clara Milich' (to 1883).	Death of Trollope.
1883	Writes 'Un Incendie en Mer' ('A Fire at Sea'). Sends a letter to Tolstoy from his death-bed, imploring him to return to literary activity from his spiritual writings. Dies in France, 3 September. Buried in St Petersburg.	Maupassant: *Une Vie*; *Clair de Lune.* Garshin: 'The Red Flower'. Fet: *Evening Lights* (4 vols, to 1891).

CHRONOLOGY

Three Emperors' League between Germany, Austria and Russia.
Narodnik (Populist) 'going to the people' campaign gathers momentum.
Young intellectuals incite peasantry to rebel against autocracy.

'Bulgarian Atrocities' (Bulgarians massacred by Turks). Founding of Land and
Freedom, first Russian political party openly to advocate revolution.

Russia declares war on Turkey (conflict inspired by Pan-Slavist movement).
Queen Victoria proclaimed Empress of India. Famous mass trial of 193
Populist agitators (to 1878).
Russian forces reach gates of Constantinople. By the Treaty of San Stefano
the Turks obliged to recognize independence of Slav nations in the Balkans.
Congress of Berlin: with Bismarck acting as 'honest broker' the Great Powers
modify the terms of San Stefano, increasing Austrian influence at the expense
of Russia. Afghan War.
Stalin born. Land and Freedom divides into terrorist organization The
People's Will, responsible for numerous political assassinations, including that
of the Tsar in 1881, and Black Repartition, which continues campaign
amongst peasantry and later the urban proletariat.
In Britain, Conservatives under Disraeli defeated in General Election;
Gladstone forms Liberal government (to 1885).

Assassination of Alexander II by Ignatius Grinevitsky. Accession of
Alexander III. Severe repression of revolutionary groups. Alexander III is
much influenced by his former tutor, the extreme conservative Pobedonostsev,
who becomes Chief Procurator of the Holy Synod. Loris-Melikov, architect
of the reforms of Alexander II's reign, resigns. Jewish pogroms.
University riots. Censorship laws strengthened.
First Russian Marxist revolutionary organization, the Liberation of Labour,
founded in Geneva by Georgi Plekhanov.

FATHERS AND CHILDREN

To the memory of
VISSARION GRIGOR'EVICH BELINSKY

I

'WELL, Pyotr? Not in sight yet?'

The question was put on 20th May 1859 by a gentleman of rather more than forty years of age as he came out, hatless and dressed in a dust-stained overcoat and check trousers, on to the low porch of the posting-house on the main road to X; he was addressing his servant, a heavy-jowled young fellow with an almost white down on his chin and small, dull eyes.

Everything about the servant – the turquoise earring in one ear, the oiled, streaky hair, the obsequious movements, in short, everything – betrayed the man of a very modern and superior generation. He glanced condescendingly down the road and replied after due deliberation: 'No, sir. Not in sight.'

'Not in sight?' repeated the gentleman.

'Not in sight,' the servant answered a second time.

The gentleman sighed and sat down on the edge of a small bench. Let us acquaint the reader with him more fully while he sits there gazing ruminatively round about, his short legs drawn up beneath him.

His name is Nikolay Petrovich Kirsanov. Some twelve miles from this little posting-house he owns a property of two hundred 'souls' or, as he himself expresses it, since he partitioned his estate among his peasantry and introduced the 'farming system', of nearly five thousand acres. His father, a general who had seen active service in 1812, a rough, semi-literate but not unkindly Russian type, had remained in harness all his life, commanding first a brigade and then a division, and had always lived in the provinces where, thanks to his rank, he figured as a person of some standing. Nikolay Petrovich was born in the south of Russia, as was his elder brother Pavel, of whom more later, and was brought up at home until the age of fourteen, surrounded by inferior tutors, over-familiar yet sycophantic adjutants, and other such characters as are to be found in every regiment and on every staff. His lady mother, of the family of Kolyazin, known when she was a girl as Agathe but after she became a general's wife as Agafokleya Kuz'minishna Kirsanova, was of the 'battle-axe' breed, wore imposing caps and rustling silk dresses, was always the first to go up to the cross at church, talked loudly and volubly, admitted her children to kiss her hand in the mornings and again to receive her blessing before they went to bed – in short, lived according to her own good pleasure. As the son of a general Nikolay Petrovich, although he was in no way remarkable for valour and had even been labelled a bit of a coward, was destined, like his brother Pavel, to take up a military career; but he broke his leg on the very day that news was received that he had been accepted for the army and, having lain in bed for two months, was left with a slight limp which remained with him for the rest of his life. His father gave him up as a hopeless case and permitted him to take up a civilian career. He took him to Petersburg as soon as he was eighteen and entered him at the university. As it happened, his brother was commissioned as an officer in a guards regiment at about the same time. The two young men shared the same rooms under the distant supervision of a cousin once removed on their mother's side, Il'ya Kolyazin, a distinguished civil servant. Their father returned to his division and to his wife, and it was only from time to time that he sent his sons large quarto sheets of grey paper closely covered by a sprawling, clerkly hand. At the bottom of these missives appeared in all their splendour, painstakingly surrounded by twirls and twists, the words 'Piyotr Kirsanoff, Major-General'. In 1835 Nikolay Petrovich graduated from the university and, in the same year, General Kirsanov, who had been retired as the result of the unsuccessful conduct of a military review, arrived with his wife to take up residence in Petersburg. He had rented a house by the Tauride Gardens and had already become a member of the English Club when he died, suddenly, of a stroke. Agafokleya Kuz'minishna soon followed him: she could not grow accustomed to her obscure existence in the capital; the nostalgic boredom of life in retirement wore her away. Meanwhile Nikolay Petrovich had found the opportunity, during the lifetime of his parents and to their considerable distress, to fall in love with the daughter of his one-time landlord, a civil servant named Prepolovensky. She was a sweet-faced and, as they say, advanced girl who read serious articles in the scientific sections of periodicals. He married her as soon as he was out of mourning and, abandoning the Ministry of Crown Lands where, with the help of higher patronage, his father had obtained employment for him, settled down to a life of bliss with his Masha, first in a private house near the Institute of Forestry, then in town, in a small and pretty apartment with a well-kept staircase and a rather chilly drawing-room and, finally, in the country, where he established himself permanently and where, not long after their arrival, a son was born to him – Arkady. Husband and wife lived together very contentedly and quietly. They were almost inseparable, read aloud to one another, played pieces written for four hands on the pianoforte and sang duets. She planted flowers and kept an eye on the fowls. He would occasionally go hunting or put in some work at the management of his estate. And Arkady grew and grew – also contentedly and quietly. Ten years passed like a dream. In 1847 Kirsanov's wife died. This blow proved almost too much for him to bear and he went grey in a few weeks; he would have made arrangements to go abroad, hoping that this would at least give his thoughts a rather more cheerful direction – but then came 1848. Reluctantly he returned to the country where, after a longish period of inaction, he began to take an interest in the management of his estate. In 1855 he accompanied his son to the university; he spent three winters with him in Petersburg, hardly going out anywhere and trying to make friends among Arkady's young fellow students. This last winter he had been unable to make the journey – and here we see him, in May 1859, already completely grey-headed, plump and slightly stooping; he is waiting for his son, who has just taken his degree at the university as he had once done himself.

The servant, either from a sense of what was fitting or perhaps not wishing to remain under his master's eye, stepped out under the gateway and lit a pipe. Nikolay Petrovich lowered his head and transferred his gaze to the steps of the porch; a well-grown, brightly coloured pullet was strutting about on them, rapping them firmly with its great yellow feet; a dirt-bespattered cat watched it furtively and inimically, flattening itself mincingly along the top of the stair rail. The sun beat down; from the dim passage between the porch and the front door of the posting-house was wafted the aroma of warm rye bread. Our Nikolay Petrovich has wandered off into a day-dream. 'My son . . . a graduate . . . dear little Arkady. . . .' The words kept revolving through his head; he tried to think of something else but kept coming back to these same thoughts. He remembered his late wife. 'She did not live to see this!' he whispered dejectedly. A fat blue-grey pigeon alighted on the road and set off hurriedly to drink from a puddle by the well. Nikolay Petrovich began to watch it, but his ear had already caught the sound of approaching wheels. . . .

'It sounds as though they were coming, sir,' reported the servant, appearing suddenly from the shelter of the gateway.

Nikolay Petrovich jumped up and looked out along the road. A tarantass[1] came into view, drawn by a team of three post-horses; in the tarantass he caught sight of the band of a student's cap, the familiar lineaments of a well-loved face.

'Arkady! Dear boy! Dear boy!' shouted Kirsanov, launching into a run and waving his arms. A few moments later his lips were already pressed against the clean-shaven, dusty and sunburnt cheek of the youthful graduate.

II

'GIVE me a chance to shake myself down, Papa dear,' said Arkady, his resonant young voice somewhat hoarse from the journey, merrily returning his father's caresses. 'I'll make you all dusty.'

---

1 A half-covered-in vehicle, the body of which is supported on two longi-tudinal wooden bars which act as springs.

'Never mind, never mind,' reiterated Nikolay Petrovich, smiling and deeply moved, and slapped once or twice at the collar of his son's greatcoat and at his own coat with his hand. 'Come on, let's have a look at you, come on,' he added, standing back, and immediately started with quick steps towards the posting-house, repeating: 'This way, this way! Horses there, and quickly!'

Nikolay Petrovich appeared to be much more overcome than his son; he seemed rather at a loss, almost as though he were shy. Arkady called him back.

'Dear Papa,' he said, 'permit me to introduce my good friend Bazarov about whom I've written you so often. He has been kind enough to agree to come and stay with us.'

Nikolay Petrovich turned back quickly and, going up to the tall man in a long, betasselled duster coat who was climbing down from the tarantass, firmly grasped the ungloved red hand which the other, not without a momentary hesitation, extended to him.

'Delighted,' he began. 'So grateful for your kind intention in coming to visit us. I hope . . . may I know your name and patronymic?'

'Yevgeny Vasil'ev,' answered Bazarov in a lazy but manly voice and, turning down the collar of his coat, showed Nikolay Petrovich the whole of his face. Long and thin, with a broad forehead and a nose flat at the bridge but pointed at the tip, with large, greenish eyes and drooping, sandy side-whiskers, it was animated by a quiet smile and expressed self-confidence and intelligence.

'I hope, my dear Yevgeny Vasil'evich, that you will not be bored with us,' continued Nikolay Petrovich.

Bazarov's thin mouth quivered almost imperceptibly, but he made no reply and merely raised his cap. His light brown hair, which was long and thick, did not hide the strongly defined irregularities of his capacious skull.

'Well, what now, Arkady?' Nikolay Petrovich hurried into speech again, turning to his son. 'Should we have the horses put to straight away, do you think? Or would you like to rest?'

'We'll rest at home, dear Papa; order them to be put to.'

'At once, at once,' his father took him up. 'Here, Pyotr, do you hear? See to it, man, quick as you can.'

Pyotr, who in his role of superior modern servant had not come up to kiss the young master's hand but had merely bowed to him from a distance, disappeared once again through the gateway.

'I came with the barouche, but there is a team of three for your tarantass as well,' fussed Nikolay Petrovich, while Arkady drank water from an iron jug brought out to him by the landlady of the posting-house and Bazarov lit a pipe and strolled over to the ostler, who was unharnessing the horses. 'Only the barouche is a two-seater and the thing is I don't know how your friend—'

'He'll take the tarantass,' interrupted Arkady. 'Please don't stand on ceremony with him. He's a wonderful fellow, so unpretentious – you'll see.'

Nikolay Petrovich's coachman led out the horses.

'There now, get a move on, bushy-beard!' Bazarov exhorted the ostler.

'Do you hear that, Mityukha?' another ostler, who was standing with his hands thrust into the back slits of his sheepskin, joined in. 'Did you hear what the gentleman here called you? Bushy-beard – just about suits you.'

Mityukha merely jerked his cap and dragged the reins from the sweating wheeler.

'Quick as you can, my lads, get on with it as quick as you can!' exclaimed Nikolay Petrovich. 'I will make it worth your while.'

Within a few minutes the horses were ready; father and son had taken their places in the barouche; Pyotr had clambered up on to the box; Bazarov had sprung into the tarantass and leant his head back on the leather cushion – and both vehicles were on their way.

III

'WELL, there we are then. At last you have your degree and have come home,' said Nikolay Petrovich, patting Arkady now on the shoulder, now on the knee. 'At last!'

'And how is Uncle? Well?' inquired Arkady, who in spite of the unaffected, almost childlike happiness which filled him wanted to turn the conversation as quickly as possible out of this exalted channel into the more everyday.

'Very well. He meant to come with me to meet you, but for some reason he changed his mind.'

'And did you have a long wait for me?' asked Arkady.

'Yes, about five hours.'

'Dear Papa!'

Arkady promptly turned to his father and kissed him resoundingly on the cheek. Nikolay Petrovich burst into a low chuckle.

'I have such a grand horse ready for you!' he began. 'You'll see. And your room has been papered.'

'But is there a room for Bazarov?'

'We'll find one for him too.'

'Please, Papa, make him feel he is welcome. I can't tell you how much I value his friendship.'

'You made his acquaintance recently?'

'Quite recently.'

'Ah, I thought I had not seen him last winter. What does he do?'

'His first subject is natural sciences. But he knows everything. Next year he means to try for his doctor's degree.'

'Oh, so he is of the medical faculty,' remarked Nikolay Petrovich, and fell silent. 'Pyotr,' he added, stretching out his arm to point, 'aren't those our peasants?'

Pyotr glanced in the direction in which his master was pointing. A few carts, harnessed to slack-reined horses, were rolling shakily along the narrow track. In each cart there sat one or more often two peasants, their sheepskin jackets hanging unbuttoned.

'Yes, sir, they are,' confirmed Pyotr.

'Where are they going, do you think? Into town?'

'Into town, it's to be assumed. To the inn,' he added contemptuously, and inclined slightly towards the coachman as
though seeking confirmation from him. However, the gesture
remained unacknowledged by so much as a movement: the
coachman was a man of the old school who had no sympathy
with modern views.

'I've had a great deal of trouble with the peasants this year,'
continued Nikolay Petrovich, addressing his son. 'They are
not paying their quit-rent.¹ What will you do about that?'

'But you are satisfied with your hired hands?'

'Yes,' conceded Nikolay Petrovich unwillingly. 'They are
under the influence of agitators though, that's the trouble;
and, well, there's still a lack of real conscientiousness. They
ruin the harness. But still, they did the ploughing quite well.
Things will come right in the end. But do the problems of the
estate really interest you now?'

'What a pity there's no shade near the house,' remarked
Arkady, ignoring the last question.

'I have put up a large awning over the veranda on the north
side,' announced Nikolay Petrovich. 'Now we will even be
able to dine in the fresh air.'

'It sounds like a summer villa – not that it matters. But how
wonderful the air is here though! How good it smells! Truly
it seems to me that there is no other place in the whole world
where the air is so sweet! And the sky here . . .'

Arkady pulled himself up suddenly, shot an oblique look
over his shoulder and fell silent.

'Of course,' remarked Nikolay Petrovich, 'you were born
here. It is only natural that everything here should seem
special to you.'

'Oh, Papa, it makes no difference where you are born.'

'But—'

'No, it makes absolutely no difference.'

Nikolay Petrovich gave his son a sidelong glance, and the

---

1 Rus. *Obrok*: payment made by serfs to their master in lieu of unpaid
labour on his fields.

barouche had covered half a mile before the conversation between them was resumed.

'I don't remember whether I wrote to you,' began Nikolay Petrovich, 'that your old nanny, Yegorovna, has died.'

'No, not really? Poor old woman! But Prokof'ich is alive?'

'Alive and quite unchanged. Still grumbling. One way and another you won't find great changes at Marino.'

'You still have the same bailiff?'

'Well, no, that is one change I have made. I decided not to keep on any more freed serfs who have been house servants, or at least not to entrust them with any position involving responsibility.' Arkady rolled his eyes inquiringly at Pyotr. '*Il est libre, en effet*,'[1] Nikolay Petrovich remarked in lowered tones, 'but of course he is really a valet. My present bailiff is lower middle class:[2] a capable fellow, I think. I pay him two hundred and fifty roubles a year. By the way,' added Nikolay Petrovich, drawing his hand across his forehead and brow, which with him was always a sign of suppressed embarrassment, 'I told you just now that you would find no changes at Marino – that is not quite true. I consider it my duty to warn you, although . . .'

He faltered for a moment, and when he continued he spoke in French.

'A strict moralist would find my frankness out of order, but in the first place it can't be kept secret, and in the second place you know I always had my own principles as to the relationship between father and son. Besides, you will, of course, be at liberty to judge me. At my age – to be brief, that – that girl, of whom you have probably heard already . . .'

'Little Fenechka?' inquired Arkady, his tone rather too familiar.

1 In French in the original.
2 Rus. *Iz meshchan*: in czarist Russia a man's class was noted on his passport. The term *meshchanstvo*, here translated as 'lower middle class', referred to the small shopkeepers and artisans, mainly town-dwellers, who were not bound to any feudal overlord. Their position at law was different from that of the peasantry or of the *kupechestvo* (the merchant class), and so in many ways were their customs, manner of life and their whole way of thinking.

Nikolay Petrovich blushed.

'Please don't say her name so loud. Well, yes – she is living with me now. I have moved her into the house. There were two modest little rooms. Besides, all that can be changed.'

'Good gracious, Papa, whatever for?'

'Your friend will be staying with us . . . the awkwardness . . .'

'As for Bazarov, please don't worry about him. He's above all that kind of thing.'

'Well, but there's you, after all,' went on Nikolay Petrovich. 'What a pity that the annexe is in such a bad state.'

'Good gracious, Papa,' Arkady took him up, 'you sound as though you are apologizing; you should be ashamed.'

'Of course I know I should be ashamed,' answered Nikolay Petrovich, growing redder and redder.

'Enough, Papa, enough, please don't!' Arkady smiled warmly. 'What a thing to apologize for!' he thought to himself, and a sentiment of indulgent tenderness for his kind and gentle father, not unmixed with a certain feeling of superiority, filled his heart. 'Let me hear no more, please,' he repeated once more, involuntarily enjoying the awareness of his own enlightenment and emancipation.

Nikolay Petrovich shot a look at him through the fingers of the hand with which he continued to wipe his forehead, and something stabbed at his heart; but he immediately took the blame on himself.

'Look, here are our fields already,' he pronounced after a long silence.

'And away to the front there, is that our wood?' asked Arkady.

'Yes, ours. Only I have sold it. It is to be cut down this year.'

'Why did you sell it?'

'I needed the money; and in any case that land goes to the peasants.'

'The ones who haven't paid you their quit-rent?'

'That is their business, and besides, they will pay some day.'

'It's a pity about the wood,' remarked Arkady, and began to look about him.

The country through which they were driving could not have been described as picturesque. Field upon field stretched to the very horizon, now billowing gently upwards, now falling away again; here and there was a glimpse of small woods; folds in the ground, filled with sparse, low bushes, twisted serpentwise across the landscape, conjuring up before the eye their own images on old maps of Catherine's time;[1] from time to time they came upon streams with underwashed banks and tiny ponds precariously dammed; little villages with squat, insignificant *izbas*[2] beneath their dark, frequently half-blown-away thatches; sheltered threshing barns with woven brushwood walls and great yawning gates giving on to deserted threshing floors; churches, sometimes of brick, the stucco peeling off in places, sometimes of wood, the crosses on their domes askew and their graveyards in a state of ruin. Gradually Arkady's heart contracted. As though specially chosen to tone with the landscape all the peasants whom they chanced to meet were shabby and worn, bestriding wretched nags; the crack willows stood like ragged beggars along the roadside, their bark hanging in strips and their twigs all broken. Thin cows, rough-coated, every bone in their bodies showing as though gnawed clean of flesh, were nibbling at the grass along the ditches. It seemed as though they had just torn themselves free of someone's terrible and deadly claws – and, evoked by the pathetic appearance of the enfeebled beasts, in the midst of the fair spring day arose the white spectre of the cheerless, endless winter with its blizzards, frosts and snows. 'No,' thought Arkady, 'this country is not rich, it impresses neither by its abundance nor by the industry of its inhabitants; it cannot, cannot be allowed to remain this way, reforms are essential – but how to put them into practice, how to begin?'

Thus mused Arkady but, while he mused, the spring began to make itself felt. Everything round about glinted golden green, everything rippled widely and gently under the soft

1 Empress Catherine the Great (1762–96).
2 Peasants' cottages made from whole pine trunks somewhat in the style of the Canadian log-cabin.

breath of the warm wind, everything – the trees, the bushes and the grasses; everywhere the skylarks were showering down the endless melodious torrents of their song; peewits were now calling over the low-lying meadows, now silently running from tussock to tussock; rooks, their blackness contrasting handsomely with the tender green, strutted about amongst the yet sprouting spring crops; in the rye, already whitening a little, they became lost to view, only their heads showing occasionally above its smoky convolutions. Arkady gazed and gazed and his thoughts, gradually losing their urgency, finally faded altogether; he threw off his overcoat and gave his father such a merry, such a little-boy look that he again embraced him.

'Not far now,' remarked Nikolay Petrovich; 'you can see the house from that little hill over there. We will rub along splendidly, Arkady; you will help me with the estate, if only it doesn't bore you. We must become really close friends now and get to know one another really well, mustn't we?'

'Of course,' murmured Arkady, 'but what a wonderful day it is today!'

'That's to welcome you home, my dear. Yes, spring in full glory. Though as a matter of fact I agree with Pushkin – do you remember in *Evgeny Onyegin*:

> How sad to me your apparition,
> Oh spring, my spring, the time of love!
> What . . .'

'Arkady!' Bazarov's voice rang out from the tarantass. 'Pass me back a match – I haven't anything to light my pipe.'

Nikolay Petrovich fell silent, and Arkady, who had begun to listen to him not without some degree of astonishment, but also not without sympathy, hastily extracted his silver matchbox from his pocket and sent Pyotr to take it to Bazarov.

'Like a cigar?' shouted Bazarov again.

'All right,' responded Arkady.

Pyotr came back to the barouche and handed him a long black cigar which Arkady promptly lit, diffusing such a strong, sour smell of stale tobacco that Nikolay Petrovich,

who had never smoked in his life, involuntarily, albeit unobtrusively so as not to offend his son, turned away his nose.

A quarter of an hour later both vehicles drew up before the
porch of a new wooden house, painted grey, with a red iron
roof. This was Marino, also the New Settlement or, as the
peasants called it, Bachelor Farm.

IV

No crowd of servants spilled out on to the porch to meet the
masters; there appeared only one little girl of about twelve
years old, and after her a young fellow very like Pyotr emerged
from the house dressed in a grey livery jacket with white
heraldic buttons, the servant of Pavel Petrovich Kirsanov.
Silently he opened the door of the barouche and unbuttoned
the apron of the tarantass. Nikolay Petrovich, together with
his son and Bazarov, crossed the dark and almost empty hall,
behind a door of which appeared for one moment the face of
a young woman, into the drawing-room, which was furnished
in the latest style.

'Well, here we are at home,' pronounced Nikolay Petrovich,
taking off his cap and shaking out his hair. 'The main thing
now is to have supper and then to rest.'

'Something to eat wouldn't come amiss, and that's a fact,'
remarked Bazarov, stretching, and sank down on to the
sofa.

'Yes, yes, let us have supper, supper at once.' Nikolay
Petrovich, without any apparent cause, stamped his feet. 'And
here is Prokof'ich.'

There entered a man of about sixty, white-haired, thin and
tanned, wearing a brown morning suit with bronze buttons
and a pink neckerchief. He grinned, came up to kiss Arkady's
hand, bowed to the guest, retreated to the door and put his
hands behind his back.

'There he is, Prokof'ich,' began Nikolay Petrovich, 'come
back to us at last. Well? How do you find him?'

'In the best of looks, sir,' pronounced the old man, and
grinned again, but immediately snapped together his thick

brows. 'Do you wish me to serve supper?' he inquired
impressively.

'Yes, yes, please. But won't you go to your room first, Yevgeny Vasil'evich?'

'No, thank you, there's no need. Just give orders for my
trunk to be hauled up there – and this old rag,' he added,
removing his dust-coat.

'Very well, Prokof'ich, take the gentleman's coat.'
Prokof'ich, apparently somewhat at a loss, took Bazarov's 'old
rag' in both hands and, raising it high above his head, tiptoed
out of the room. 'And you, Arkady, will you go to your room
for a minute?'

'Yes, I must clean up a little,' replied Arkady, and would
have made for the door had not at that very moment a man
entered the drawing-room. Pavel Petrovich Kirsanov was of
middle height, dressed in a dark English suit, a fashionable
low cravat and patent-leather half-boots. He looked to be
about forty-five years of age: his short grey hair gave off a dull
glint like new silver; his face, irritable but unlined, remarkably
regular and clean-cut as though worked by a light and sensi-
tive chisel, still showed traces of remarkable beauty: particularly fine were the bright black almond-shaped eyes. Elegant
and aristocratic, the whole figure of Arkady's uncle had
retained a youthful slenderness and that *élan* which usually
disappears as men grow out of their twenties.

Pavel Petrovich drew out his beautiful hand with its long
pink nails from the pocket of his trousers – a hand which
seemed even more beautiful against the snowy whiteness of
his cuff, linked by a single large opal – and extended it to his
nephew. Having first gone through the rite of the European
'shake hands',[1] he then kissed him three times according to
the Russian custom, that is to say he brushed his cheek three
times with his scented moustaches, and pronounced: 'I bid
you welcome.'

Nikolay Petrovich introduced him to Bazarov: Pavel Petrovich accorded him a slight inclination of his supple figure and

1 In English in the original.

a slight smile. However, he did not offer his hand but actually put it back into his pocket.

'I had already decided that you would not come today,' he opened the conversation in a pleasant voice, swaying amiably, jerking his shoulders and showing his fine white teeth. 'Could it be that something happened on the road?'

'Nothing happened,' replied Arkady, 'we just loitered a bit on the way. But now we're as hungry as hunters. Hurry up Prokof'ich, Papa, and I will be back in a minute.'

'Wait, I'll come with you!' exclaimed Bazarov, heaving himself up abruptly from the sofa. Both young men left the room.

'Who is that?' inquired Pavel Petrovich.

'A friend of little Arkady's. A very clever man according to him.'

'Will he be staying here?'

'Yes.'

'That unkempt specimen?'

'Well, yes.'

Pavel Petrovich beat a tattoo on the table with his nails. 'I find that Arkady *s'est dégourdi*,'[1] he remarked. 'I am thankful that he has come home.'

Over supper there was little conversation. Bazarov, particularly, said almost nothing, but ate a great deal. Nikolay Petrovich recounted some incidents from his, as he put it, farmer's existence, and delivered his opinion on several pending governmental measures, on committees, on deputies, on the necessity of introducing machinery and so on. Pavel Petrovich paced slowly up and down the dining-room (he never ate supper), infrequently taking a sip from a glass of red wine, and still less frequently giving vent to some remark or rather exclamation such as 'Ah!' 'Er!' 'Hem!' Arkady recounted some of the latest Petersburg gossip, but he was experiencing a slight feeling of awkwardness, the awkwardness which usually overcomes a young man when he has just ceased to be a child and has come back to a place where people are used to seeing him as and to accounting him a child. He spoke with an

1 In French in the original (= 'has let himself go').

unnecessary drawl, avoiding the word papa, for which he once even substituted the word father, albeit pronounced through gritted teeth. With an exaggerated assumption of ease he poured himself out much more wine than he really wanted, and drank it all. Prokof'ich never took his eyes off him and merely chewed on his lip. After dinner the party immediately broke up.

'A bit of an eccentric, your uncle,' said Bazarov to Arkady, seated on his friend's bed clad in a dressing-gown and sucking at a short pipe. 'What dandyism to find in the country to be sure! His nails, now, his nails. Why, they're fit for an exhibition!'

'Ah, but you don't know,' replied Arkady. 'You see he was a society lion in his time. I will tell you his story some day. He was a beau, you see, and turned the ladies' heads.'

'Oh, so that's it! For old times' sake then. A pity there's no one to fascinate here. I was watching him all the time: such an extraordinary little collar, as stiff as stone, and his chin so precisely clean-shaven. Arkady Nikolayevich, surely all that is ridiculous?'

'Perhaps; only he really is a good person.'

'An archaic phenomenon! But your father is a grand fellow. It's a pity he recites poetry and he doesn't seem to understand much about estate management, but he's kind.'

'My father has a heart of gold.'

'Did you notice how shy he was?'

Arkady nodded his head, just as though he had not felt shy himself.

'A remarkable thing,' continued Bazarov, 'these funny old romantics! They work up their nervous system into a state of agitation, then, of course, their equilibrium is upset. However, I'll take my leave! There's an English wash-basin in my room but the door doesn't lock. Still, that's something to be encouraged – English wash-basins. Progress, in other words!'

Bazarov took himself off and Arkady was left to indulge a mounting feeling of delight. It is pleasant to fall asleep in the house where one was born, on a familiar bed under a counterpane worked by beloved hands, the hands of one's nanny perhaps, those gentle, kind and tireless hands. Arkady remembered Yegorovna and sighed, and wished her the kingdom of heaven. He said no prayers for himself.

He and Bazarov both fell asleep quickly, but there were others in the house who were not sleeping. Nikolay Petrovich was excited by his son's return. He went to bed but did not put out the candle and, propping his head on his hands, thought long thoughts. His brother sat long after midnight in his study in a wide armchair of English manufacture before the fireplace in which the coal glowed faintly. Pavel Petrovich had not undressed, except that red, heelless Chinese slippers had replaced the patent half-boots on his feet. He held in his hand the latest number of *Galignani*,[1] but he was not reading; he gazed fixedly into the fire where, now dying down and now leaping up again, a bluish flame trembled. God knows where his thoughts were wandering, but their wanderings were not confined to the past: the expression on his face was concentrated and sombre, which is not so when a man is occupied with nothing but memories. And, in a little back room, clad in a pale blue quilted jacket, a white kerchief thrown over her dark hair, the young woman Fenechka was sitting on a large chest, now listening, now dozing, now glancing across at the open door through which could be seen a child's cot and the even breathing of a sleeping child could be heard.

V

THE next morning Bazarov woke before the others and went outside. 'Aha!' he thought, looking round about him. 'Not much to look at, this place.' When Nikolay Petrovich had divided up his land with his peasants he had no choice but to set aside four acres of completely flat and unplanted grassland for the site of his new farmstead. He had built the house, outbuildings and farm, laid down a garden and excavated a

1 *Galignani's Messenger*: a daily newspaper of liberal orientation published in English in Paris.

pond and two wells; but the young trees were doing badly, very little water had collected in the pond and the wells had turned out to have a somewhat brackish taste. Only the arbour of lilac and acacia had grown up as it should; sometimes they drank tea or took luncheon there. In a few minutes Bazarov had explored all the garden paths, looked in at the yard where the cattle were kept, at the stable, discovered two servant boys with whom he at once made friends, and set off with them towards a small marshy patch rather more than a mile from the farmstead in search of frogs.

'What do you want frogs for, master?' asked one of the boys.

'Well, I'll tell you,' answered Bazarov, who was gifted with a particular talent for gaining the confidence of people of inferior station, although he never flattered them and treated them with scant consideration. 'I split the frog open and take a look at what's going on inside him; and, as you and I are just these same frogs, except that we walk on two legs, I shall get to know what's going on inside us too.'

'I see, but why do you want to know?'

'So as not to make any mistake if you get ill and I have to cure you.'

'Are you a doctor then?'

'Yes.'

'Vas'ka, do you hear that, the gentleman says that we're them same frogs. Queer!'

'I'm afraid of 'em, them frogs,' remarked Vas'ka, a bare-footed boy of about seven with a head white as flax, dressed in a grey smock with a high standing collar.

'What's there to be afraid of? They don't bite surely?'

'Come on, into the water with you, you philosophers!' said Bazarov.

In the meantime Nikolay Petrovich had also woken and had gone to look in on Arkady, whom he found already dressed. Father and son strolled out to the veranda under the overhang of the awning; by the railing, on the table between two large bunches of lilac, the samovar was already boiling. A little girl appeared, the same one who had met the new arrivals on the porch the previous evening, and announced in a thin, high voice:

'Feodos'ya Nikolayevna isn't very well, she can't come; she gave orders to inquire whether you would be pleased to pour out tea yourself or whether she should send Dunyasha?'

'I'll pour out myself, myself.' Nikolay Petrovich took her up hastily. 'How do you take your tea, Arkady, with cream or lemon?'

'With cream,' answered Arkady and, having refrained from speech for a moment, ventured, on a note of inquiry, 'Papa?'

Nikolay Petrovich glanced up at his son in some embarrassment.

'What?' he said.

Arkady lowered his eyes.

'Forgive me, Papa, if my question seems out of place,' he began, 'but you yourself by your frankness of yesterday have led me on to be frank. You won't be angry. . . ?'

'Go on.'

'You give me the courage to ask you – is it that Fen – is it that she won't come here to pour out the tea because I am here?'

Nikolay Petrovich turned away slightly.

'It may be,' he pronounced finally, 'she supposes – she is ashamed. . . .'

Arkady cast a quick glance at his father.

'She has no reason to be ashamed. In the first place you know my views' – it gave Arkady great pleasure to pronounce these words – 'and in the second – how could I ever wish to disturb your life, your habits, even in the least little thing? And then I am certain that you could not make a bad choice; if you permit her to live under the same roof with you, then it is to be assumed that she is worthy to do so. In any case a son is not his father's judge, and more particularly I am not, and particularly not of such a father as you, who have never restricted my freedom in any way.'

To begin with Arkady's voice was trembling: he felt himself to be behaving magnanimously, yet at the same time realized that he was subjecting his father to something like a lecture;

but the sound of his own voice works a powerful charm on any man, and Arkady pronounced the last words firmly, even with pathos.

'Thank you, Arkady, dear boy,' said Nikolay Petrovich in a toneless voice, and his fingers again ran over his brow and forehead. 'Your suppositions are in fact well founded. Of course, if the girl had not been worthy – it is no frivolous whim. It is not easy for me to speak to you about it; but you understand that it would have been difficult for her to come here when you were here, especially on the first day of your return.'

'In that case I shall go to her myself,' exclaimed Arkady with a new onrush of magnanimous feelings, and he jumped up from the table. 'I shall explain to her that she has no reason to feel ashamed in front of me.'

Nikolay Petrovich also got up.

'Arkady,' he began, 'do me the favour ... how can you ... there ... I haven't warned you. ...'

But Arkady was already out of hearing and had run from the veranda. Nikolay Petrovich was left looking after him and sank back in his seat in confusion. His heart began to thud. Whether he foresaw in that moment the inevitable strangeness of his future relationship with his son, whether he realized that Arkady might well have shown him more respect had he not mentioned the matter at all, whether he reproached himself for weakness, it is difficult to say: all these sentiments were present in him, but in the guise of feelings – and confused feelings at that; but the flush did not leave his face and his heart thudded.

Came the sound of hurrying feet, and Arkady reappeared on the veranda.

'We've made each other's acquaintance, Father!' he cried, an expression of a kind of tender and benevolent triumph on his face. 'Feodos'ya Nikolayevna really isn't quite well today and will come later. But why didn't you tell me that I had a brother? I would have gone and given him a good hug and kiss yesterday evening, as I've just done now.'

Nikolay Petrovich tried to say something, tried to stand up and open his arms. Arkady flung himself on his neck.

'What is all this? Embracing again?' Pavel Petrovich's voice sounded from behind them.

Father and son were equally glad of his appearance at that moment; there are situations from which, however touching, one wishes to extricate oneself as quickly as possible.

'What's so surprising in that?' demanded Nikolay Petrovich merrily. 'Here have I been waiting for goodness knows how many ages for my little Arkady. I haven't even had my fill of looking at him since yesterday.'

'I am not in the least surprised,' remarked Pavel Petrovich. 'In fact I don't even have anything against embracing him myself.'

Arkady went up to his uncle and again felt his scented moustaches brush his cheek. Pavel Petrovich took his place at the table. He wore an elegant morning suit in the English style; on his head a small fez sat jauntily. This fez and the carelessly knotted tie suggested the informality of country life; but the tight wings of his shirt collar – not white, it is true, but striped as is fitting for morning dress – pressed into the clean-shaven chin with customary inexorability.

'Where has this new friend of yours disappeared to?' he asked Arkady.

'He's not in the house; he usually gets up early and goes off somewhere. The main thing is not to pay any attention to him: he dislikes formality.'

'Yes, that is obvious.' Pavel Petrovich began unhurriedly to spread butter on a slice of bread. 'Is he going to stay with us long?'

'As long as it suits him. He has stopped off with us on his way to his father.'

'And where does his father live?'

'In our province, about sixty-five miles from here. He has a small property there. He used to be a regimental surgeon.'

'Tee – tee-tee – tee – that was why I kept on asking myself where I had heard that name Bazarov. Nikolay, I seem to remember, in our good father's division, wasn't there a leech called Bazarov?'

'I believe there was.'

'Precisely, precisely. So that leech is his father. Hem!' Pavel Petrovich caressed his moustaches. 'Well then, and Mr Bazarov himself, who is he exactly?' he inquired deliberately.

'Who is Bazarov?' Arkady grinned ironically. 'My dear uncle, do you want me to tell you who exactly he is?'

'Humour me thus far, my dear nephew.'

'He's a nihilist.'

'What?' demanded Nikolay Petrovich, and Pavel Petrovich raised his knife with a bit of butter on the end of the blade and remained poised.

'He's a nihilist,' repeated Arkady.

'A nihilist,' pronounced Nikolay Petrovich. 'To the best of my judgment that comes from the Latin *nihil*; presumably this word signifies a man who – who recognizes nothing?'

'Say, who respects nothing,' Pavel Petrovich took him up, and applied himself again to the butter.

'Who approaches everything in a critical spirit,' Arkady amended.

'But doesn't it all come to the same?' inquired Pavel Petrovich.

'No, it does not come to the same. A nihilist is a man who bows before no authorities, who accepts no principle whatsoever as an article of faith, however great the respect in which that principle may be generally held.'

'And what of it? Is it a good thing?' interrupted Pavel Petrovich.

'It affects different people differently, Uncle. For some it is good, for others very bad.'

'So that's the way of it. Well, I see that it is not our province. We are people of the old school, we consider that without principles' – Pavel Petrovich affected the soft French pronunciation of this foreign word principles whereas Arkady stressed the first syllable, pronouncing the initial 'i' hard in the Russian manner – 'without principles accepted, as you put it, as articles of faith it is impossible to undertake one single step, even to breathe. *Vous avez changé tout cela*,[1] God grant

1 In French in the original.

you health and the rank of general, and we are destined merely
to sit back and admire these gentlemen. What did you say
they were called?'

'Nihilists,' pronounced Arkady distinctly.

'Yes. Before there were Hegelians and now Nihilians.
It will be interesting to see how you will go on existing in a
void, in an airless vacuum; and now ring the bell, please,
brother Nikolay Petrovich, it is time for me to drink my
chocolate.'

Nikolay Petrovich ran and called out 'Dunyasha!' but
instead of Dunyasha Fenechka herself came out on to the
veranda. She was a young woman of about twenty-three years
of age, all white and yielding, with dark hair and eyes, red
childishly pouted lips and a delicate colour. She was wearing
a neat cotton dress; a new pale blue triangular kerchief lay
lightly over her rounded shoulders. She was carrying a large
cup of chocolate and, having put this down before Pavel
Petrovich, she became covered in confusion: the hot blood
rose in a scarlet wave under the delicate skin of her sweet face.
She lowered her eyes and stood by the table, leaning lightly
on the very tips of her fingers. It seemed that she felt as
though she ought not to have come and at the same time that
she had the right to come.

Pavel Petrovich frowned severely and Nikolay Petrovich
looked embarrassed.

'Good morning, Fenechka,' he said between his teeth.

'Good morning, sir,' she responded in a quiet, melodious
voice and according Arkady, who was smiling at her in a
friendly way, a sidelong glance, she went quietly out. She
swayed slightly as she walked, but this also suited her.

On the veranda silence reigned for the space of several
minutes. Pavel Petrovich was sipping his chocolate and suddenly raised his head.

'And now Mr Nihilist is coming to favour us with his
company,' he muttered, half to himself.

Indeed, across the garden, striding over the flower-beds,
Bazarov was coming towards them. His linen coat and
trousers were bespattered with dirt; a clinging plant from the

marshes had wound itself round the crown of his old round hat; in his right hand he held a small bag; in the bag something alive was moving. He quickly came up on to the veranda, nodded his head and said:

'Good morning, gentlemen, excuse my being late for tea; I'll be back in a moment, I must find somewhere to put my prisoners.'

'What have you there – leeches?' inquired Pavel Petrovich.

'No, frogs.'

'Do you eat them or breed them?'

'I use them for experiments,' replied Bazarov indifferently, and went on into the house.

'That means he's going to cut them up,' remarked Pavel Petrovich. 'No faith in principles, but believes in frogs.'

Arkady gave his uncle a disappointed look and Nikolay Petrovich shrugged his shoulders unobtrusively. Pavel Petrovich himself felt that his joke had fallen flat and began to talk of the estate and of the new manager, who had come to him yesterday to complain that the labourer Foma 'was debauching' and had got out of hand. 'He's such an Aesop,'[1] the manager had said among other things. 'He has protested himself everywhere to be a bad man; he'll be a fool to his dying day.'

VI

BAZAROV came back, took his seat at the table and addressed himself hastily to the tea. Both brothers regarded him in silence, and Arkady darted surreptitious glances now at his father, now at his uncle.

'Did you go far?' asked Nikolay Petrovich at last.

'You've got a little patch of marsh over there by the aspen grove. I put up five snipe; you can slaughter them, Arkady.'

'But don't you shoot?'

'No.'

---

1 Aesop: this proper name is quite commonly used in peasant dialect to mean 'a queer fellow'.

'Your chief interest is, in fact, physics?' inquired Pavel Petrovich in his turn.

'Physics, yes; and natural science in general.'

'They say that lately the Teutons have been making great progress in that field.'

'Yes, the Germans are our masters there,' Bazarov returned indifferently.

Pavel Petrovich had used the word Teutons instead of Germans in a spirit of irony which had, however, passed unnoticed by anyone.

'Have you so high an opinion of the Germans?' inquired Pavel Petrovich with exquisite deference. He had begun to feel secretly annoyed. The way in which Bazarov made himself so completely at home outraged his aristocratic nature. The leech's son not only showed no shyness, he even answered questions abruptly and reluctantly, and in the tone of his voice there was something rough, almost insolent.

'Their scholars know their business.'

'I see, I see. Then your opinion of Russian scholars is presumably somewhat less flattering?'

'Maybe. Yes.'

'That shows most admirable selflessness,' pronounced Pavel Petrovich, drawing himself up and throwing back his head. 'But how is it that Arkady Nikolayevich has just said that you recognize absolutely no authorities? That you do not believe in them?'

'Why should I recognize them? And in what am I supposed to believe? People talk sense to me, I agree, and that's all there is to it.'

'And do all Germans talk sense?' inquired Pavel Petrovich, and his face took on such a disinterested, remote expression that he appeared to have withdrawn into some distant height above the clouds.

'Not all,' Bazarov replied with a slight yawn; he obviously had no wish to pursue the argument.

Pavel Petrovich glanced at Arkady as one who would say: 'How respectful your friend is, I must say.'

'As far as I am concerned,' he began again, not without an

effort, 'I, for my sins, have no great liking for the Germans. Russian Germans I prefer to pass over in silence – everyone knows what they are. But German Germans don't appeal to me either. Formerly they were still tolerable; then they had – well, Schiller, for instance, Goethe – my brother favours them particularly. But now they seem to produce nothing but various chemists and materialists—'

'A decent chemist is twenty times more useful than any poet,' interrupted Bazarov.

'Really,' pronounced Pavel Petrovich, and as though about to drop off to sleep raised his brows a fraction. 'Then you do not recognize art?'

'The art of making money, or pink pills for piles,' exclaimed Bazarov with a contemptuous sneer.

'Doubtless, doubtless. So that is your style of humour. You abjure everything then. Let us assume so. In fact you believe in science alone?'

'I have already informed you that I believe in nothing; and what is science – science in the abstract? There are sciences, as there are trades, professions; but science in the abstract simply does not exist.'

'Very well, sir. And now, in so far as other values normally accepted as obligatory in human society are concerned, do you take an equally negative attitude?'

'What is this, a cross-examination?' asked Bazarov.

Pavel Petrovich turned rather white. Nikolay Petrovich found it expedient to enter the conversation.

'Some time we will have another chat on this subject with you, my dear Yevgeny Vasil'evich; we'll get to know your opinion and tell you ours. For my part I am very glad that you are a natural scientist. I have heard that Liebig has made some remarkable discoveries about the fertilization of fields. You will be able to help me in my agrarian undertakings: perhaps you will be able to give me some good advice.'

'I am at your service, Nikolay Petrovich, but Liebig is far above your head! You must learn the alphabet before starting to read books, and you don't know "a" from "b" yet.'

'Well, now I see you really are a nihilist, my lad,' thought

Nikolay Petrovich. 'Nevertheless give me leave to appeal to you if the occasion arises,' he added aloud. 'And now, brother, I believe it is time we went and talked to the bailiff.'

Pavel Petrovich rose from his chair.

'Yes,' he said, not looking at anyone, 'it's a tragedy to have rusticated for five years like this in the country, far from the great minds! You are shown up as the most complete fool. You try not to forget what you were taught, and there – just like that! – it appears that it was all nonsense and you are told that sensible people don't occupy themselves with such trifles any longer and that you yourself are, as they say, old hat. What can we do? Evidently the young really are cleverer than we.'

Pavel Petrovich turned slowly on his heel and went slowly out; Nikolay Petrovich followed him.

'Is he always like that?' Bazarov asked Arkady unfeelingly as soon as the door had closed behind the two brothers.

'Listen, Yevgeny, you were rather too sharp with him,' remarked Arkady. 'You hurt his feelings.'

'I can just see myself kowtowing to them, these provincial aristocrats! All that is nothing but vanity, you know, lionizing habits, foppishness. Well, he should have kept his *pied-à-terre* in Petersburg, if that's the way he's made. Anyway he's no concern of ours, bless him! I found quite a rare specimen of water-beetle, *Dytiscus marginatus*, do you know? I'll show it to you.'

'I promised to tell you his story,' began Arkady.

'The story of the beetle?'

'Oh, stop it, Yevgeny. The story of my uncle. You will see that he is not the kind of man you imagine. He deserves pity rather than sneers.'

'I don't dispute it; but why is he worrying you so?'

'One must be just, Yevgeny.'

'From what does that follow?'

'No, listen. . . .'

And Arkady told him the story of his uncle. The reader will find it in the next chapter.

VII

To begin with, Pavel Petrovich Kirsanov had been educated at home, like his brother, and then in the cadet corps. From childhood he had been distinguished by exceptional good looks; in addition he was self-confident, slightly sarcastic and quick-tempered in a way which was somehow amusing; he could not fail to please. From the moment he became an officer he was received everywhere. He was generally made much of and he also indulged himself, even played the fool, even cultivated a certain affectation of manner; but this also suited him. The women lost their wits over him, the men called him a fop and secretly envied him. He lived, as has already been established, in the same rooms as his brother, to whom he was sincerely attached, although not in the least resembling him. Nikolay Petrovich was slightly lame, had small, pleasant but rather melancholy features and fine, scanty hair; he delighted in idleness, but also in reading, and was afraid of going into society. Pavel Petrovich was never at home in the evenings, had a reputation for boldness and physical prowess (he almost succeeded in starting a fashion for gymnastics among the young men of society), and had read five or six French books. At twenty-eight years of age he was already a captain; a brilliant career lay before him. Suddenly all this was changed.

At that time Petersburg society was enlivened by the infrequent appearances of a woman who is still remembered to this day, Princess R. She had a well-bred, correct but somewhat stupid husband and there were no children. She was accustomed to leave suddenly for abroad, to return suddenly to Russia, and in general pursued a strange way of life. She had the reputation of a frivolous coquette, abandoned herself with passion to pleasure of all kinds, danced until ready to drop, giggled and joked with young men whom she received before dinner in the half dark of her drawing-room, yet at night wept and prayed, found no peace anywhere and would often pace about her room until morning, wringing her hands drearily, or would sit, all pale and cold, poring over her psalter. Day

would come and she would again be transformed into a society lady, would again go visiting, laugh, chatter and positively
fling herself into anything which promised her the least diver-
sion. She had a striking figure; her single braid, golden in
colour and heavy as gold, fell beneath her knees, but no one
would have called her a beauty; in the whole of her face the
only good feature was the eyes, and not even the eyes themselves, which were grey and not large, but their expression,
glancing and profound, carefree to dare-devilry and thoughtful to the point of melancholy – an enigmatic expression.
Something exceptional shone in these eyes, even when her
lips were murmuring the most empty nothings. She dressed
with elegance. Pavel Petrovich met her at a ball, danced the
mazurka with her, during which she uttered not one word to
the point, and fell passionately in love with her. Having the
habit of success, here also he soon achieved his goal; but the
ease of his conquest did not cool his passion. On the contrary:
still more tormentingly, still more irresistibly, was he drawn
to this woman, in whom, even when she surrendered herself
irrevocably, there yet still seemed to remain something sacred
and unapproachable, into which no one could penetrate. What
had made its home in that soul, God knows. It seemed as
though she were in the thrall of mysterious powers of whose
true nature she herself was ignorant; they played with her as
they would; her small mind could not control their whims.
All her behaviour represented a series of inconsistencies; the
only letters which might have awakened just suspicions on
the part of her husband she wrote to a man who was almost a
stranger to her, while her love found expression in sadness:
she no longer laughed or joked with the man of her choice,
but listened to him and looked at him as one bewildered.
Sometimes, most often quite suddenly, this bewilderment
gave way to cold horror; her face took on a wild and dreadful
expression; she locked herself in her room, and her maid, by
laying her ear to the keyhole, could hear her stifled sobbing.
On more than one occasion, on returning home after a tender
meeting, Kirsanov experienced that lacerating and bitter frustration which wells up in the heart after some final failure.

'What more do I want?' he would ask himself, but his heart still ached. Once he gave her a ring with a sphinx carved on the stone.

'What is that?' she asked. 'A sphinx?'

'Yes,' he replied, 'and that sphinx is you.'

'I?' she queried, and slowly raised her enigmatic eyes to his. 'Do you know that that is very flattering?' she added with an empty, ironical smile, but the eyes continued to look strangely.

It was hard for Pavel Petrovich even when Princess R. loved him; but when she began to tire of him – and this happened quite soon – he almost went out of his mind. He suffered torments and grew jealous, gave her no peace and followed her wherever she went; she grew weary of his importunate suit and left for abroad. He retired from the service, in spite of the pleas of his friends, of the exhortations of his superiors, and set off after the princess; for about four years he remained in foreign parts, now pursuing her, now purposely losing her from sight; he was ashamed of himself, was indignant at his own poor-spirited behaviour – but nothing helped. Her image, that incomprehensible, almost meaningless, yet enchanting image, had taken root too deeply in his heart. In Baden he somehow came together with her again as before; it seemed that never before had she loved him with such passion – but a month later all was at an end: the flame had leapt up for the last time and had been quenched for ever. Foreseeing the inevitable separation, he wished at least to remain her friend, as though friendship with such a woman were possible. She left Baden quietly and from that time consistently avoided Kirsanov. He returned to Russia, tried to take up his old life, but found it impossible to return to his former routine. Like one infected he wandered from place to place; he continued to take part in the life of society and retained all the habits of a man of the world; he could boast two or three new conquests; but already he expected nothing, either from himself or from others, and undertook nothing new. He had aged, grown grey; to sit in a club in the evenings, irritable and bored, and to argue apathetically in bachelor society became a necessity to him – a bad sign, as everyone knows. Of marriage

he naturally did not even think. Ten years passed in this fashion, uneventfully, fruitlessly and swiftly, terribly swiftly.
Nowhere does time pass so quickly as in Russia; in prison, so
they say, it passes even quicker. Then, at dinner in the club,
Pavel Petrovich heard of the death of Princess R. She had
died in Paris in a state near to madness. He rose from the table
and wandered for a long time through the rooms of the club,
pausing, as if rooted to the ground, by the card-players, but
returned home no earlier than usual. Some time later he
received a parcel addressed in his name; in it was the ring
given by him to the princess. She had made a cross-shaped
mark over the sphinx and had requested that he be told that
the cross was the solution of the enigma.

   This happened in 1848 at the very time when Nikolay Petrovich, having lost his wife, came to Petersburg. Pavel Petrovich
had scarcely seen his brother since he went to live in the
country: Nikolay Petrovich's marriage had coincided with
the very first days of Pavel Petrovich's acquaintanceship
with the princess. On his return from abroad he had gone to
visit Nikolay Petrovich with the intention of staying for
about two months to feast his eyes on his brother's happiness,
but had found he could support life with him for no more
than one week. The difference in the situations of the two
brothers was too great. In 1848 that difference had decreased:
Nikolay Petrovich had lost his wife, Pavel Petrovich had lost
his memories; after the princess's death he tried not to think
of her. But Nikolay was left with the feeling of a life well
spent – his son was growing up under his eye; Pavel, on the
other hand, a lonely bachelor, had entered that dim twilight
season, the season of regrets which are like hopes, hopes
which are like regrets, when youth is over and old age has
not yet set in.

   This time was harder for Pavel Petrovich than for anyone
else: having lost his past he had lost everything.

   'I won't tease you to come to Marino,' Nikolay once said to
him (he had given the village that name in honour of his wife).
'You were bored there even when my wife was alive, and now,
I think, you would die of depression.'

'I was still stupid and restless then,' answered Pavel Petrovich. 'Since then I have settled down, even if I haven't grown any wiser. Now, on the contrary, if you would permit it, I am ready to move in with you for good.'

Instead of answering, Nikolay Petrovich embraced him; but a year and a half went by after that conversation before Pavel Petrovich made up his mind to put his intention into practice. However, once having settled in the country he did not leave it even during those three winters which Nikolay Petrovich spent in Petersburg with his son. He began to read, mainly in English; in general he organized his whole life on the English pattern, seeing little of the neighbours and going out only to elections, where for the most part he remained silent, only now and again provoking and alarming landlords of the old school by his liberal freaks yet not making friends among the representatives of the younger generation. Both factions considered him arrogant; both respected him for his excellent aristocratic manners, for the rumours of his amorous conquests; because he dressed very well and invariably stayed in the best room at the best hotel; because he always dined well and had once dined with Wellington on the invitation of Louis Philippe; because he took with him wherever he went a real silver *nécessaire* and a field bath; because he smelt of some exceptional and remarkably 'aristocratic' scent; because he played a brilliant game of whist and invariably lost; finally, he was also respected for his impeccable integrity. The ladies considered him an enchanting melancholic; but he did not cultivate the society of ladies. . . .

'So you see, Yevgeny,' said Arkady, finishing his story, 'how unfairly you jump to conclusions about Uncle! Quite apart from the fact that he has often helped my father out of trouble and given him all his money – the estate, as perhaps you know, isn't divided between them – he is always glad to help anybody and, by the way, he always stands up for the peasants; it's true that when he talks to them he wrinkles his nose and sniffs eau-de-Cologne—'

'A common complaint: nerves,' interrupted Bazarov.

'Perhaps, but he has the kindest heart. And he is far from

stupid. He has given me such good advice – especially – especially about relations with women.'

'Aha! Having burnt his tongue on his own milk he blows on other people's water. We've heard that one before!'

'Well, in short,' persevered Arkady, 'he is deeply unhappy, believe me; it's a sin to despise him.'

'But who's despising him?' objected Bazarov. 'However, I would still say that a man who staked his whole life on the card of a woman's love, and when that card took no tricks went all limp and degenerated to such an extent that now he's no longer capable of anything – that that man is no man, he's not male. You say he's unhappy: you ought to know; but he hasn't had all the nonsense knocked out of him. I am certain that he seriously believes he is a man of affairs because he reads that wretched *Galignani* and once a month gets a peasant out of a flogging.'

'But remember his upbringing, the times in which he lived,' remarked Arkady.

'Upbringing?' Bazarov took him up. 'Everybody should look after their own upbringing – as I did, if you like, for one instance. And as to the times – why should I be subject to them? They should rather be what I make them. No, brother, all that is lack of discipline, futility! And what are these mysterious relations between man and woman? We physiologists know all about such relations. Try studying the anatomy of the eye: from where will you get your enigmatic expression, as you call it? All that is romanticism, nonsense, rot, art. We'd much better go and look at the beetle.'

And the two friends went off to Bazarov's room, which had already acquired a kind of medicinal-surgical smell, mixed with the smell of cheap tobacco.

VIII

PAVEL PETROVICH did not attend for long at his brother's interview with the bailiff, a tall thin man with a honeyed, consumptive voice and knavish eyes, whose invariable reply to all Nikolay Petrovich's comments was 'Gracious me, sir, the old story, sir,' and who tried to represent the peasants as thieves and drunkards. The administration of the estate, which had so lately been organized along new lines, creaked like unoiled wheels, like home-carpentered furniture made from un-seasoned wood. Nikolay Petrovich did not lose hope but quite often he would sigh and become thoughtful; he felt that with-out money there was little chance of success and he had almost run out of funds. Arkady had spoken the truth: Pavel Petrovich had frequently come to his brother's rescue; more than once, seeing how he was struggling and racking his brains over the problem of how to make ends meet, Pavel Petrovich had slowly walked over to the window and, thrusting his hands into his pockets, had muttered between his teeth '*Mais je puis vous donner de l'argent*,'[1] and had given him money; but on this particular day he had none himself and preferred to withdraw. The petty unpleasantnesses of estate management depressed him; and in addition it always seemed to him that Nikolay Petrovich, in spite of all his zeal and diligence, did not go about his business as he should, although he could not have said where exactly he was at fault. 'My brother is not sufficiently practical,' he would reason to himself, 'he is being cheated.' Nikolay Petrovich, on the other hand, had a high opinion of Pavel Petrovich's practical qualities and always asked his advice. 'I am a weak, soft-hearted man who has lived all his life in the depths of the country,' he used to say, 'and it isn't for nothing that you have lived so much among people; you're a good judge of them, you have an eagle eye.' Pavel Petrovich merely turned away in reply to such words as these, but he did not disillusion his brother.

Having left Nikolay Petrovich in his study, he walked off along the passage which separated the front part of the house from the back and, finding himself opposite a low door, paused for a moment lost in thought, pulled at his moustaches and knocked.

'Who's there? Come in,' called Fenechka's voice.

1 In French in the original.

'It is I,' announced Pavel Petrovich, and opened the door.

Fenechka jumped up from the chair on which she was seated with her child and, handing him over to the maid, who immediately carried him out of the room, hastily tidied her braids.

'Forgive me if I am disturbing you,' began Pavel Petrovich, not looking at her. 'I just wanted to ask you – I believe someone is being sent into town today – ask them to buy me some green tea.'

'Yes, sir,' answered Fenechka. 'How much do you wish to have bought?'

'Oh, half a pound should be enough, I suppose. But I see you have been making changes here,' he added, casting a rapid glance at his surroundings which took in Fenechka's face while appearing to scour the room. 'Those curtains,' he added, seeing that she had not understood him.

'Oh yes, sir, the curtains: Nikolay Petrovich kindly gave them to me; but they've been hung for quite a time now.'

'Yes, and it's quite a time since I've been to see you. It is very pleasant here now.'

'Thanks to the kindness of Nikolay Petrovich,' whispered Fenechka.

'Are you more comfortable here than in the annexe where you were before?' inquired Pavel Petrovich politely but without the shadow of a smile.

'Of course, sir, much more comfortable.'

'Who has been moved into your place?'

'The washerwomen are there now.'

'Ah!'

Pavel Petrovich fell silent. 'Now he will go away,' thought Fenechka, but he did not go away and she remained standing before him as though rooted to the ground, fidgeting feebly with her fingers.

'Why did you have your little boy carried out?' Pavel Petrovich eventually broke the silence. 'I am fond of children: let me see him.'

Fenechka blushed all over from confusion and pleasure. She was afraid of Pavel Petrovich: he hardly ever talked to her.

'Dunyasha,' she called, 'bring Mitya here.' (Fenechka addressed everyone in the house with the polite form 'you', avoiding the familiar 'thou'.) 'Or rather wait a minute, we must put his dress on.'

Fenechka started towards the door.

'That doesn't matter,' remarked Pavel Petrovich.

'I will only be a moment,' answered Fenechka, and hurried out.

Pavel Petrovich was left alone and this time he looked round the room with particular attention. The small low room in which he was standing was very clean and homely. There was a scent of freshly washed floor, daisies and whitewash. Along the walls stood chairs with lyre backs: they had been bought by the late general in Poland during a campaign; in one corner stood a little bed with muslin curtains and beside it an iron-bound chest with a round lid. In the opposite corner a *lampada*[1] was burning before a large dark icon of Nicholas the Miracle-worker; a tiny porcelain Easter egg on a red ribbon hung on the saint's chest, attached to his halo; on the window-sills jars of last year's jam with carefully tied-on lids filtered a green light; on their paper tops Fenechka herself had written 'Goossberry' in large letters. Nikolay Petrovich was particularly fond of this jam. From the ceiling on a long cord hung a cage with a short-tailed greenfinch; he was always fluttering and chirruping and the cage was always rocking and trembling; hemp seeds dropped pattering to the floor. On the wall between the windows, over a small chest of drawers, hung some rather bad photographs of Nikolay Petrovich in various poses taken by some itinerant photographer; there also hung a photograph of Fenechka herself, which was a complete failure; an anonymous, eyeless face smiled self-consciously from the dark frame, and nothing more could be distinguished; but above Fenechka Ermolov[2] in a felt coat frowned threateningly

1 A small candle like a night-light which is set or hung in a glass holder before the icons in Russian homes. Sometimes the candle is replaced by a tiny oil-lamp.
2 A popular Russian general, hero of the campaign of 1812 and later commander-in-chief of the Russian Army in the Caucasus.

at the distant Caucasian heights from beneath a silk pin-cushion in the form of a boot which hung down right over his forehead.

Five minutes passed; in the next room there was a sound of rustling and whispering. Pavel Petrovich picked up a well-thumbed book from the chest of drawers, an odd volume of Masallsky's *Strelitzes*,[1] and turned a few pages. The door opened and in came Fenechka carrying Mitya. She had dressed him in a red shirt with lace on the collar, brushed his hair and wiped his face: he was breathing heavily, wriggling with his whole body and threshing about with his little arms as do all healthy children; but the smart shirt had evidently had its effect on him: his whole plump little figure exuded an aura of satisfaction. Fenechka had tidied her own hair as well and put up her braids more becomingly, but she might just as well have remained as she was. And in very truth is there anything in the world more enchanting than a beautiful young mother with a healthy child in her arms?

'What a chubby little fellow,' said Pavel Petrovich condescendingly, and tickled Mitya's double chin with the tip of the long nail of his index finger; the child caught sight of the greenfinch and burst out laughing.

'That's your uncle,' said Fenechka, bending her face over him and shaking him lightly as Dunyasha quietly stood a lighted candle on a coin on the window-sill in case Pavel Petrovich should wish to smoke.

'How many months did you say he was?' asked Pavel Petrovich.

'Six months; soon it will be seven, on the eighteenth.'

'Are you sure it won't be eight, Feodos'ya Nikolayevna?' Dunyasha broke in, not without timidity.

'No, seven; how could I be mistaken?' The child laughed again, fixed his eyes on the chest and suddenly seized his mother with all five fingers by the nose and mouth. 'Naughty,' said Fenechka, not moving her face away from his fingers.

'He resembles my brother,' remarked Pavel Petrovich.

1 A colourful historical romance in four volumes.

'Who else could he be like?' thought Fenechka.

'Yes,' continued Pavel Petrovich as though speaking to himself. 'A distinct resemblance.' He regarded Fenechka attentively, almost sadly.

'That's your uncle,' she repeated, this time in a whisper.

'Ah, Pavel! So this is where you are!' Nikolay Petrovich's voice rang out suddenly.

Pavel Petrovich spun round frowning; but his brother was surveying him with such pleasure, with such gratitude, that he could not but return his smile.

'You've got a grand little boy here,' he said, and glanced at his watch. 'But I dropped in about some tea....'

And, assuming an expression of indifference, Pavel Petrovich there and then walked out of the room.

'Did he come in of his own accord?' Nikolay Petrovich asked Fenechka.

'Yes; he just knocked and came in.'

'Well, and my Arkady hasn't been to see you again?'

'No. Are you sure that I should not remove to the annexe, Nikolay Petrovich?'

'Why should you?'

'I think that perhaps it might be better just to begin with.'

'N – no,' pronounced Nikolay Petrovich with a slight hesitation, and wiped his forehead. 'We should have thought before. Hallo, bubble!' he exclaimed with sudden animation and, going up to the child, kissed him on the cheek; then he bent a little and pressed his lips to Fenechka's hand, which showed white as milk against Mitya's bright red shirt.

'Nikolay Petrovich! Get along with you, do!' she murmured, and dropped her eyes, then stealthily raised them. Her eyes held the most charming expression when she looked up suspiciously in this fashion and at the same time gave a little laugh, caressing and rather stupid.

Nikolay Petrovich had made Fenechka's acquaintance in the following way. Once, three years ago, he had had to spend the night at the coaching inn of a distant district town. He had been pleasantly surprised by the cleanliness of the room

which was offered to him and by the freshness of the bed
linen. 'I wonder if the landlady is a German?' had been his
first thought; but the landlady turned out to be a Russian,
about fifty years of age, with a respectable, clever face and a
sedate manner of speaking. He got into conversation with her
over tea; she pleased him extremely. At that time Nikolay
Petrovich had only just moved into his new farmstead and,
not wishing to run his home with serf labour, was on the look-
out for hired servants; the landlady, for her part, complained
of the scarcity of custom in that town and of hard times; he
suggested that she should enter his service as housekeeper;
she agreed. Her husband had long since died, leaving her with
one daughter, Fenechka. In two weeks' time Arina Savishna
(so the new housekeeper was called) arrived at Marino
together with her daughter and established herself in the
annexe. Nikolay Petrovich's choice proved a happy one. Arina
brought order into the household. Of Fenechka, who was then
just past seventeen, no one had a word to say, and very few
ever saw her: she lived quietly, modestly, and only on Sundays
did Nikolay Petrovich catch a glimpse of the tender profile
and the whiteness of her face in some unobtrusive corner of
the parish church. So more than a year passed.

One morning Arina appeared in his study and, bowing low
as usual, asked whether he would not help her daughter who
had got a spark from the stove in her eye. Nikolay Petrovich,
like all stay-at-homes, dispensed home cures and had even
laid in a stock of herbs worthy of a small homoeopathic
chemist's. He immediately requested Arina to bring the
patient to him. When she heard that the master has sent for
her Fenechka was very unnerved. However, she followed her
mother. Nikolay Petrovich led her to the window and took
her head in both hands. Having carefully examined the
reddened and swollen eye, he prescribed a bathing lotion
which he made up himself on the spot and, ripping up his
own handkerchief, showed her how to apply it. Fenechka
heard him out and would have taken her leave. 'Kiss the
master's hand, stupid,' Arina said to her. Nikolay Petrovich
would not give her his hand and, thoroughly embarrassed,

kissed her himself on her bent head, on the parting.
Fenechka's eye soon got better, but the impression which she
had made on Nikolay Petrovich did not pass off so soon. He
was haunted all the time by that pure, tender, shyly raised
face; he felt the soft hair under his palms, saw the innocent
slightly parted lips, behind which the pearly teeth shone
moistly in the sun. He began to look at her more attentively
in church, tried to engage her in conversation. At first she
was very shy of him and once, towards evening, seeing him
coming towards her along a narrow path made by people
walking through a ryefield, she stepped off into the high,
close-standing rye, wound about with wormwood and corn-
flowers, just so that he should not see her. He caught sight of
her pretty head behind a golden mesh of ears through which
she was peering like a little animal and called softly to her.

'Good day, Fenechka! I don't bite.'

'Good day,' she answered in a whisper, making no move to
come out of her ambush.

Little by little she grew used to him, but was still shy in his
presence when her mother died suddenly of cholera. What
was to become of Fenechka? She had inherited her mother's
love of order, her discretion and sedate manner; but she was
so young, so lonely; Nikolay Petrovich was himself so kind
and simple. It is hardly necessary to tell the rest. . . .

'And so my brother came to see you just like that?'
Nikolay Petrovich asked her. 'Just knocked on the door and
walked in?'

'Yes.'

'Well, that's very nice. Here, let me have my game with
Mitya.'

And Nikolay Petrovich began throwing him up almost to
the ceiling, to the enormous delight of the baby and the considerable anxiety of his mother, who, each time he flew
upwards, stretched out her hands after his little bare legs.

But Pavel Petrovich returned to his elegant study, the walls
of which were hung with fine wallpaper of an extraordinary
colour, with weapons hanging against the brilliant Persian

carpet, with walnut furniture, with the Renaissance bookcase in old black oak, with bronze statuettes on the magnificent writing-desk, with the open fireplace. He cast himself down on to the sofa, linked his hands behind his head and remained motionless, staring at the ceiling with something like despair. Whether it was that he wished to hide what was taking place on his face from the very walls, or whether for some other reason, he got up, unfastened the heavy window curtain and again cast himself down on the sofa.

IX

THAT same day Bazarov also made the acquaintance of Fenechka. He was walking round the garden with Arkady explaining to him why certain trees, the young oaks in particular, were not doing well.

'They should plant more silver poplars here, and spruce and perhaps limes, digging in some black earth. The arbour over there is doing well,' he added, 'because it's all acacia and lilac – good children who need no attention. Bah! Look, there's somebody there.'

In the arbour was seated Fenechka with Dunyasha and Mitya. Bazarov halted and Arkady nodded to Fenechka as to an old friend.

'Who's that?' asked Bazarov as soon as they had passed by. 'What a pretty girl!'

'Which one are you talking about?'

'You know which: only one of them is pretty.'

Arkady, not without embarrassment, gave him a brief explanation of who Fenechka was.

'Aha!' pronounced Bazarov. 'Your father obviously knows what's good for him. But I like him, your father. He-he! He's a fine fellow. But we must make each other's acquaintance,' he added, and set off back towards the arbour.

'Yevgeny!' Arkady called after him in some trepidation. 'Mind what you say, for heaven's sake.'

'Don't get excited,' said Bazarov. 'We've seen a thing or two, we have: been about the town.'

Approaching Fenechka, he doffed his cap.

'Allow me to introduce myself,' he began with a polite bow. 'A friend of Arkady Nikolayevich's and a peaceable man.'

Fenechka rose from the bench and surveyed him in silence.

'What a splendid child!' continued Bazarov. 'Don't be afraid, I've never ill-wished anyone yet. Why are his cheeks so red? Cutting teeth, is he?'

'Yes, sir,' answered Fenechka. 'He's already cut four teeth and now his gum is all swollen again.'

'Let's have a look – don't be afraid though. I'm a doctor.'

Bazarov lifted up the child, who, to the surprise of Fenechka and Dunyasha, made no resistance and did not take fright.

'I see. I see – that's all right, nothing the matter there: he'll have a mouthful of teeth. If anything happens let me know. And you yourself, are you in good health?'

'I am well, praise be to God.'

'Praise be – that's the most important thing. And you?' added Bazarov, turning to Dunyasha.

For answer Dunyasha, a girl of most forbidding demeanour above stairs and a giggler below, merely snorted at him.

'Well, that's fine. Here is your hero.'

Fenechka received the child into her arms.

'How still he sat with you,' she ventured softly.

'All children sit still with me,' answered Bazarov. 'I have a knack for that sort of thing.'

'Children feel who is fond of them,' remarked Dunyasha.

'That is true,' confirmed Fenechka. 'Our Mitya here wouldn't go to anyone else for anything.'

'And will he come to me?' asked Arkady, who, having stood for some time at a distance, had come up to the arbour.

He tried to lure Mitya to him, but Mitya threw back his head and began to squeal, much to Fenechka's confusion.

'Another time, when he's got used to me,' said Arkady indulgently, and both the friends took themselves off.

'What did you say she was called?' asked Bazarov.

'Fenechka – Feodos'ya,' answered Arkady.

'And her patronymic? One needs to know that too.'

'Nikolayevna.'

'*Bene.*[1] What I like about her is that she doesn't seem too embarrassed. Another might disapprove of that in her. What nonsense! What is there to be embarrassed about? She's a mother – and quite right too!'

'*She* may be quite right,' remarked Arkady, 'but as for my father—'

'He's right too,' interrupted Bazarov.

'Well no, I don't think so.'

'Evidently a superfluous heir is not to our taste?'

'You should be ashamed of yourself to think such a thing of me,' Arkady took him up hotly. 'It's not from that point of view that I consider my father in the wrong; I think that he should have married her.'

'Oh-ho!' pronounced Bazarov calmly. 'How very generous we are, to be sure! You still attach importance to marriage; I didn't expect that of you.'

The friends took several steps in silence.

'I've been round all your father's establishments,' Bazarov began again. 'The cattle are poor and the horses break-downs. The buildings are pretty poor too, and the labourers look like inveterate idlers; and the bailiff is either a fool or a knave – can't quite make him out yet.'

'You're very severe today, Yevgeny Vasil'evich.'

'And the good peasants will most certainly swindle your father. You know the proverb, "A Russian peasant will gobble up God Himself".'

'I am beginning to agree with my uncle,' remarked Arkady; 'you most certainly have a poor opinion of Russians.'

'As if that mattered! The Russian's only good point is that he holds the poorest conceivable opinion of himself. All that matters is that twice times two makes four and everything else is nonsense.'

'Is nature nonsense too?' asked Arkady, gazing thoughtfully away over the colourful fields, softly and beautifully illuminated by a sun which was already low in the sky.

1 In Latin in the original (= 'Good').

'Nature is nonsense too in the way in which you understand it. Nature is not a temple but a workshop, and man is there to work in it.'

At that very moment the lazy notes of a violoncello floated out to them from the house. Someone was playing with feeling, although with unpractised hand, Schubert's 'Expectation', and the sweet melody poured over the air like honey.

'What's that?' demanded Bazarov in amazement.

'That is my father.'

'Your father plays the violoncello?'

'Yes.'

'But how old is your father?'

'Forty-four.'

Bazarov suddenly burst out laughing.

'What are you laughing at?'

'For pity's sake! At forty-four years of age a man, a *pater familias*,[1] in the province of X, plays the violoncello!'

Bazarov continued to laugh heartily but this time Arkady, however much he might revere his mentor, did not even smile.

X

NEARLY two weeks had passed. Life at Marino went on in the usual way; Arkady idled sybaritically, Bazarov worked. Everyone in the house had grown accustomed to him, to his careless manners, to his monosyllabic and abrupt speech. Fenechka in particular had begun to feel so at home with him that once in the night she sent to awaken him: Mitya had had a convulsion; and he came, the same as ever, half joking and half yawning, sat with her for two hours and helped the child. Pavel Petrovich, on the other hand, had conceived for Bazarov an obsessive hatred: he considered him arrogant, impertinent, cynical and plebeian. He suspected that Bazarov held him in scant respect, that he almost despised him – him, Pavel Kirsanov! Nikolay Petrovich stood rather in awe of the young 'nihilist' and was doubtful of the desirability of his influence

1 In Latin in the original.

on Arkady; but he enjoyed listening to him and enjoyed watching his experiments in physics and chemistry. Bazarov had brought a microscope with him and would mess about with it for hours on end. The servants also became attached to him, although he was always chaffing them; they felt that in spite of everything he was one of them, not a gentleman born. Dunyasha was very ready to giggle with him and gave him significant sidelong glances, whisking past him with a darting movement like a quail. Pyotr, a singularly vain and stupid man whose brow was always furrowed by lines of concentration and whose whole merit consisted in looking respectful, in being able to spell out written words and in frequently going over his jacket with a little brush – even he lit up and grinned when Bazarov took any notice of him. The servant lads trailed after the 'doctor' like little dogs. Only the old man Prokof'ich disliked him, served him with food at table with an air of disapproval, called him a 'blood-sucker' and a rogue, and maintained that he and his side-whiskers resembled nothing so much as a boar in a bush. Prokof'ich, in his own way, was quite as much of an aristocrat as Pavel Petrovich.

Came the best days of the year – the first days of June. The weather was set fine; true there were distant rumours of cholera, but the inhabitants of the province of X had already grown accustomed to its visitations. Bazarov rose very early and walked two or three miles, not for the sake of exercise – he could not bear walking without a purpose – but to collect grasses and insects. Sometimes he took Arkady with him. On the way home they usually started an argument from which Arkady, although he talked more than his companion, usually came off worse.

Once they had somehow loitered for longer than usual. Nikolay Petrovich had come out into the garden to meet them and, having walked as far as the arbour, suddenly heard the quick steps and voices of both young men. They were passing by on the other side of the arbour and could not see him.

'You don't know my father well enough,' said Arkady.

Nikolay Petrovich kept a discreet silence.

'Your father's a good fellow,' pronounced Bazarov, 'but he's a retired man – it's time he was off the forest.'

Nikolay Petrovich pricked up his ears. Arkady returned no reply.

The 'retired man' remained standing for a minute or two and slowly drifted back towards the house.

'The other day I saw him reading Pushkin,' Bazarov continued in the meantime. 'I wish you'd explain to him that that will get him nowhere: it's time he gave up such nonsense. And why anyone should want to be a romantic in these days! Give him something worth while to read.'

'What should I give him?' asked Arkady.

'Well, I think Büchner's *Stoff und Kraft* for a beginning.'

'I think so too,' Arkady agreed approvingly. '*Stoff und Kraft* is written for the general reader.'

'And so you and I are just "retired people",' Nikolay Petrovich told his brother that same day after dinner as they were sitting together in his study. 'It's time we were off the forest. What do you make of that? Perhaps Bazarov is right; but I confess it's very painful to me: just as I had hoped to establish a real, close friendship with Arkady it turns out that I have been left behind; he's gone on ahead and we can't understand one another.'

'But why do you say he's gone on ahead? And wherein is he so different from us?' exclaimed Pavel Petrovich impatiently. 'It's that *signor* who has put all these ideas into his head, that nihilist. I detest that wretched little leech; in my opinion he's nothing but a charlatan! I am convinced that for all his frogs he hasn't got very far in physics.'

'No, brother, don't say that: Bazarov is both clever and a good scholar.'

'And he's so disgustingly pleased with himself,' interrupted Pavel Petrovich again.

'Yes,' agreed Nikolay Petrovich, 'he is pleased with himself. Only I suppose that's essential, in a way, but here's what I can't understand. It would seem that I do all I can not to fall behind the times: I've given the peasants land, introduced the farming system,[1] so that I even have a reputation as a Red throughout the province; I read and study and generally make every effort to keep up with modern demands – and they say that it's time I was off the forest. And indeed, brother, I'm beginning to think myself that it really must be true.'

'Why so?'

'This is why. Today I was sitting reading Pushkin – I remember I had opened it at "The Gipsies" – when suddenly up comes Arkady and without a word, but with such a look of affectionate compassion on his face, quietly took the book away from me as though I had been a child and put down another one in front of me, a German one – smiled and went off, and took Pushkin away with him.'

'Really! What was the book he gave you?'

'This one here.'

And Nikolay Petrovich produced from the back pocket of his jacket Büchner's famous brochure, the ninth edition.

Pavel Petrovich turned it about in his hands.

'Hm!' he muttered. 'Arkady Nikolayevich has taken it upon himself to see to your education. Well, have you tried reading it?'

'I've tried.'

'Well, and what came of it?'

'Either I am stupid or the whole thing's nonsense. I suppose I must be stupid.'

'You haven't forgotten your German, have you?' asked Pavel Petrovich.

'I understand German.'

Pavel Petrovich again turned the book about in his hands and glanced doubtfully at his brother. Neither found anything to say.

'Oh, by the way,' began Nikolay Petrovich, obviously wishing to change the subject, 'I had a letter from Kolyazin.'

'From Matvey Il'ich?'

'Yes. He has arrived in X to inspect the province. He's

---

1 The farming system on the English model, using hired hands rather than serf labour.

become a real bigwig now and writes that he would like to see us *en famille* and invites you and me and Arkady to come to town.'

'Will you go?' asked Pavel Petrovich.

'No; and you?'

'I won't go. Much good it will do me to go on a wild-goose chase of forty miles. Mathieu[1] wants to show himself off to us in all his glory, deuce take him! He'll have his fill of provincial sycophancy without our adding our mite. Anyway, what has he to be so proud of – a privy councillor! If I had continued in the service, had gone on in the same idiotic harness, I would be an adjutant-general by now! But then you and I are retired people.'

'Yes, brother; it begins to look as though we should order our coffins and fold our hands on our breasts,' remarked Nikolay Petrovich with a sigh.

'Well, I shan't give up as easily as that,' muttered his brother. 'We'll come to grips yet with this leech; I can see it coming.'

They came to grips on that very day over late evening tea. Pavel Petrovich came down to the drawing-room already prepared for battle, irritable and uncompromising. He was only waiting for a pretext to have at the enemy; but for a long time no such pretext was offered! In the usual course of things Bazarov spoke little in front of 'the poor old Kirsanovs' (so he called the two brothers), and that evening he was feeling out of sorts and drank cup after cup in silence. Pavel Petrovich positively smouldered with impatience; in the end his hopes were fulfilled.

The talk had turned to one of the neighbouring landlords. 'Good-for-nothing, pretentious little aristocrat,' coolly remarked Bazarov, who had met him in Petersburg.

'May I inquire,' began Pavel Petrovich, and his lips quivered, 'whether, according to your lights, the words "good-for-nothing" and "aristocrat" are synonymous?'

'I said "pretentious little aristocrat",' pronounced Bazarov, lazily sipping at his tea.

---

1 In French in the original. Matvey is the Russian version of Matthew.

'Precisely; but I assume that your opinion of aristocrats is the same as your opinion of pretentious aristocrats. I consider it my duty to inform you that I do not share that opinion. I think I am entitled to say that all know me as a man of liberal views and as a lover of progress; but for that very reason I respect aristocrats – the genuine ones. Remember, my good sir' – at these words Bazarov raised his eyes and looked full at Pavel Petrovich – 'remember, my good sir,' he repeated, his tone hardening, 'the English aristocrats. They refuse to cede one jot or tittle of their own rights and therefore they respect the rights of others; they insist on the fulfilment of obligations owed to them and therefore they themselves fulfil their *own* obligations. The aristocracy gave England freedom and now maintains it.'

'We've heard all that many times before,' returned Bazarov, 'but what do you hope to prove by it?'

'By *dat* I hope to prove, my good sir' (Pavel Petrovich purposely pronounced 'that' as 'dat' when he lost his temper, although he knew perfectly well that it was against the rules of literate speech. This odd habit was a reflection of some leftover traditions from the time of Alexander I. At that period men of great consequence, on the rare occasions when they spoke their mother tongue, would affect certain popular local mispronunciations of this kind as if to say: 'We are dyed-in-the-wool Russians, and at the same time we are noblemen who can afford to ignore classroom rules.'), 'by *dat* I hope to prove that without a sense of one's own dignity, without self-respect – and in the aristocrat these feelings are highly developed – there can be no solid foundation to the common – *bien public*[1] – common weal. Personality, my good sir, that is the main thing; the individual personality should be as firm as a rock, for it is the foundation of everything. I, for instance, am perfectly well aware that it pleases you to ridicule my habits, my dress and, finally, the care I lavish upon my person, but all that is the outward expression of my sense of self-respect and sense of duty – yes, indeed, sir, duty! I live in the country, in

1 In French in the original.

the back of beyond, but I do not let myself go, I keep my respect for myself as a human being.'

'But really, Pavel Petrovich,' returned Bazarov, 'you have just said that you respect yourself, yet you sit about with folded hands; in what way does that contribute to the *bien public*? If you did not respect yourself you could still do just that.'

Pavel Petrovich turned pale.

'That is quite another question. I am under absolutely no obligation to explain to you now why I sit with folded hands, as you please to put it. I merely wish to say that aristocratism is a principle, and that in our day only immoral or superficial people can live without principles. I said so to Arkady the day after his arrival, and now I am saying it again to you. Isn't that right, Nikolay?'

Nikolay Petrovich nodded his head.

'Aristocratism, liberalism, progress, principles,' Bazarov was saying meanwhile. 'Just think of it, all these foreign, and quite futile, words! They would be of no use as a gift to the ordinary Russian.'

'Then what would be of use to him in your opinion? Listening to you one might think that we Russians are outside humanity, outside her laws. For pity's sake, the logic of history demands—'

'And what has that logic to do with us? We get along all right without it.'

'And how do you manage that, pray?'

'It's quite simple. You, I hope, have no need of logic in order to put a piece of bread in your mouth when you're hungry. What need have we of such abstractions?'

Pavel Petrovich threw up his hands.

'I fail to understand you after that. You insult the Russian people. I fail to understand how it is possible not to acknowledge rules and principles! What then is the motive force behind your actions?'

'I told you already that we do not acknowledge authorities, Uncle,' broke in Arkady.

'The motive force behind our actions is that which we

recognize to be useful,' pronounced Bazarov. 'At the present time the most useful thing is negation – so we deny—'

'Everything?'

'Everything.'

'How can that be? Not only art, poetry – but also – terrible to say—'

'Everything,' repeated Bazarov with indescribable composure.

Pavel Petrovich gaped at him. This he had not expected, and Arkady actually flushed with pleasure.

'But by your leave,' spoke up Nikolay Petrovich, 'you deny everything, or to put it more precisely you destroy everything; but when all is said and done it is also necessary to construct.'

'That already goes beyond our task. The first thing is to clear the field.'

'The present state of the people makes it necessary,' added Arkady pompously. 'We must bow to that necessity, we have no right to abandon ourselves to the satisfaction of personal egoism.'

This last sentence was evidently not to Bazarov's liking; it smacked of philosophy, that is of romanticism, for Bazarov designated even philosophy as romanticism; but he did not consider it necessary to refute his young pupil.

'No, no!' exclaimed Pavel Petrovich in a sudden outburst. 'I will not believe that you, my fine sirs, really know the Russian people, that you are representatives of their needs, of their aspirations! No, the Russian people is not as you imagine. It is a people who have the deepest reverence for tradition, a patriarchal people who cannot live without faith—'

'I don't deny it,' Bazarov broke in, 'I am even ready to agree that *there* you are right.'

'But if I am right—'

'Then it still doesn't prove anything.'

'Exactly, it doesn't prove anything,' repeated Arkady with the confidence of an experienced chess player who has foreseen an apparently dangerous move on the part of his opponent and has therefore remained quite unruffled.

'What do you mean, "it doesn't prove anything"?' muttered

Pavel Petrovich, quite confounded. 'Then I suppose you will go against your own people?'

'And even if we would?' cried Bazarov. 'The people believe that when there is a clap of thunder it is Elijah the prophet riding about the sky in a chariot. So what? Must I agree with them? And for all that they are Russian, am not I myself a Russian?'

'No! You are not a Russian after all that you have just said. I cannot consider you as a Russian.'

'My father walked behind the plough,' Bazarov replied, arrogant with pride; 'ask any one of your peasants in which of us, in you or in me, he would sooner recognize the compatriot. You don't even know how to talk to him.'

'And you talk to him and despise him at the same time.'

'And why not, if he deserves to be despised? You censure my attitude but how do you know that it has come to me fortuitously, that it isn't called into being by that very popular spirit which you are so hot to champion?'

'How could that be! We have no use for nihilists.'

'Whether or not they are of any use is not for us to decide. After all, you consider yourself not altogether useless.'

'Gentlemen, gentlemen, please let us leave personalities out of it!' exclaimed Nikolay Petrovich, and half rose from his seat.

Pavel Petrovich smiled and, laying his hand on his brother's shoulder, compelled him to sit down again.

'Have no fear,' he pronounced, 'I shall not forget myself; thanks precisely to that feeling of dignity which is an object of such unkind mockery to this worthy – er – worthy doctor. Permit me,' he continued, again addressing Bazarov, 'you perhaps believe that your doctrine is something new? You are quite out there, you know. Materialism, which is what you are preaching, has been in vogue before more than once, and has always been found wanting—'

'Still another foreign word,' interrupted Bazarov. He was beginning to lose his temper, and his face had taken on an unpleasant bronzish colour. 'In the first place we preach nothing. That is not our way.'

'What do you do then?'

'Here is what we do. Before, not so long ago, we said that our civil servants took bribes, that we have neither roads nor trade, nor equitable justice—'

'Why, yes, yes! You are accusers – so it is called, I believe. With many of your accusations I agree myself, but—'

'And then we realized that to talk, and to do nothing but talk, about the evils of our society was not worth the trouble, that that led only to banality and to doctrinairianism; we saw that even our bright boys, our so-called progressive element, and our accusers, were good for nothing; that we were wasting our time on rubbish, airing our opinions on something we called art, on unconscious creation, on parliamentarianism, on legal representation and the devil knows what, when the root of the matter is our daily bread, when we are being choked by the most gross superstition, when all our share companies collapse for the sole reason that there are not enough honest people, when even this same freedom which the Government is striving to bring about[1] will hardly be of any lasting benefit to us because the peasant is only too happy to embezzle his own funds in order to go and drink himself stupid at the inn.'

'So,' interrupted Pavel Petrovich, 'so you have convinced yourselves of all this and have made up your minds to undertake nothing on your own account.'

'And have made up our minds to undertake nothing on our own account,' repeated Bazarov grimly. He had suddenly begun to feel annoyed with himself at having so poured out his heart before this 'gentleman'.

'And just to sit back and to hurl abuse?'

'And to hurl abuse.'

'And that is called nihilism?'

'And that is called nihilism,' again repeated Bazarov, this time with deliberate insolence.

Pavel Petrovich narrowed his eyes slightly.

1 The reference is to the preparations for the Government Bill of 1861 providing for the liberation of the serfs.

'So that's it!' he enunciated in a strangely calm voice. 'Nihilism is a cure for every ill and you are our saviours and heroes. But why then do you abuse all the others, be it only those same accusers? Do you not waste your time talking, just like everyone else?'

'We may have our faults, but that is not one of them,' pronounced Bazarov between his teeth.

'Well, what then? You are putting your ideas into action, are you? Or you're preparing to act?'

Bazarov made no reply. Pavel Petrovich twitched slightly but immediately regained command of himself.

'Hmm! To go into action, to break things up,' he continued; 'but how can you break things up without even knowing why?'

'We break things because we are a force,' remarked Arkady.

Pavel Petrovich glanced at his nephew and smiled ironically.

'Yes, a force – a force which counts no cost,' pronounced Arkady, and drew himself up.

'Unhappy youth!' cried Pavel Petrovich; he was definitely in no condition to contain himself any longer. 'If you would only think just *what* in Russia you were supporting with your banal maxim! No, really, it's enough to put an angel out of patience! A force! There's a force in the barbarian Kalmuk and in the Mongol – but what need have we of it? We value our civilization; yes, good sir, yes! we value its fruits. And do not tell me that its fruits are negligible: the last dauber, *un barbouilleur*,[1] a hack of a pianist who gets fivepence an evening for playing at a dance, even these are of more use than you because they are representatives of civilization and not of brute Mongol force! You imagine yourselves to be progressives and your place is in Kalmuk tents! A force! Well, remember finally, my forceful gentlemen, that there are only four and a half of you in all, and of those who will not permit you to trample underfoot their most sacred beliefs and who will eventually crush you there are millions!'

'If we are to be crushed then that is our deserts,' said

1 In French in the original.

Bazarov. 'However, that's as may be; we are not so few as you think.'

'How is that? Surely, surely you cannot think to gain the sympathy of the whole people?'

'From a penny candle, you know, the whole of Moscow went up in flames,' retorted Bazarov.

'I see, I see! First pride – almost satanic pride – and then cynical mockery. So this, this is the latest craze of youth; this is the doctrine that enslaves the inexperienced hearts of little boys! There, look, one of them is sitting there next to you; why, he almost worships you, just look at him!' (Arkady turned away and frowned.) 'And that infection is already widely spread. I have heard that our artists refuse to set foot in Rome. Raphael is considered a fool, for the simple reason that he is, as they say, an authority; and they themselves are weak and impotent to the point of nausea and their own imagination doesn't stretch beyond "The Maiden at the Fountain",[1] whatever you may say! And the maiden is painted extraordinarily badly. In your opinion they are splendid fellows, am I not right?'

'In my opinion,' corrected Bazarov, 'Raphael is not worth a brass farthing, and they are no better than he is.'

'Bravo! Bravo! Listen, Arkady, that is the way modern young men ought to talk! And how shouldn't they follow you, when you come to think of it. Before, young men had to study; they didn't want to be known for ignoramuses so they had to work, whether they liked it or not. And now all they have to do is to say "Everything in the world is rubbish!" – and it's all in the bag for them. The young men are delighted. And indeed previously they were just ordinary blockheads, whereas now they have suddenly become nihilists.'

1 Pavel Petrovich is probably referring to a picture of this title by the artist Novokovich which appeared in an exhibition in the year 1859. During the late fifties and sixties a new movement began to gather way in Russian art which sought to break with the academical tradition and to find its inspiration and its public among the Russian people. Novokovich was most probably an early pioneer of this didactic and realistic tendency which culminated, in 1869, in the formation of the Society of Ambulants and which was to dominate Russian art until the aesthetic reaction of the late nineties.

'There now, your famous regard for your own dignity has let you down,' remarked Bazarov phlegmatically, whereas Arkady's whole figure appeared to bridle with indignation and his eyes took on an angry sparkle. 'Our argument has gone too far. It would be better, it seems, to put an end to it. And I will be ready to agree with you,' he added, rising from his chair, 'when you are able to show me even one institution in our present way of life which does not call forth the most complete and absolute negation.'

'I can show you millions of such institutions,' exclaimed Pavel Petrovich, 'millions! Why, take the peasants' commune[1] for instance.'

Bazarov's lips curled in a cold sneer.

'Well, as to the commune,' he pronounced, 'you would do better to have a chat with your brother. He, it seems, has now found out by experience what they in fact represent – the commune, the system of mutual guarantees, sobriety and suchlike!'

'The family then, the family as it exists among our peasantry!' cried Pavel Petrovich.

'That question also, I should think, would be better not examined in detail – for your own sake! I suppose you have heard about the fathers-in-law carrying on with their sons' wives. Listen to me, Pavel Petrovich, give yourself two or three days' grace, you'll scarcely hit on anything without pause for thought; go over every walk of life in our society and really think about each one, and meanwhile Arkady and I will—'

'Make a mockery of everything,' Pavel Petrovich took him up.

'No, dissect frogs! Come on, Arkady; goodbye, gentlemen!'

Both friends left the room. The brothers remained alone, and for the first time ventured to look at one another.

---

1 The commune (*obshchina* or *mir*) was a kind of village council, primarily concerned with the distribution of land, which had existed before the introduction of serfdom as a generally accepted system. Some Russian intellectuals, notably Alexander Herzen, idealized it as an example of natural, popular, socialist democracy.

'There,' finally began Pavel Petrovich, 'there's the youth of today for you! There they are – our successors!'

'Our successors,' repeated Nikolay Petrovich with a melancholy sigh. He had sat throughout the argument as though on hot bricks, merely stealing an occasional furtive and painful glance at Arkady. 'You know what I've just remembered, brother? Once I had a quarrel with our mother; she started shouting and wouldn't listen to me. In the end I told her: you, I said, cannot understand me; we, said I, belong to two different generations. She was terribly affronted but I thought, what can one do? The pill is bitter – but it has to be swallowed. So now here is our turn, and our successors can say to us: you, they can say, are not of our generation; swallow the pill.'

'You are really too good-natured and modest,' returned Pavel Petrovich. 'I, on the other hand, am convinced that we have far more right on our side than those young gentlemen, even if we do express our thoughts in a somewhat old-fashioned idiom, *vieilli*,[1] and haven't their degree of insolent self-confidence. And how high and mighty they are, the youth of today. You ask one of them "What wine will you take, red or white?" "I have formed the habit of preferring red!" he answers in a bass voice and with such a solemn face that you might think the whole universe were watching him in that moment.'

'Will you be requiring more tea?' inquired Fenechka, poking her head round the door; she had not dared enter the drawing-room while voices had still been raised in argument.

'No, you may give orders for the samovar to be removed,' answered Nikolay Petrovich, and rose to meet her. Pavel Petrovich wished him a jerky *bonsoir*[1] and retired to his own study.

[1] In French in the original.

XI

HALF an hour later Nikolay Petrovich went out into the garden, to his beloved arbour. His thoughts had taken a melancholy direction. For the first time he had realized fully the degree of estrangement between himself and his son; he foresaw that it would increase day by day. In vain had he tried to listen to the young men's talk; in vain had he been glad of every opportunity to put in a word of his own amid their seething declamations. 'My brother says that we are right,' he thought, 'and, putting all vanity aside, it seems to me, too, that they are farther from the truth than we are; yet at the same time I feel that they have something on their side, something which we lack, some advantage over us. Youth? No! Not youth only. Could their superiority be that they bear fewer of the characteristics of the ruling classes than we do?'

Nikolay Petrovich bent his head and wiped his hand across his face.

'But to renounce poetry?' he thought again. 'To have no feeling for art, for nature?' And he gazed around him as though seeking to understand how it was possible to have no feeling for nature.

Evening was already falling; the sun was hidden behind a small grove of aspens which lay about a quarter of a mile from the garden, its shadow stretching endlessly over the still fields. A peasant on a white pony was jogging along the dark, narrow path which skirted the grove; his whole figure was clearly visible, right down to the patch on his shoulder, even though he rode in the shadow. The pony's legs twinkled with a pleasing distinctness. The sun's rays, for their part, shone through the grove and, penetrating even the thickest part, inundated the aspen stems with such a warm light that they began to resemble the trunks of pine-trees, while their foliage appeared almost blue, and above them rose the pale, pale blue sky, scarcely flushed by the sunset. The swallows were flying high; the wind had died completely; belated bees were buzzing lazily and sleepily in the lilac blossom; midges had swarmed together in a cloud above one lonely, far-protruding bough.

'My God, how lovely!' thought Nikolay Petrovich, and some favourite lines of verse came to his lips; then he remembered Arkady, *Stoff und Kraft*, and fell silent, but sat on and continued to abandon himself to the melancholy and delightful play of solitary thoughts. He loved to day-dream; life in the country had developed this capacity in him. Not so long ago he had been dreaming in just such a fashion as he awaited his son at the coaching inn, but since then things had changed; their relationship, then so hazy, had taken definite form – and what a form! The image of his late wife came again into his mind, not as he had known her over the course of many years, not as a kind, domesticated chatelaine, but as a young girl with a slender figure, an innocent yet searching gaze and a plait tightly knotted above a childlike neck. He remembered how he had seen her for the first time. He had been still a student then. They had first met on the staircase of the apartment house where he lived, when he had bumped into her by mistake and, turning, would have apologized but could only mutter '*Pardon, monsieur!*'[1] She had inclined her head and smiled mockingly, but suddenly seemed to take fright and ran on, yet looked back at him again from the turn of the stairs, becoming suddenly serious and blushing. And then the first shy visits, half-words, half-smiles and bewilderment, and sadness, and sudden outbursts, and finally that breathless joy.... Whither was all that sped? She had become his wife, he had been happy, like few other men on this earth. 'But,' he thought, 'those first sweet moments, why can we not live in them – an eternal and immortal life?'

He did not try to analyse his own thoughts, but he felt that he wanted to recapture that blissful time by means more potent than memory; he wanted to see again the nearness of his Mariya, to feel her warmth and her breathing, and already it seemed to him as though above him ...

1 In French in the original.

'Nikolay Petrovich,' Fenechka's voice sounded close by him, 'where are you?'

He started. He felt neither grieved nor conscience-stricken. . . . He did not admit even the possibility of comparison between his wife and Fenechka, but he was sorry that she had thought of coming to seek him out. Her voice immediately reminded him of his grey hairs, his age, his present. . . .

The enchanted world into which he had already stepped, which had already risen up from the misty waves of the past, quivered – and vanished.

'I'm here,' he answered. 'I'm coming, you go on in.'

'There they are, the characteristics of the ruling classes,' flashed through his head. Without a word Fenechka looked into the arbour where he sat and passed on out of sight, and he noticed with astonishment that since he had first begun to dream night had fallen. Everything had grown dark and silent round about and Fenechka's face had glimmered briefly before him, very pale and small. He half rose with the intention of going back into the house; but his mellowed heart could not settle down in his breast and he began to walk slowly about the garden, now gazing thoughtfully at the ground beneath his feet, now raising his eyes to the heavens where the first stars had already woken and were winking one to the other. He walked long, almost to the point of weariness, and a sense of foreboding within him, a kind of searching, ill-defined, despondent foreboding, still would not leave him. Oh! how Bazarov would have laughed at him had he known what was going on in his mind. Arkady himself would have disapproved of him. He, a man of forty summers, an agriculturist and a landlord, walked with tears in his eyes, causeless tears; this was a hundred times worse than the violoncello.

Nikolay Petrovich went on walking and could not make up his mind to go into the house, into that peaceful and homely nest which appeared to be looking out at him so hospitably from all its lighted windows; he could not bring himself to part with the darkness, the garden, the sense of fresh air on his face, and with this feeling of sadness, with this foreboding.

At a turn in the path he came upon Pavel Petrovich.

'What's the matter with you?' he asked Nikolay Petrovich. 'You are as white as a ghost; you're not well, why aren't you in bed?'

Nikolay Petrovich explained his state of mind to him in a few short words and went on his way. Pavel Petrovich walked on to the end of the garden and he too became lost in thought and he too raised his eyes to the heavens. But in his fine dark eyes nothing was reflected but the starlight. He was no born romantic and his dryly fastidious and passionate soul, misanthropic in the French tradition, did not know how to dream.

'Do you know what?' Bazarov was saying that same night to Arkady. 'I've had a magnificent idea. Your father was saying today that he had received an invitation from this important relative of yours. Your father won't go; what about you and I slipping over to X? After all, the gentleman invited you too. You see how the weather's set in here; but you and I will go for a ride and take a look round the town. We can mess about for five or six days and *basta*!'[1]

'And from there would you return here?'

'No, I must go and see my father. You know he is twenty-five miles from X. I haven't seen him for a long time, nor my mother either; one must cheer up the old 'uns. They're good people, my parents, especially my father – he's priceless. I'm the only one they've got.'

'And will you stay long with them?'

'I shouldn't think so, I expect it will be boring.'

'And will you drop in on us on the way back?'

'Don't know – I'll see. Well, what about it! Shall we go?'

'I should think so,' remarked Arkady languidly. In his heart of hearts he was really delighted with Bazarov's suggestion, but considered it his duty to conceal his feelings. Not for nothing was he a nihilist!

The next day he and Bazarov set off for X. The young people at Marino regretted their departure; Dunyasha even shed a few tears; but their elders breathed more freely.

1 In Italian in the original.

XII

THE town of X, whither our friends were bound, was admin-
istered by a governor of the younger generation, a progressive
and a despot, a combination often to be met with in Russia.
In the course of the first year of his administration he had
succeeded in quarrelling not only with the provincial Marshal
of the Nobility, a retired captain of the guards, second grade,
a horse-breeder with large ideas of hospitality, but also with
his own officials. The strife which arose as a result of this
eventually took on such proportions that the ministry in
Petersburg found it politic to dispatch a delegate with orders
to sort things out on the spot. The choice of the administration fell on Matvey Il'ich Kolyazin, the son of that Kolyazin
whose protection had sometime been enjoyed by the brothers
Kirsanov. He was also one of the 'younger generation', that is
he was not long since turned forty, but he already had his eye
on governmental status and sported a star on either side of his
chest. One, it is true, was a foreign order of no particular
merit. Like the governor whom he had come to judge he
was considered a progressive and he was already a person of
consequence, although he did not resemble the majority of
the breed. He had the highest opinion of himself; his vanity
knew no bounds; but he bore himself simply, cultivated a
benevolent expression, was an indulgent listener and laughed
with such good humour that on first acquaintance it was even
possible to take him for a 'splendid fellow'. At the right
moment, however, he was able, as the expression goes, 'to lay
it on thick'. 'Energy is indispensable,' he would say at such
times. '*L'énergie est la première qualité d'un homme d'état.*'[1] But
for all that he was habitually imposed upon and any more or
less experienced civil servant could twist him round his little
finger. Matvey Il'ich spoke with the greatest admiration of
Giseau and did his best to impress on all and sundry that he
was not to be numbered among the rigid upholders of routine
and the retrograde bureaucrats, that there was no significant

[1] In French in the original.

phenomenon of public life which did not command his attention. All such phrases came most readily to his tongue. He even attended, albeit with a certain negligent stateliness, to the development of modern literature; thus a grown man, meeting a procession of boys in the street, may sometimes join it for a while. In fact, Matvey Il'ich had not progressed far beyond those statesmen of Alexander's day[1] who in preparation for an evening spent at the *salon* of Madame Svechina,[2] then resident in Petersburg, would set themselves to read a page of Condillac every morning; only his manner was different, more modern. He was an accomplished courtier, a great schemer, and nothing more. He had neither brain nor sound judgment in matters of business, but he did know how to manage his own affairs; here no one could twist him round their finger, and that, after all, is the main thing.

Matvey Il'ich received Arkady with the good nature – nay, more, with the playfulness – peculiar to the enlightened statesman. He was, however, amazed when he heard that the relatives whom he had invited had remained behind in the country.

'Your papa always was an eccentric,' he remarked, playing with the tassels of his magnificent velvet dressing-gown, and, suddenly swinging round with a preoccupied air to a young civil servant in the most respectably buttoned-up uniform, barked 'What?'

The young man, who had been sitting silent for so long that his lips had stuck together, half rose and stared at his superior in astonishment. However, having thus reduced his subordinate to a state of complete bewilderment, Matvey Il'ich paid no further heed to him. In general our statesmen enjoy bewildering their subordinates, and the methods which they employ to attain this end are sufficiently varied. The following method is, incidentally, very widely applied – 'is quite a favourite',[3] as the English say. The statesman suddenly

1 Alexander I (1801–25).
2 A lady famous for her *salon* and for her writings on mystic subjects.
3 In English in the original.

ceases to grasp the meaning of the most simple words, affects to be deaf. He asks, for instance, what day it is today.

He is answered with the utmost politeness. 'It is Friday today. Your H–h–h–ness.'

'Eh? What? What's that? What did you say?' repeats the statesman with strained attention.

'Today is Friday, Your H–h–ness.'

'How's that? What? What do you mean, Friday? What Friday?'

'Friday, Your H–hhh–hhh–ness, is a day of the week.'

'So–ho, you really think I need to be told that, do you?'

Matvey Il'ich was after all a statesman, even though he was considered a liberal.

'My advice to you, my friend, is to go and call on the governor,' he said to Arkady. 'You understand, I am not advising this because I hold the old-fashioned view that it is essential to go and pay homage to the powers that be, but simply because the governor is a very good sort of fellow; and then most probably you would like to make the acquaintance of society here – after all, you're not a bear, I hope? And the day after tomorrow he is giving a large ball.'

'Will you be at this ball?' asked Arkady.

'He is giving it for me,' pronounced Matvey Il'ich, almost with regret. 'Do you dance?'

'I do, only badly.'

'How deplorable. There are pretty girls here, and anyway a young man should be ashamed not to dance. Again I do not say that from old-fashioned prejudice, I by no means assume that a man's mind is in his legs, but Byronism is ludicrous, *il a fait son temps*.'[1]

'But, dear Uncle, it's nothing to do with Byronism nor—'

'I will introduce you to the local young ladies, I will take you under my wing,' interrupted Matvey Il'ich, and chuckled complacently. 'You will be comfortable there, uh?'

A servant entered and announced the arrival of the chairman of the Commission on Crown Lands, a gentle-eyed old

1 In French in the original.

man with wrinkled lips who was a great admirer of nature, especially of a summer's day, when, in his own words, 'every little bee takes sweet bribes from every little flower'. Arkady took his leave.

He found Bazarov in the inn where they were staying and set himself to persuade him to visit the governor.

'Since there's no way out of it!' said Bazarov at last. 'It's no good turning back half way! We came to have a look at the landlords, so let's go and have a look at them!'

The governor received the young men affably but neither invited them to be seated nor sat down himself. He was always bustling and hurrying, wore a closely fitting uniform and an extremely tight tie from the moment he first rose in the morning, never finished anything he was eating or drinking and never stopped giving orders. In the province he was nicknamed Bourdalou, not from the famous French preacher but from the Russian word *burdà*, meaning 'wishy-washy'. He invited Kirsanov and Bazarov to his ball and two minutes later repeated the invitation, this time addressing them as the brothers Kaysarov.

They were making their way back to the inn on foot when suddenly from a passing cab there jumped out a rather short man in a Slavophile[1] frogged jacket, who with a cry of 'Yevgeny Vasil'evich!' came rushing up to Bazarov.

'Oh, it's you Herr Sitnikov,' remarked Bazarov, continuing to stride along the pavement. 'How do you come to be here?'

'Just imagine, quite by chance,' answered the other and, turning to the cab, waved his hand five or six times and shouted: 'Follow along after us, follow along! My father has business here,' he continued, jumping over the gutter, 'and, well, since he asked me ... I got to hear about your arrival today and have already been to call on you.' (Indeed, when the friends returned to their room they found a dog-eared visiting-card inscribed with the name Sitnikov, in French on

---

1 The Slavophiles were a section of the Russian intelligentsia who held that the salvation of Russia would be brought about by a return to all that was best in the purely national traditions of the past.

one side and on the other in Slavonic script.) 'I hope you are not coming from the governor's!'

'Then don't hope, we've just left him.'

'Ah! In that case I shall call on him as well. Yevgeny Vasil'evich, introduce me to your – to this . . .'

'Sitnikov – Kirsanov,' muttered Bazarov grudgingly, not pausing in his stride.

'Such an honour,' began Sitnikov, edging sideways, smirking and hurriedly dragging off his too elegant gloves. 'I have heard so much – I am an old acquaintance of Yevgeny Vasil'evich's and, I may say, his pupil. I owe to him the beginning of an entirely new life. . . .'

Arkady looked at Bazarov's pupil. The small but pleasant features of his smooth face wore an expression at once anxious and obtuse; the small eyes, which looked as though they had been squashed into his head, looked out fixedly and apprehensively and his laugh too was apprehensive: a brief, wooden laugh.

'Would you believe it,' he went on, 'the first time that Yevgeny Vasil'evich said in my hearing that it is wrong to recognize authorities I felt such enthusiasm – as though I had suddenly seen a great light! "There," I thought, "at last I have found the man!" By the way, Yevgeny Vasil'evich, you must come and call on a lady who lives here, who will be perfectly able to understand you and for whom your visit will be a real treat; you, I think, have probably heard of her?'

'Who is she?' Bazarov inquired grudgingly.

'Kukshina, Eudoxie[1] – Yevdoksiya Kukshina. She is a remarkable character, *émancipée*[1] in the true sense of the word, a progressive woman. Do you know what? Let's all go to call on her now, together. She lives just near here. We'll have luncheon there. You haven't eaten yet, have you?'

'Not yet.'

'Well, that's settled then. She is separated from her husband, you understand, and is quite independent.'

'Is she pretty?' interrupted Bazarov.

1 In French in the original.

'N – no, you couldn't say that.'

'Well, why the devil do you want us to go and see her then?'

'Oh, naughty, naughty! She will stand us a bottle of champagne.'

'So that's how it is! There speaks the practical man. Incidentally, is your old man still farming?'[1]

'Still farming,' confirmed Sitnikov impatiently, and gave a shrill laugh. 'Well? Does it appeal to you?'

'I don't know what to say really.'

'You wanted to see people, you'd better go,' remarked Arkady in a low voice.

'And what about you then, Mr Kirsanov?' Sitnikov took him up. 'Do us the pleasure of joining us. We can't go without you.'

'But how can we all descend on her at once?'

'It won't matter. Kukshina is a wonderful person.'

'And there'll be a bottle of champagne?' inquired Bazarov.

'Three!' exclaimed Sitnikov. 'I will answer for that!'

'With what?'

'My head.'

'Better with your father's purse! However, let's go.'

XIII

The small house, of the type of town residence favoured by the Moscow nobility, in which lived Avdot'ya Nikitishna (or Yevdoksiya) Kukshina, was situated in one of the streets of the town of X but lately destroyed by fire; it is a well-known fact that our provincial towns burn every five years or so. A visiting-card had been nailed somewhat askew beside the door and above this hung the bell-pull.

In the entrance hall the friends were met by a personage of indeterminate station, not quite a maid and not quite a companion, wearing an indoor cap: indisputable evidence of the progressive tendencies of the lady of the house.

1 Sitnikov's father 'farmed' the Crown monopoly on the sale of spirits.

Sitnikov asked whether Avdot'ya Nikitishna were at home.

'Is that you, Victor?' a thin voice sounded from the next room. 'Come in.'

The woman in the cap promptly effaced herself.

'I'm not alone,' announced Sitnikov, dashingly throwing off his coat, under which was disclosed a long-waisted garment in the nature of a 'sack coat', and casting a knowing look at Arkady and Bazarov.

'It doesn't matter,' replied the voice. '*Entrez!*' [1]

The young people went in. The room in which they found themselves was more like a study than a drawing-room. Papers, letters, volumnous numbers of Russian periodicals, many of which had not yet been cut, were scattered over the dusty tables; everywhere were scattered white cigarette ends.

On the leather sofa a lady was half reclining, still young, blonde and slightly dishevelled. She wore a silk dress, not altogether clean, large bracelets on her short arms and a lace kerchief on her head. She rose from the sofa and, carelessly pulling about her shoulders a velvet stole trimmed with yellowing ermine, drawled languidly: 'How do you do, Victor,' and shook Sitnikov's hand.

'Bazarov, Kirsanov,' he pronounced abruptly, in imitation of Bazarov.

'You are very welcome,' answered Kukshina, and, fixing Bazarov with her round eyes, between which her tiny snub nose shone red and childishly pathetic, she added: 'I know you,' and extended her hand to him also.

Bazarov frowned. In the small and unsightly figure of the emancipated woman there was nothing exactly repulsive; yet the expression of her face had an unpleasant effect on the beholder. Involuntarily you wanted to ask her: 'What's the matter, are you hungry? Or bored? Or shy? Why are you so strung up?'

She, like Sitnikov, appeared always to have something grating on her soul. She spoke and moved in an extremely free-and-easy manner which was yet at the same time constrained:

1 In French in the original.

it was obvious that she considered herself to be a good-natured and simple being yet, in spite of this, it constantly kept occurring to you that everything she undertook was just exactly what she had not meant to do; it turned out as children say 'like on purpose', that is, not simply, not naturally.

'Yes, yes! I know you, Bazarov,' she repeated. Like many provincial and Muscovite ladies she had the habit of addressing men by their surname from the first day of her acquaintance with them. 'Have a cigar?'

'A cigar's all very well,' Sitnikov, who had already flung himself into an armchair and put up his feet, took her up, 'but better give us some lunch, we're terribly hungry; and order a bottle of champagne for us.'

'Sybarite,' remarked Yevdoksiya, and laughed. (When she laughed you could see the upper gum over her teeth.) 'It's true, isn't it, Bazarov, he's a sybarite?'

'I like the comforts of life,' pronounced Sitnikov portentously. 'That does not prevent my being a liberal.'

'No! It does prevent you, it does!' cried Yevdoksiya, but nevertheless she ordered her servant to make arrangements both for the luncheon and for the champagne. 'What do you think?' she added, turning to Bazarov. 'I am sure that you must be of my opinion.'

'Well, no!' objected Bazarov. 'A slice of meat is better than a slice of bread, even from the chemical point of view.'

'And are you interested in chemistry? It is my passion. I have even invented a new kind of mastic.'

'Mastic? You?'

'Yes, I! And do you know what for? To make dolls, their heads, so that they won't break. You see I am practical too. But all that isn't ready yet. I have still to read Liebig; by the way, have you read Kislyakov's article on women's work in the *Moscow News*? Do read it! You are interested in the feminist movement, surely? And in schools too? What does your friend do? What is his name?'

Madame Kukshina let fall her questions one after the other with a pampered capriciousness, not waiting for answers; spoilt children take this tone with their nannies.

'I am called Arkady Nikolayevich Kirsanov,' stated Arkady, 'and I don't do anything.'

Yevdoksiya burst out laughing.

'But how charming! Why aren't you smoking? Victor, you know I am angry with you.'

'What for?'

'I have been told that you have begun to enthuse over George Sand again. She has fallen behind the times and there's no more to be said! How could you compare her to Emerson! She has no idea either of education or of physiology or of anything. I'm sure she never even heard of embryology and in our times what can you expect without that?' Yevdoksiya even flung out her hands. 'Oh, what a remarkable article Elisevich wrote about that! What a genius that gentleman is!' Yevdoksiya was always using the word 'gentleman' instead of 'man'. 'Bazarov, sit down beside me on the sofa. Perhaps you don't know it but I'm terribly afraid of you.'

'And why is that, if I may ask?'

'You are a dangerous gentleman; you're such a critic. Oh, good heavens! how funny it sounds – here am I talking like some female landowner from the Steppes. Not but what I really am a landowner. I administer the estate myself and, just imagine, the village elder Yerofey is the most *remarkable* man, just like Cooper's Pathfinder: there's something so ingenuous about him! I have finally settled in here; an unbearable town, isn't it? But what can one do!'

'It's much like any other town,' Bazarov commented phlegmatically.

'But always such petty interests, that is the dreadful thing! Before I used to live in Moscow in the winter – but now the house is occupied by my lord and master, Monsieur Kukshin. And then even Moscow nowadays – I really don't know – it isn't what it used to be. I am thinking of going abroad; and last year I really did very nearly go.'

'To Paris, of course?' asked Bazarov.

'To Paris and to Heidelberg.'

'Why to Heidelberg?'

'Good gracious, that's where Bunsen lives!'

To this Bazarov found nothing to reply.

'Pierre Sapozhnikov – do you know him?'

'No, I don't.'

'Good gracious, Pierre Sapozhnikov – he still visits Lidiya Khostatova regularly.'

'I don't know her either.'

'Well, he offered to go with me. Thank heaven I'm free, I have no children. Now why did I say *thank heaven*! Not that it matters.'

Yevdoksiya rolled a cigarette between her tobacco-stained fingers, drew her tongue along it, sucked at it and lit it. The maid came in carrying a tray.

'And here is luncheon! Would you like something before-hand? Victor, open the bottle! That's in your department.'

'Yes, yes – in my department,' murmured Sitnikov, and burst again into a shrill laugh.

'Are there any pretty women here?' inquired Bazarov, drinking off his third glass.

'Oh yes!' answered Yevdoksiya. 'But they are all so empty-headed. For example, *mon amie*[1] Odintsova is not bad-looking. A pity that her reputation is somewhat . . . Not that that would matter, but she has no freedom of outlook, no breadth, none of – all that. The whole system of upbringing ought to be changed. I have already given it some thought; our women are very badly brought up.'

'There's nothing to be done about them,' Sitnikov took her up. 'They are to be despised, and I despise them completely and utterly!' (The opportunity to despise and to express his contempt was one of the most agreeable feelings known to Sitnikov; he was particularly virulent against women, all unsuspecting that in a few months' time he would be fawning on his own wife for no better reason than that she was born a Princess Durdoleosova.) 'Not one of them would be capable of understanding our conversation; not one of them is worthy that we, serious men, should discuss her.'

1 In French in the original.

'But it's not necessary that they should understand our conversation,' pronounced Bazarov.

'Who are you talking about?' interjected Yevdoksiya.

'About pretty women.'

'How is this! Can it be that you share the opinion of Prud'hon?'

Bazarov drew himself up.

'I share no one's opinions. I have my own.'

'Down with authorities!' cried Sitnikov, delighted by this opportunity to express himself forcibly in the presence of a man who was for him a very idol.

'But Macaulay himself—' began Kukshina.

'Down with Macaulay!' thundered Sitnikov. 'You stand up for that crew of women?'

'Not for the women, but for female rights, which I have sworn to defend to the last drop of blood.'

'Down with them!' But here Sitnikov pulled himself up. 'However, I don't deny them,' he pronounced.

'No, I see that you are a Slavophile!'

'No, I am not a Slavophile, though of course—'

'No, no, no! You are a Slavophile – an adherent of *Domostroy*.[1] You only need a lash in your hands!'

'The lash is not such a bad thing,' observed Bazarov, 'only now we've got down to the last drop—'

'What of?' interrupted Yevdoksiya.

'Champagne, most worthy Avdot'ya[2] Nikitishna, champagne – not your blood.'

'I cannot listen calmly when women are criticized,' continued Yevdoksiya. 'It is terrible, terrible! Instead of criticizing them you would do much better to read Michelet's book

1 A medieval Russian treatise on household and family management which in the nineteenth century was taken to symbolize the view that a man's wife and children are little more than his chattels. In fact the treatise, written by a priest, teaches a stern but benevolent patriarchal approach to the family and, far from advocating wife-beating, as is still popularly supposed, actually exhorts the husband never to strike his wife in the presence of other members of his household.

2 Avdot'ya: Bazarov deliberately substitutes the common Russian variant of the somewhat *recherché* name Yevdoksiya.

De l'Amour. It's wonderful! Gentlemen, let us talk about love,'
Yevdoksiya added, allowing her arm to rest languidly on the
crumpled sofa cushion.

A sudden silence fell.

'No! Why should we talk about love?' said Bazarov. 'But
you were saying about Odintsova – that's what you called her,
isn't it? Who is the lady?'

'Charming, charming!' squeaked Sitnikov. 'I will introduce
you. So clever, so rich – and a widow! Unfortunately she is not
yet sufficiently progressive: she ought to see more of Yevdoksiya here. Your health, Eudoxie! Come and clink glasses! "Et
toc, et toc, et tin-tin-tin! Et toc, et toc, et tin-tin-tin." '

'Victor, you are naughty!'

The luncheon went on for a long time. After the first bottle
of champagne came another, a third and even a fourth.
Yevdoksiya chattered without a pause; Sitnikov played second
fiddle to her. They talked a lot about marriage – whether it be
a prejudice or a crime. And about heredity – whether people
are all born alike or not. And what exactly goes to make up
personality.

In the end Yevdoksiya, all flushed from the wine which she
had drunk and banging the keys of the piano with her flat
nails, started to sing in a husky voice, first a gipsy song and
then Seymour Schiff's romance 'Sleepy Granada Dozes',
while Sitnikov bound a scarf round his head and gave an
impersonation of the swooning lover on the words:

> And in a passionate kiss
> My lips with thine I'll join.

Finally Arkady could bear it no longer.

'Gentlemen! This is beginning to resemble a madhouse,'
he remarked aloud.

Bazarov, who had contented himself with interjecting an
occasional ironic word into the conversation – he had rather
concentrated on the champagne – yawned loudly, rose to his
feet and, omitting to take leave of his hostess, walked out,
together with Arkady. Sitnikov came bouncing after them.

'Well, how was it? How was it?' he asked, making little

darts now to the left, now to the right, in his eagerness to
please. 'You see, I told you: a remarkable person! If only more
women were like that! In her own way she is a highly moral
phenomenon.'

'And that institution of your father's is also a moral phenomenon, I suppose, Victor my boy?' inquired Bazarov, poking his finger in the direction of an inn which they happened
to be passing at that moment.

Sitnikov again went off into a squeal of laughter. He was
very ashamed of his origin and did not know whether to feel
flattered or insulted by Bazarov's unexpected familiarity.

XIV

THE ball at the governor's took place a few days later. Matvey
Il'ich was the true hero of the hour. The Marshal of the
Nobility informed all and sundry that he had consented to
come out of respect for him; the governor, even during the
ball, even when remaining outwardly motionless, continued
to make arrangements. The kindliness of Matvey Il'ich's
manner was only matched by his stateliness. He was pleasant
to all – to some with an inflection of repulsion, to others
with an inflection of respect; he overwhelmed the ladies with
compliments, *en vrai chevalier français*,[1] and laughed continually – a big resounding, monotonous laugh, most suitable to a
statesman. He clapped Arkady on the back and hailed him
loudly as 'nephew'; honoured Bazarov, who was wearing a
rather old tailcoat, with an absent-minded but condescending
look which somehow slipped past his eyes to focus on his
cheek, and an incoherent but affable bleat in which the only
distinguishable words were 'I . . .' and ' 'sstremely'; to Sitnikov he offered one finger and a smile, but his gaze was already
directed elsewhere; even to Kukshina, making her appearance
at the ball without so much as the suggestion of a crinoline
and wearing dirty gloves, but with a bird of paradise in her
hair – even to Kukshina he expressed himself *enchanté*.[1]

1 In French in the original.

There was a great crush of people and no shortage of gentlemen. The civilians tended to crowd together round the walls, but the military danced with enthusiasm, more particularly one of their number who had spent six weeks in Paris, where he had picked up several dashing expressions such as '*Zut!*' '*Ah, fichtrrre*', '*Pst, pst, mon bibi*', etc.[1] He pronounced them perfectly, with real Parisian chic, yet at the same time said '*si j'aurais*' instead of '*si j'avais*', '*absolument*'[1] when he meant 'certainly' and, in a word, spoke that Russo-French dialect of which the French themselves make such fun when they wish to make any of us believe that we speak their language like angels, '*comme des anges*'.[1]

Arkady, as we already know, was a poor dancer, and Bazarov did not dance at all. They both installed themselves in a quiet corner, where they were joined by Sitnikov. Assuming an expression of contemptuous mockery and letting fall various barbed comments, he stared boldly about him and, it seemed, was thoroughly enjoying himself. Suddenly his face changed, and turning to Arkady he said almost shyly:

'Odintsova has come.'

Arkady looked round and saw a tall woman in a black dress hesitating in the doorway of the ballroom. He was struck immediately by the dignity of her bearing. Her bare arms lay gracefully against her slender sides; delicate sprays of fuchsia fell gracefully from her shining hair on to her sloping shoulders; tranquilly and discerningly, really tranquilly and not thoughtfully, her clear eyes looked out from under a white, slightly protuberant forehead and her lips smiled a scarcely definable smile. Her face radiated a force of character which was somehow wholly gentle and tender.

'Are you acquainted with her?' Arkady asked Sitnikov.

'Intimately; shall I introduce you?'

'All right. After this quadrille.'

Bazarov had also noticed Odintsova.

'Who might that be over there?' he remarked. 'She's not like the other females.'

---

1 In French in the original.

Having waited till the end of the quadrille Sitnikov led Arkady over to Odintsova; but he had hardly any acquaintance with her and got himself so tangled up in his own phrases that she looked at him in some astonishment. However, her face took on a cordial expression when she heard Arkady's surname. She asked him whether he were not the son of Nikolay Petrovich.

'Yes, ma'am.'

'I have seen your papa twice and heard much about him,' she continued. 'I am very happy to meet you.'

At that moment some adjutant came flying up to her and invited her to stand up for the quadrille. She accepted.

'Do you dance then?' asked Arkady respectfully.

'I do. But why should you think I don't dance? Or do I seem too old to you?'

'Good heavens, how can you. . . ? But in that case may I ask you for the mazurka?'

Odintsova permitted herself a tolerant smile.

'If you wish,' she said, and looked at Arkady not precisely with condescension but in the way that married sisters look at their youthful brothers.

Odintsova was only a little older than Arkady, she was entering her twenty-ninth year yet, in her presence, he felt himself a schoolboy, a scruffy student, just as though the difference in their ages had been much greater.

Matvey Il'ich descended on her with a stately mien and flattering speeches. Arkady yielded his place at her side but continued to observe her: he never took his eyes off her throughout the quadrille. She talked to her partner just as naturally as she had to the statesman, quietly tilting her face and raising her eyes, and once or twice she laughed quietly. Her nose was a little broad, as with almost all Russians, and her complexion was not quite perfect; even so Arkady decided that he had never before met so enchanting a woman. The sound of her voice still rang in his ears; even the folds of her dress seem to fall differently on her than on others, more harmoniously and fully, and her movements were peculiarly smooth and flowing yet entirely natural.

Arkady felt in his heart a certain timidity when at the first sounds of the mazurka he seated himself beside his lady and, with every intention of engaging her in conversation, merely sat running his hand through his hair without finding a word to say.

But he did not remain shy or nervous for long; Odintsova's calm communicated itself to him: not a quarter of an hour had passed before he was already telling her quite freely all about his father, his uncle, his life in Petersburg and in the country. Odintsova listened to him with polite sympathy, slightly opening and shutting her fan. His chatter broke off only when she was claimed by other partners; Sitnikov, incidentally, asked her to dance twice. She would return, sit down again, take up her fan, even her breath seeming to come no faster, and Arkady would take up his chatter anew, wholly immersed in the happiness of being near her, of talking to her, of looking into her eyes, at her beautiful forehead, into her whole sweet, dignified and intelligent face. She herself said little, but her words told of experience; from some of her remarks Arkady concluded that this young woman had already been through much, both mentally and emotionally.

'Who was that you were standing with,' she asked him, 'when Mr Sitnikov brought you over to me?'

'And so you noticed him?' asked Arkady in his turn. 'He has a fine face, hasn't he? It's a fellow called Bazarov, a friend mine.'

Arkady began to talk about this 'friend of his'. He spoke of him in such detail and with such enthusiasm that Odintsova turned towards him and looked at him with interest.

Meanwhile the mazurka was coming to an end. Arkady was loath to part with his lady, so happily had he passed nearly an hour in her company. True, all this time he had felt as though she were condescending towards him, as though he ought to be grateful to her; but young hearts are not resentful of this feeling.

The music stopped.

'*Merci*,'[1] said Odintsova, rising to her feet. 'You promised

---

1 In French in the original.

to call on me – bring your friend with you. I am very curious to see a man who has the courage to believe in nothing.'

The governor came up to Odintsova, announced that supper was served and, with a preoccupied expression, offered her his arm. As she walked away she looked back to give Arkady a last smile and a nod. He bowed low, gazed after her (how slender her figure appeared to him, the black silk cascading about it in a sheen of grey), and thinking 'In this moment she has already forgotten my existence', he felt in his heart some strange refinement of humility.

'Well, how did you get on?' demanded Bazarov as soon as Arkady had returned to him in their corner. 'Did you enjoy yourself? A gentleman here has just been telling me that that lady is oo-la-la! But I must say he seemed a fool. Come on, what's your impression? Is she really oo–la–la?'

'I don't altogether understand that definition,' replied Arkady.

'Don't you indeed! What an innocent!'

'In that case I don't understand your gentleman. Odintsova is very sweet, not a doubt, but she conducts herself so coolly and properly that—'

'Still waters, you know!' Bazarov took him up. 'You say she's cold. That's just where the piquancy lies. After all, you like ice-cream, don't you?'

'Perhaps,' muttered Arkady. 'I'm no judge of that. She wants to meet you and asked me to bring you to see her.'

'I can imagine what a portrait you must have drawn of me! Not but what you didn't do quite right. Take me to her, whoever she may be – just a provincial belle or an "*emancipée*" like Kukshina – she has shoulders the like of which I haven't seen for many a long day.'

Arkady was taken aback by Bazarov's cynicism, but as so often happens he reproached his friend for something other than that which had actually displeased him.

'Why will you not admit the possibility of free-thinking women?' he said in a low voice.

'Because, little brother, according to my observations the only free-thinking women are monstrously unattractive.'

On this the conversation ended. Both young men left immediately after the supper. Kukshina laughed at their retreating backs with nervous malice, but not without shyness: her vanity had been deeply wounded by the fact that neither the one nor the other had paid the least attention to her. She remained at the ball later than anyone else and at four o'clock in the morning she danced a polka-mazurka with Sitnikov in the latest Parisian style.

With this edifying spectacle the governor's party was over.

XV

'LET us see to which breed of mammal this person may belong,' said Bazarov to Arkady on the following day as together they mounted the stairs of the hotel where Odintsova was staying. 'I smell something suspicious.'

'I am surprised at you!' exclaimed Arkady. 'How is this? You! You, Bazarov, are coming out in support of that narrow morality which—'

'What an odd fellow you are!' Bazarov broke in unceremoniously. 'Don't you know that in peasant dialect "suspicious" means "promising"? Some profit to be had, that's what it means. Didn't you say yourself today that she had made a strange marriage, although in my opinion to marry a rich old man is not strange in the least but on the contrary most reasonable. I don't believe town gossip; but I like to think, as our enlightened governor says, that there is something to it.'

Arkady made no reply to this and knocked at the door of the room.

The room into which a young liveried servant showed the two friends was large, badly furnished like all Russian drawing-rooms, but full of flowers. Soon Odintsova herself made her appearance in a simple morning dress. She seemed still younger in the light of the spring sun.

Arkady presented Bazarov to her, and with some unacknowledged surprise noticed that he appeared to be embarrassed, whereas Odintsova remained completely at ease, just as she had been on the previous evening. Bazarov for his part felt that he had betrayed embarrassment and was annoyed. 'Here's a pretty state of affairs! Me to be intimidated by a woman!' he thought and, lounging in his armchair in a manner to rival Sitnikov, he began to talk in an exaggeratedly free-and-easy fashion; but Odintsova's clear eyes never wavered from his face.

Anna Sergeyevna Odintsova was born of Sergey Nikolaye-vich Loktev, a famous beau, adventurer and gambler who, having maintained himself with some little noise in Moscow and Petersburg for roughly fifteen years, had finally lost all he had at the tables and had been obliged to remove to the country where, as it happened, he soon died, bequeathing a minute estate to his two daughters, Anna aged twenty and Katerina aged twelve years. Their mother, an offspring of the impoverished family of the Princess Kh ..., had died in Petersburg when her husband was still in the full flush of his strength. Anna's position on the death of her father had been extremely difficult. The brilliant education which she had received in Petersburg had in no way prepared her for the responsibilities of estate and household management, or for a quiet life in the country. She knew absolutely no one in the whole neighbourhood and had no one to advise her. Her father had done his best to avoid contact with his neighbours. He despised them and they despised him, each in their own fashion.

She did not, however, lose her head but sent immediately for her mother's sister, Princess Avdot'ya Stepanovna Kh ..., an ill-tempered and self-conceited old woman who, having installed herself in her niece's house, proceeded to annex all the best rooms for her own use, to grumble and complain from morning till night and even to decline to walk about the garden unless accompanied by her only serf, a surly footman in worn-out pea-green livery and a blue-braided tricorn.

Anna bore with all her aunt's eccentricities patiently, little by little set about the education of her sister and, it seemed, had already resigned herself to the prospect of withering away in the depths of the country. But fate had decided otherwise. A certain Odintsov happened to make her acquaintance – a very rich man of about forty-six years of age, eccentric, hypochondriac, puffy, heavy and sour, but neither stupid nor unkind; he fell in love with her and offered her his hand in marriage. She consented to become his wife – and he lived with her for six years and on his death bequeathed to her all his worldly goods.

For almost a year after his death Anna Sergeyevna remained in the country; then she went abroad with her sister, but only visited Germany; she grew homesick and returned to live in her beloved Nikol'skoye, situated about thirty-five miles distant from the town of X. There she was mistress of a magnificent, excellently appointed house with a beautiful garden and conservatories: the late Odintsov had denied himself nothing.

Anna Sergeyevna came to town very seldom, usually on business and then not for long at a time. She was not well liked in the province and there had been a great outcry over her marriage to Odintsov. All kinds of legends were told about her. People said that she had helped her father in his various sharp practices, that it was not for nothing that she had gone abroad, but from necessity in order to conceal the unhappy results 'of what you will understand', the righteously indignant speakers would finish their story.

'She has passed through fire and water,' people would say of her; and a well-known provincial wit would usually add 'and through bronze pipelines'. She was aware of all these rumours but turned a deaf ear to them; her character was independent and fairly decisive.

Odintsova sat leaning against the back of her armchair, her hands folded, listening to Bazarov. He talked, contrary to his custom, rather loquaciously and was patently endeavouring to interest his listener, which again surprised Arkady. He could not decide whether or not Bazarov was achieving his aim. It was difficult to judge Anna Sergeyevna's reactions from her face: she preserved always the same expression, pleasant, responsive, her lovely eyes alight with attention, but with detached attention. The way in which Bazarov had put on airs during the first few minutes of the visit had affected her unpleasantly like a bad smell or a raucous noise; but she had understood at once that he was feeling embarrassed, and this even flattered her. Only genuine banality repulsed her and no one could accuse Bazarov of banality. It was Arkady's lot to be ceaselessly surprised on that day. He had expected that Bazarov would talk to Odintsova of his convictions and views, as to an intelligent woman: she herself had expressed the wish to hear the man 'who had the courage to believe in nothing', but instead of this Bazarov talked of medicine, of homoeopathy, of botany.

It appeared that Odintsova had not wasted her time in retirement: she had read a few good books and expressed herself in correct Russian. She led the talk on to music but, remarking that Bazarov had no respect for the arts, gradually returned to botany, although Arkady was quite ready to hold forth on the significance of folk-songs. Odintsova continued to behave to him as to a younger brother: it seemed that in him she valued his good nature and youthful simplicity – nothing more. The talk continued for more than three hours, unhurried, varied and animated.

At last the friends rose and began to take their leave. Anna Sergeyevna surveyed them affectionately, extended her beautiful white hand to each in turn and, after a moment's thought, with a hesitant but friendly smile ventured:

'If, gentlemen, you are not afraid of being bored, come and visit me in Nikol'skoye.'

'How can you speak so, Anna Sergeyevna?' exclaimed Arkady. 'I should think myself extraordinarily happy . . .'

'And you, Monsieur Bazarov?'

Bazarov merely bowed – and Arkady was subjected to a last surprise: he noticed that his friend was blushing.

'Well?' he asked him outside in the street. 'Do you still hold the same opinion, that she's oo–la–la?'

'God knows! I can't make her out. Just look how she's put herself on ice!' retorted Bazarov, and, having remained silent for a moment, added:

'A duchess, a *maîtresse-femme*. All she needs is a train behind and a crown on her head.'

'Our duchesses don't talk Russian like that,' observed Arkady.

'She's had her ups and downs, brother mine, had a taste of our bread.'

'Anyway, she's charming,' pronounced Arkady.

'Such a magnificent body!' continued Bazarov. 'Just perfect for the anatomical theatre.'

'Stop it, for goodness' sake, Yevgeny! That's going too far.'

'Come now, don't be angry, tenderfoot. I mean she's first-class. We must go and visit her.'

'When?'

'The day after tomorrow if you like. What is there for us to do here – drink champagne with Kukshina? Listen to that relative of yours, the liberal statesman? We'll slip over there the day after tomorrow. By the by, my father's cottage isn't far from there. That Nikol'skoye's on the X road, isn't it?'

'Yes.'

'*Optime*.[1] No reason to hang about. Only fools delay – and wise men! I'm telling you: a magnificent body.'

Three days later both friends were trundling along the road to Nikol'skoye. The day was fine and not too hot and the well-fed coach horses trotted on merrily, gently whisking their looped and plaited tails. Arkady had his eyes on the road and was smiling for some reason not known even to himself.

'Congratulate me,' Bazarov exclaimed suddenly. 'Today is the twenty-second of June, my saint's day. We'll see what he will do for me. They expect me home today,' he added, sinking his voice. 'Well, they'll wait. As though it mattered?'

XVI

THE country seat in which Anna Sergeyevna lived stood on a steep open hillside, not far from a yellow stone church with a green roof, white columns and an *al fresco*[2] painting over the main door representing the Resurrection of Christ in the 'Italian' style. Particularly remarkable for his rounded contours was the prostrate figure of a warrior in a spiked helmet

1 In Latin in the original (= 'excellent').
2 In Italian in the original (= 'wall-painting').

in the foreground. Behind the church stretched the long village in a double line of houses with here and there a chimney
rising from the thatched roofs. The manor-house was built
in the same style as the church, a style known to us as the
Alexandrine; the house was also painted a yellow colour and
the roof was supported on green and white pillars, the pedi-
ment embellished by a coat of arms. A provincial architect
had erected both these edifices with the approval of the late
Odintsov, who had no patience with any empty and capricious
novelties, as he was pleased to call them. The dark trees of the
old garden grew right up to the house on either side and an
avenue of trimmed spruce led up to the front entrance.

Our friends were met in the hall by two well-grown foot-
men in livery, one of whom promptly hurried off to fetch the
butler. The butler, a fat man in a black tailcoat, appeared
without delay and conducted the guests up a carpeted staircase and into the room which had been set aside for their use,
where two beds and all the requisites of a gentleman's toilet
had already been prepared for them. It was evident that order
reigned in the house: everything was clean and the whole
house had a respectable kind of smell just like that in minis-
ters' reception-rooms.

'Anna Sergeyevna will receive you in half an hour,'
announced the butler. 'Will there be anything further in the
meantime?'

'Nothing more, thank you, old fellow,' answered Bazarov,
'unless, that is, you would be good enough to bring a swig of
vodka.'

'Certainly, sir,' enunciated the butler, not without astonishment, and took himself off, his shoes squeaking protestingly.

'What *grand genre*!'[1] remarked Bazarov. 'That, I believe, is
your word for it? A duchess, and that's all there is to it.'

'A fine duchess,' argued Arkady, 'to invite two such mighty

1 In French in the original, but written, like all Bazarov's gallicisms, in
Russian letters. An English Bazarov would probably have pronounced
foreign words with the same deliberate and humorous Anglo-Saxon intona-
tion as that affected by Sir Winston Churchill in the famous war-time
speeches.

aristocrats as you and me to stay at her home on first acquaintance.'

'Especially me, a future doctor, a doctor's son and the grandson of a church deacon. Did you know that I was the grandson of a deacon? Like Speransky,'[1] added Bazarov after a moment's pause, his lip curling. 'But be that as it may, she knows how to make herself comfortable; oof, how she knows, that great lady! Perhaps we should put on evening dress?'

Arkady merely shrugged his shoulders; but he too felt slightly ill at ease.

Half an hour later Bazarov and Arkady went down to the drawing-room. It was a spacious, high room, decorated with some luxury but with no particular taste. The heavy, expensive furniture was ranged in the usual formal order along the walls, which were hung with brown wallpaper with golden arabesques which the late Odintsov had had sent from Moscow through an acquaintance always ready to do commissions for him, a wine merchant. Over the divan in the middle hung the portrait of a flabby, blond man who, it appeared, regarded the guests with some disfavour.

'That must be *him*,' whispered Bazarov to Arkady and, wrinkling his nose, added: 'Shall we make a bolt for it?' But at that moment their hostess entered. She was wearing a light dress of barathea; her hair, pulled smoothly back behind her ears, lent her pure, fresh face a virginal expression.

'Thank you for keeping your word to come and stay with me,' she began. 'It is really very pleasant here. You must meet my sister, she plays the piano well. To you, Monsieur Bazarov, that is a matter of indifference, but you, Monsieur Kirsanov, like music, I believe. Apart from my sister I have an aunt living with me, an old lady, and there is a neighbour who sometimes drives round for a hand of cards: that is all the society we can provide. And now let's sit down.'

Odintsova articulated all this little 'speech'[2] with particular

---

1 A brilliant Russian statesman of middle-class origin who for a time enjoyed high favour at the court of Alexander I.
2 In English in the original.

distinctness, as though she had learnt it off by heart; then she turned to Arkady. It came out that her mother had known Arkady's mother and had even been the recipient of confidences about her love for Nikolay Petrovich. Arkady spoke of his mother with great warmth, while Bazarov sat flicking over the pages of some albums. 'How meek and mild I have become,' he thought to himself.

A handsome borzoi dog with a pale blue collar came rushing into the drawing-room, its nails tapping the floor, and in its wake a young girl of about eighteen, black-haired and tanned, with a rather round but pleasant face and small dark eyes. She held in her hands a basketful of flowers.

'And here is my Katya,' stated Odintsova, indicating her by an inflection of the voice.

Katya curtsied slightly, sat down beside her sister and began to sort out the flowers. The borzoi, whose name was Fifi, went up to each guest in turn wagging her tail, and pressed her cold nose into their hands.

'Did you pick all those yourself?' asked Odintsova.

'All by myself,' answered Katya.

'And Aunt will come down for tea?'

'Yes, she'll come.'

When Katya spoke she smiled most endearingly, shyly and frankly, and looked up from under her brows in a manner at once comical and severe. Everything about her was still green and young: her voice, the down over her whole face, the pink hands with the whitish circles on the palms, the very slightly hunched shoulders; she blushed the whole time and breathed quickly.

Odintsova turned to Bazarov.

'You are just looking at those pictures out of politeness, Yevgeny Vasil'evich,' she began. 'They do not really interest you. You had better come and sit by us and then we can have an argument about something.'

Bazarov came over to them.

'What do you wish to argue about, ma'am?' he inquired.

'Anything you like. I must warn you that I enjoy arguing.'

'You?'

'Yes, I. That seems to surprise you. Now why?'

'Because, so far as I can judge, your style is calm and cool, and for an argument one should be capable of being carried away.'

'How have you managed to get to know me so soon? In the first place I am impatient and stubborn, you had better ask Katya; and in the second I am very easily carried away.'

Bazarov stared at Anna Sergeyevna.

'Possibly, you should know. So you want an argument – delighted. I was looking at views of Saxon Switzerland in your album, and you remarked to me that these could not really interest me. You said that because you assume me to have no taste for art – and indeed I haven't. But those views might have interested me from the point of view of geology, from the point of view of the formation of mountains, for instance.'

'Forgive me, but as a geologist surely you would rather turn to a book, to some special work, rather than to a sketch?'

'The sketch shows me by visual demonstration what could take up ten pages of description in a book.'

Anna Sergeyevna digested this in silence.

'And so you have absolutely no feeling for art whatsoever?' she demanded, putting her elbows on the table and by this very gesture bringing her face closer to Bazarov's. 'How do you get along without it?'

'But of what use is it, pray?'

'Why, even if only to be able to understand and to study people.'

Bazarov smiled wryly.

'In the first place, that is the province of experience. In the second, I have to inform you that the study of individuals is a waste of time. All people are just like one another, in body as in soul. In each one of us the brain, the spleen, the heart and the lungs are formed in just the same way. And the so-called moral qualities are the same in everyone: slight modifications mean nothing. One human specimen is enough to enable us to reach conclusions about all the others. People are like trees in the forest; no botanist would dream of making a special study of each particular birch-tree.'

Katya, who was unhurriedly selecting the blooms which blended best together from among her flowers, raised her eyes to Bazarov in amazement – and, meeting his swift and casual glance, coloured up to her ears. Anna Sergeyevna shook her head.

'Trees in the forest,' she repeated. 'Then according to you there is no difference between the clever person and the stupid one, the good and the evil?'

'No, there is a difference: as between the hale and the sick. The lungs of a consumptive are not in the same condition as mine and yours, although they are formed in the same way. We know more or less what causes our physical ailments; but our moral ailments spring from bad upbringing, from all sorts of trifles which are drummed into people's heads from infancy – from the disgraceful state of society, in a word, improve society and there will be no more diseases of this sort.'

Bazarov said all this as though he were thinking to himself at the same time: 'Believe it or not, it's all one to me!' He slowly stroked his side-whiskers with his long fingers, and his eyes wandered from corner to corner.

'And do you assume,' pronounced Anna Sergeyevna, 'that when society has been put right there will be no more stupid or evil people?'

'At least when society is properly organized it will be a matter of complete indifference whether a person is stupid or clever, good or evil.'

'Yes, I see; you will all have one and the same spleen.'

'Precisely so, madam.'

Odintsova turned to Arkady.

'And what is your opinion, Arkady Nikolayevich?'

'I agree with Yevgeny,' he answered.

Katya shot him a look from beneath her eyebrows.

'You surprise me, gentlemen,' said Odintsova, 'but we shall talk of this again. And now I can hear Aunt coming for her tea. We must spare her ears.'

Anna Sergeyevna's aunt, Princess Kh ..., a skinny little woman with a face screwed up like a small fist and with eyes that looked out from beneath a grey toupee in an unwavering, malicious stare, entered and, scarcely bowing to the guests, lowered herself into a wide plush armchair in which no one but herself had the right to sit. Katya pushed a footstool beneath her feet. The old lady did not thank her, did not even look at her, only moved her hands beneath the yellow shawl which almost entirely enveloped her puny body. The princess was fond of yellow: she had bright yellow ribbons in her cap as well.

'How did you sleep, Auntie?' inquired Odintsova, raising her voice.

'That dog's here again,' the old lady muttered in reply, and, noticing that Fifi had taken two hesitant paces in her direction, cried out: 'Shoo! Shoo!'

Katya called Fifi and opened the door for her. Fifi joyfully bounced out hoping that she was to be taken for a walk but finding herself alone on the other side of the door began to scratch and whine. The princess frowned; Katya made as if to go out.

'I think that tea is ready,' Odintsova intervened. 'Let us go, gentlemen; Auntie, come and take tea with us.'

The princess rose from her chair in silence and led the way from the drawing-room. They all followed her into the dining-room. A liveried page noisily pulled out another equally sacrosanct well-cushioned armchair and the princess sat down. Katya, who was pouring out the tea, served her first in a cup with a painted coat of arms. The old lady put honey into her cup (she considered that to drink tea with sugar was both sinful and extravagant, although she herself never spent a penny on anything) and suddenly demanded in a hoarse voice:

'And what has Prince Ivan to say in his letter?'

Nobody answered her. Bazarov and Arkady soon realized that nobody took any notice of her, although they treated her with respect. 'Just so as to keep up her dignity because she's born a princess,' thought Bazarov. After tea Anna Sergeyevna suggested they should go for a walk; but it had begun to spot with rain and the whole company, with the exception of the princess, returned to the drawing-room. Came the neighbour, the lover of cards, whose name was Porfiry Platonovich, a plump, grey-headed little man, with short legs that looked as though they had been whittled away, very polite and much given to laughter. Anna Sergeyevna, who spoke more and more with Bazarov, asked him if he would not like to take them on at an old-fashioned game of preference. Bazarov consented, saying that he must prepare himself in advance for his *métier* of provincial doctor.

'Be careful,' warned Anna Sergeyevna, 'Porfiry Platonovich and I will make mincemeat of you. And you, Katya,' she added, 'play something for Arkady Nikolayevich. He likes music and we can listen as we play!'

Katya moved unwillingly across to the piano; and Arkady, although it was true that he loved music, followed her unwillingly. It seemed to him as though Odintsova were sending him away and that his heart, as that of any other young man of his age, was already swelling with an ill-defined and oppressively expectant feeling like a presentiment of love. Katya raised the lid of the piano and, not looking at Arkady, inquired in a low voice:

'What shall I play to you?'

'Whatever you like,' answered Arkady indifferently.

'What kind of music do you like best?' persisted Katya, not shifting her position.

'Classical,' answered Arkady in the same tone of voice.

'Do you like Mozart?'

'Yes, I like Mozart.'

Katya got out Mozart's Fantasy Sonata in C minor. She played very well indeed, though perhaps a little too strictly and dryly. Not taking her eyes from the notes and tightly compressing her lips, she sat straight and still, and only towards the end of the sonata did her face become animated and a tiny lock of waving hair fall over her dark brow.

Arkady was particularly struck by the last part of the sonata, that part where, in the midst of the enchanting gaiety of the carefree refrain, there awake sudden gusts of such bitter, almost tragic sorrow; but the thoughts which Mozart awoke in his heart had nothing to do with Katya. Watching her he thought merely: 'This young lady doesn't play so badly after all, and she's not a bad sort herself.'

Having finished the sonata Katya, without raising her hands from the keys, asked: 'Enough?' Arkady declared that he would not presume to trouble her any further and began to talk to her about Mozart, asking her whether she herself had chosen to learn that sonata or whether someone had recommended it to her. But Katya replied in monosyllables: she was hiding from him, had retired into her shell. When this happened with her she was not quick to re-emerge; at such times her face would take on a stubborn, almost a stupid, expression. She was not exactly shy, but mistrustful and somewhat intimidated by the sister who had brought her up and who, of course, had no suspicion that this might be so. Arkady was finally reduced to calling up Fifi, who had been allowed into the room again, and to stroking her head with a benevolent smile in order to appear at his ease. Katya went back to her flowers.

Meanwhile Bazarov was suffering reverse after reverse. Anna Sergeyevna played an excellent game of cards; Porfiry Platonovich could also stand up for himself. Bazarov remained the loser, though not by much, but still by more than his vanity could relish. Over dinner Anna Sergeyevna again introduced the subject of botany.

'Let us go for a walk tomorrow morning,' she said to him. 'I would like to learn all the Latin names of the wild flowers from you, and all their special characteristics.'

'What good will the Latin names be to you?' asked Bazarov.

'Method is necessary in everything,' she replied.

'What a wonderful woman Anna Sergeyevna is,' exclaimed Arkady on finding himself alone with his friend in the room appointed for them.

'Yes,' agreed Bazarov, 'a female with a mind of her own. Well, she's seen some sights, you may be sure of that.'

'In what sense do you say that, Yevgeny Vasil'evich?'

'In the best sense, the best, little father mine, Arkady

Nikolayevich! I am sure that she even administers her estate quite excellently. But the miracle's not her, but her sister.'

'What? That little brown creature?'

'Yes, that little brown creature. There you have something fresh and untouched and wild and silent and – anything you like. There's someone who would be worth taking in hand. You could still make anything you like out of her; but the elder – she already knows her way about.'

Arkady did not answer Bazarov, and each lay down to sleep busy with his own thoughts.

Anna Sergeyevna, too, was thinking about her guests that evening. She liked Bazarov for his absence of affectation and for the very abruptness with which he expressed his opinions. She saw in him a novelty which had not before come her way and her curiosity was aroused.

Anna Sergeyevna was rather a strange being. Having no prejudices, no strong convictions even, she shrank from nothing and was going nowhere. Many things she perceived clearly, many interested her, and nothing completely satisfied her; indeed, she probably did not even desire complete satisfaction. Her mind was curious and indifferent at the same time: her doubts were never completely lulled into oblivion and never grew to perturbation. Had she not been rich and independent she might perhaps have been caught up in the struggle for existence, have experienced passion. But her life was easy, although she occasionally suffered boredom, and she continued to live from day to day, not hurrying and only occasionally stirred by emotion. Rainbow colours sometimes played before her eyes, too, but she felt relieved when they began to fade and did not regret them. Her imagination would sometimes carry her beyond the borders of that which according to the laws of accepted morality is considered permissible; but even then the blood flowed tranquilly as ever in that enchantingly slender and tranquil body. Sometimes, on emerging from her scented bath all warm and deliciously relaxed, she begins to dream of the futility of life, of its sorrows, labours and evils. Her heart, filled with sudden courage, seethes with noble ambition; but let a draught blow in from

the half-open window and Anna Sergeyevna will shrink, complain, grow almost pettish – and in that moment she wants
only one thing: that that revolting draught should stop blowing in on her.

Like all women who have never loved she wanted something without knowing exactly what. In actual fact she wanted
nothing, although it seemed to her that she wanted everything. She had scarcely been able to endure the late Odintsov
(she had married him for convenience although she probably
would not have agreed to become his wife had she not
considered him a good man), and had acquired a secret repulsion to all men, whom she could not imagine otherwise than
as slovenly, heavy, flaccid, feebly importunate beings. Once
when abroad she had met a young and handsome Swede with
a knightly expression and honest blue eyes beneath an open
forehead. He had made a great impression on her, but this
had not stopped her returning to Russia.

'A strange man, that doctor!' she thought, lying in her magnificent bed on lacy pillows beneath a light silk coverlet. Anna
Sergeyevna had inherited a part of her father's love of luxury.
She had loved her sinful but kindly father very dearly, and he
had adored her, joking with her in a friendly way as with an
equal, and had taken her completely into his confidence and
counsels. She scarcely remembered her mother.

'A strange man, that doctor!' she repeated to herself. She
stretched, smiled, flung back her arms behind her head, then
ran her eyes over a page or two of a foolish French novel,
dropped the book on to the floor – and fell asleep, all chaste
and cold in her chaste and sweet-scented linen.

The next morning Anna Sergeyevna set out to 'botanize'
with Bazarov immediately after breakfast and did not return
until lunch time; Arkady did not go out anywhere and spent
about an hour with Katya. He was not bored in her company;
she herself offered to repeat the sonata she had played the day
before. But when Odintsova finally returned, when he set eyes
on her, his heart contracted for a moment. She was walking
up the garden with a slightly weary gait; her cheeks glowed

and her eyes sparkled more brightly than usual under her round straw hat. She was twirling the slender stem of a wild flower between her fingers, a light lace shawl fell to her elbows and the broad grey ribbons of her hat lay flat against her breast. Bazarov was walking behind her, self-confident and casual as always, but the expression on his face, although merry and even tender, displeased Arkady. Muttering 'Good morning!' between his teeth, Bazarov went off to his own room and Odintsova absent-mindedly shook Arkady by the hand and also went straight on past him.

'Good morning,' thought Arkady. 'Has he forgotten we've seen each other already today?'

XVII

TIME, as everyone knows, sometimes flies like a bird and sometimes crawls like a worm; yet it is a sign of particular well-being when a man does not even notice whether it passes quickly or slowly. Arkady and Bazarov spent a fortnight with Odintsova in just this fashion. The illusion was in part created by the routine which she maintained in her household as in her life. She kept to it strictly and compelled others to do the same. Everything that happened in the course of the day had its allotted time. In the morning, punctually at eight, the whole household met for breakfast. From breakfast till luncheon everyone did as they wished; their hostess issued her orders to her bailiff (the estate worked on the system of *obrok*),[1] to her butler, to her housekeeper. Before luncheon they all met again for discussion or reading aloud; the evening was devoted to walking, playing cards, music; at half past ten Anna Sergeyevna would retire to her room, give her orders for the following day and go to bed. Bazarov did not approve of this measured, rather solemn regularity of their day-to-day existence. 'You get into a rut,' he insisted; liveried lackeys and pompous butlers offended his democratic feelings. He thought that, since they had already gone so far in this

1 *See* note on p. 12.

direction, they should have dined like the English in evening
dress and white ties. One day he explained this to Anna
Sergeyevna. Her manner was such that everyone confided his
opinion to her without a moment's hesitation. She heard him
out, answered 'From your point of view you are right, and
perhaps in this case I am too much the lady of leisure; but you
cannot lead an unmethodical life in the country, you would be
overcome with boredom,' and continued to go her own road.
Bazarov grumbled, but both he and Arkady found life at
Odintsova's so pleasant precisely because they were 'in a rut'!
Yet in spite of this both young men had changed since they
came to Nikol'skoye. In Bazarov, whom Anna Sergeyevna evidently held in high esteem although she seldom found herself
in agreement with him, a hitherto unprecedented malaise
became apparent; he easily grew irritated, spoke reluctantly,
looked cross and would not sit still in one place, as though he
were being eaten away by some unsatisfied longing. But
Arkady, who had finally made up his mind that he was in love
with Odintsova, began to fall into a quiet melancholy. Not
that this melancholy prevented him from making friends with
Katya; it even helped him to establish an affectionate and
friendly relationship with her. '*She* doesn't appreciate me! So
be it! But here's a kind soul who won't repulse me' – so he
thought, and knew again in his heart the sweetness of generous sentiments. Katya dimly perceived that he sought some
kind of comfort in her company, and denied neither him nor
herself the pleasure of a half-bashful, half-trusting friendship.
In the presence of Anna Sergeyevna they did not talk to one
another: Katya always shrank into herself under her sister's
penetrating gaze and Arkady, as behoves a man in love, could
not pay attention to anything else when near the object of his
passion; but he got on very well with Katya alone. He felt
himself to be incapable of engaging Odintsova's interest; he
was shy and at a loss whenever he found himself alone with
her; and she did not know what to say to him – he was too
young for her. On the other hand, with Katya Arkady felt
completely at home; he treated her with kindly superiority,
allowed her to tell him her impressions of music she had

heard, of stories she had read, of poetry and suchlike frivolities, not noticing, or at least not fully realizing, that these
same *frivolities* interested him as well. On her side Katya made
no attempt to tease him out of his melancholy. Arkady got on
well with Katya, Odintsova with Bazarov, and so what usually
happened was this: both couples, having kept together for a
little while, would then go their separate ways, especially
when out for a walk. Katya *adored* the country, and Arkady
also loved it although he would never have dared to admit it;
Odintsova was fairly indifferent to the beauties of nature, as
was Bazarov. This almost constant separation was not without
its effect on our friends: their relations began to change. Bazarov no longer discussed Odintsova with Arkady and even
stopped inveighing against her 'aristocratic tricks'. True, he
praised Katya no less than before, merely advising that her
sentimental leanings should be checked, but his praises were
skimped, his advice dry, and in general he talked to Arkady
much less than before; it was as though he were avoiding him,
as though he felt guilty towards him.

   Arkady noticed all this but kept his impressions to himself.

   The real reason for all this 'novelty' was the feeling which
Odintsova inspired in Bazarov – a feeling which tortured and
exasperated him and which he would have repudiated with
scornful laughter and cynical abuse if anyone had even
remotely hinted at the possibility of what was happening to
him. Bazarov was a great connoisseur of women and of female
beauty, but idealistic or, as he called it, romantic love he dis-
missed as sheer nonsense, as unforgivable folly, considered
chivalrous feelings something in the nature of a deformity or
a disease and had more than once been heard to express surprise that no one had thought to clap Toggenburg, together
with all the troubadours and minnesingers, into the nearest
lunatic asylum. 'If a woman attracts you,' he would say, 'see
what's to be got out of her; if nothing – well, don't persist, go
your ways, there are plenty more fish in the sea.' Odintsova
did attract him: the rumours rife about her, her freedom and
independence of thought, her obvious liking for him – all this,
it seemed, spoke in his favour; however, he soon realized that

he 'would get nothing out of her', yet found to his consterna-
tion that he had not the strength to turn from her. His blood
caught fire whenever she entered his thoughts. He would have
dealt with his blood easily enough, but something else had
taken root in him, something the existence of which he had
never acknowledged, at which he had always mocked, and
which revolted his pride. In conversation with Anna Sergeyevna he was louder than ever in his frigid scorn for everything
romantic; but left alone he was brought indignantly face to
face with the romantic in himself. Then he would set off into
the forest and walk through it with great strides, snapping off
branches which came in his way and swearing *sotto voce* at
both her and himself; or he would seek refuge in the hayloft
or the barn and, stubbornly closing his eyes, would will himself to sleep, at which, needless to say, he was not always
successful. Suddenly he would imagine that those chaste arms
would some time be wound about his neck, that those proud
lips would respond to his kisses, that those intelligent eyes
would look with tenderness – yes, with tenderness – into his,
and his head would spin and he would forget himself for a
moment until indignation flared up in him anew. Sometimes
it seemed to him that Odintsova herself was changing, that
there was something peculiar in her expression, that perhaps
. . . But at this stage he usually stamped his foot or ground his
teeth and menaced himself with his fist.

But in fact Bazarov was not altogether mistaken. He had
captured Odintsova's imagination; he interested her and she
often thought about him. In his absence she did not miss him,
did not find herself waiting for him, but in his presence she at
once grew more animated. She liked to be alone with him,
and enjoyed talking to him, even when he annoyed her and
insulted her taste, her elegant habits. It was as though she
wished to test him and to find out something about herself.

Once, walking in the garden with her, he had suddenly
announced in a sullen voice that he had formed the intention
of leaving shortly for the country to go to his father. She
turned pale, as though something had stabbed at her heart,
and had stabbed so deep that she herself was astonished and

the thought of what it might signify haunted her for some time to come. Bazarov had not told her of his forthcoming departure with the intention of testing her or to see what would come of it; he never 'made things up'. On the morning of that day he had had an interview with his father's bailiff, Timofeyich, who had looked after him as a boy. This Timofeyich, a worldly-wise, nimble old man with faded yellow hair, a weathered red face and tear-drops in his shrunken eyes, had unexpectedly materialized before Bazarov clad in his short jacket of thick blue-grey cloth, belted with the broken-off end of a leather strap, and tarred boots.

'Hallo, old man, how do you do?' exclaimed Bazarov.

'How do you do, Yevgeny Vasil'evich, sir,' began the old man, and beamed with delight, with the result that his whole face was suddenly covered with wrinkles.

'What have you come for? Have they sent you to fetch me?'

'Good gracious, sir, how can you say such a thing,' stammered Timofeyich (he remembered the strict orders he had received from his master before leaving). 'I was on my way to town on the master's business and happened to hear about your honour and went out of my road to come and see how your honour was doing – how could you think I'd come to disturb you!'

'Come now, don't fib,' Bazarov interrupted him. 'Are you telling me this is really on your way to town?'

Timofeyich collapsed and did not answer.

'Is my father well?'

'Praise be, sir.'

'And my mother?'

'And Anna Vlas'evna, the Lord be praised.'

'And they're expecting me, are they?'

The old man cocked his diminutive head.

'Eh, Yevgeny Vasil'evich, how shouldn't they be expecting you! As God's my witness, your parents' hearts are sore for the sight of you.'

'Well, all right, all right! You needn't go into detail. Tell them that I'll be there soon.'

'Very good, sir,' answered Timofeyich with a sigh.

Leaving the house, he slammed his cap down on his head with both hands, clambered up on to the dilapidated light pony-trap which he had left at the gates and set off at a trot, but not in the direction of the town.

In the evening of that same day Odintsova was sitting with Bazarov in her study while Arkady was pacing up and down the drawing-room listening to Katya's playing. The princess had retired upstairs; she heartily disliked guests in general and in particular these 'new profligates' as she called them. In the reception-rooms she merely sulked, but in the privacy of her bedchamber with only her maid to hear her she would sometimes work herself up into such a fury of abuse that her cap would jump about on her head together with her toupee. Odintsova was perfectly well aware of this.

'How can you mean to leave,' she began. 'What of your promise?'

Bazarov pricked up his ears.

'What promise, ma'am?'

'Have you forgotten? You were going to give me some lessons in chemistry.'

'What can I do, ma'am? My father is expecting me. I can't delay any longer. Anyway you can read Pelouse et Frémy, *Notions générales de chimie*,[1] a good, clear book. You'll find all you need there.'

'But don't you remember, you assured me that a book cannot replace ... I've forgotten what exactly it was you said, but you know what I mean – don't you remember?'

'What can I do!' repeated Bazarov.

'Why must you go?' asked Odintsova, lowering her voice.

He looked up at her. She had tilted her head back against the back of her chair and crossed her arms, which were bare to the elbows, on her breast. She seemed paler by the light of the single lamp shaded by a cut-out paper net. Her full-skirted white dress enveloped her from top to toe in soft folds; only the very tips of her feet, also crossed, were to be seen.

'And why should I stay?' retorted Bazarov.

1 In French in the original.

Odintsova turned her head a little.

'How is this? Aren't you enjoying yourself with me? Or do you think that we shall not regret your going?'

'I am convinced you will not.'

Odintsova did not speak at once.

'You have no cause to think that. Not that I believe you. You couldn't mean that.' Bazarov continued to sit motionless. 'Yevgeny Vasil'evich, why are you silent?'

'What can I say to you? There's no point in regretting anybody, and me still less than others.'

'Why do you say that?'

'I am a stolid, uninteresting type. I can't talk.'

'You are fishing for compliments, Yevgeny Vasil'evich.'

'That is not one of my habits. Don't you know yourself that the elegances of life are out of my reach, those elegances which you value so much?'

Odintsova bit on the corner of her handkerchief.

'You may think what you will, but I shall be bored after you leave.'

'Arkady will stay,' remarked Bazarov.

Odintsova shrugged slightly.

'I shall be bored,' she repeated.

'Truly? In that case you won't be bored for long.'

'Why should you suppose that?'

'Because you told me yourself that you are only bored when your routine is broken. You have organized your life with such infallible regularity that there can be no place in it for boredom, or longing – or any unpleasant feelings.'

'And you find that I am infallible – that is, in that I have organized my life with such regularity?'

'And what regularity! For instance, now: in a few minutes it will strike ten and I know in advance that you will send me packing.'

'No I won't, Yevgeny Vasil'evich. You may stay. Open that window a little – somehow it feels stuffy.'

Bazarov stood up and pushed the window. It swung open at once with a bang. He had not expected it to open so easily; also his hands were trembling. The dark, soft night looked into the room with its almost black sky, softly rustling branches and the fresh smell of the free pure air.

'Pull down the blind and sit down,' said Odintsova. 'I want to have a talk with you before you go. Tell me something about yourself; you never talk about yourself.'

'I try to talk to you on useful subjects, Anna Sergeyevna.'

'You are very modest. But I should like to learn something of you, of your family, of your father for whom you are deserting me.'

'Why does she talk like that?' thought Bazarov.

'None of that is of any interest,' he said aloud, 'especially for you. We are obscure people—'

'And do you think I am an aristocrat then?'

Bazarov raised his eyes to Odintsova's face.

'Yes,' he said with deliberate harshness.

She smiled wryly.

'I see that you know little of me, although you maintain that all people are alike and that it is not worth while to study them. Some time I will tell you my life – but first tell me yours.'

'I do know little of you,' repeated Bazarov. 'Perhaps you are right. Perhaps every human being is indeed a mystery. You yourself, for instance: you avoid company, you are wearied by it – and you invited two students to come to stay with you. Why, with your brain and with your beauty, do you live in the country?'

'What? What was that you said?' Odintsova took him up with animation. 'With my – beauty?'

Bazarov frowned.

'That's of no matter,' he muttered. 'I meant to say that I don't completely understand why you settled in the country.'

'You don't understand that, but you explain it to yourself somehow?'

'Yes – I assume that you always remain in one place because you have pampered yourself to such a degree – because you are very fond of your own convenience, of comfort, and are very indifferent to everything else.'

Odintsova again smiled her wry smile.

'You definitely refuse to believe me capable of being carried away?'

Bazarov shot her a look from under his brow.

'By curiosity, possibly; but not otherwise.'

'Really? Well, now I understand why you and I have become such friends. You are the same sort of person as I am.'

'We have become friends . . .' pronounced Bazarov in a hollow voice.

'Yes! But I was forgetting that you mean to go away.'

Bazarov stood up. The lamp burned dully in the middle of the darkening, sweet-scented, isolated room: through the lightly swaying Venetian blind the disturbing freshness of the night came pouring in and they could hear its mysterious whisperings. Odintsova did not move a muscle, but a secret excitement was gradually taking hold of her. It communicated itself to Bazarov. Suddenly he was conscious that he was alone with a young and beautiful woman.

'Where are you going?' The words came slowly.

He did not answer and dropped back into his chair.

'And so you think me a placid, coddled and pampered creature,' she continued in the same voice, never taking her eyes from the window. 'And yet I know of myself that I am very unhappy.'

'You unhappy! Why should you be? Surely you don't pay any heed to worthless rumours?'

Odintsova frowned. She was annoyed that he should have understood her thus.

'Those rumours don't even amuse me, Yevgeny Vasil'evich, and I am too proud to allow them to disturb me. I am unhappy because I have no wishes, no desire to live. You look at me mistrustfully. You think: that is the "aristocrat" talking, all dressed in lace and sitting in a velvet chair. I don't dissemble; I do enjoy what you call comfort, but at the same time I have little wish to live. Reconcile that contradiction if you can. Not but that in your eyes all that is romanticism.'

Bazarov shook his head.

'You are healthy, independent, rich. Whatever more? What is it that you want?'

'What is it that I want,' repeated Odintsova, and sighed. 'I am very tired, I am old, it seems to me that I have been living a very long time. Yes, I am old,' she added, softly adjusting the ends of her lace stole so that they covered her bare arms. Her eyes met Bazarov's and she blushed very slightly. 'Already there are so many memories behind me: life in Petersburg, wealth, then poverty, then my father's death, marriage, then the trip abroad, as was fitting – so many memories, but nothing worth remembering, and before me a long, long road and nowhere to make for. I do not even want to set out.'

'Are you so disillusioned?' asked Bazarov.

'No,' pronounced Odintsova after a moment's thought, 'but I am not fulfilled. I think that had I been able really to attach myself to something—'

'What you want is to fall in love,' interrupted Bazarov, 'and you're incapable of it: there's all your misfortune for you.'

Odintsova set herself to examine the lace of her sleeves.

'Could I really not fall in love?' she asked.

'Hardly! But I was wrong to call that a misfortune. On the contrary, the one to be pitied is the one who has it happen to him.'

'What happen to him?'

'To fall in love.'

'But how do you know?'

'By hearsay,' answered Bazarov angrily.

'You're flirting,' he thought. 'You're bored and you're teasing me because you've got nothing better to do, but I . . .' He really did feel as though his heart was being torn to shreds.

'Then perhaps you are too fastidious,' he pronounced, leaning forward with his whole body and playing with the fringe of his armchair.

'Perhaps. My way it is either all or nothing. A life for a life. You have taken mine, so give me yours, and that without regret or returning. Otherwise it is better not to begin!'

'What of that?' remarked Bazarov. 'It is a fair condition and I am surprised that you haven't yet found what you have been wishing for.'

'And do you think it is easy to give yourself without reservations to anything whatsoever?'

'Not easy if you stop to think about it, to put it off, to set a value on yourself, to care for yourself that is; but if you don't stop to think it's very easy to give yourself.'

'How can one not care about oneself? If I am of no value, then who needs my devotion?'

'That's not my affair; it's the other's affair to decide my value. The only thing that matters is to be able to give yourself.'

Odintsova sat up away from the back of her chair. 'You talk,' she began, 'as though you had been through all that.'

'The subject just happened to come up, Anna Sergeyevna, you know all that isn't in my line.'

'But you would be able to give yourself?'

'I don't know. I wouldn't like to boast.'

Odintsova said nothing and Bazarov fell silent. The sounds of the piano were wafted to their ears from the drawing-room.

'How late Katya is playing,' remarked Odintsova.

Bazarov rose.

'Yes, it really is late now. Time for you to get some sleep.'

'Wait, where are you going in such a hurry – I have something to say to you.'

'What?'

'Wait,' whispered Odintsova.

Her eyes were fixed on Bazarov; she appeared to be looking him over with great attention.

He paced about the room, then suddenly came up to her, hastily said goodbye, pressed her hand so that she almost cried out, and left the room. She raised her crushed fingers to her lips, blew on them and suddenly, rising impulsively from her chair, went with quick steps towards the door as though to call back Bazarov. The maid came into the room with a jug of water on a silver tray. Odintsova halted, ordered her to go, sat down again and again began to think. Her plait had come loose and fallen like a dark snake on to her shoulders. The lamp burned late that night in Anna Sergeyevna's room and for a long time she remained motionless, only from time to time drawing her hands over her arms, which were slightly nipped by the chill of the night.

Two hours later Bazarov returned to his room, his boots wet with dew, shock-headed and sullen. He found Arkady seated at the writing-table with a book in his hand and his jacket still done up to the top button.

'Haven't you gone to bed yet?' he demanded with something like irritation.

'You sat late tonight with Anna Sergeyevna,' stated Arkady, ignoring the question.

'Yes, I was sitting with her all the time you and Katerina Sergeyevna were playing the piano.'

'I wasn't playing . . .' began Arkady, and stopped. He felt tears coming to his eyes, and he did not want to break down and cry in front of his sardonic friend.

XVIII

ON the following day when Odintsova came down to breakfast Bazarov sat for a long time bent over his cup, then suddenly he looked across at her. She turned sharply towards him as though he had pushed her and it seemed to him that her face had grown somewhat paler overnight. She soon retired to her own room and did not reappear until lunch time. The weather had been rainy all morning and there had been no possibility of getting out for a walk. The whole party assembled in the drawing-room. Arkady took up the latest number of a periodical and began to read aloud. The princess, as was her wont, at first schooled her expression to register pained astonishment, as though he had ventured on some unseemly occupation, and then continued to stare at him with concentrated malice; but he took no notice of her.

'Yevgeny Vasil'evich,' uttered Anna Sergeyevna, 'let us go up to my room. I wanted to ask you – yesterday you mentioned a certain handbook. . . .'

She rose and made for the door. The princess gazed about her as though to say 'Just look, just look how I am lost in amazement!' and once more fixed her eyes on Arkady, but he merely raised his voice and, exchanging glances with Katya, next to whom he was sitting, continued his reading.

Odintsova went with swift steps to her study. Bazarov was prompt to follow her, not raising his eyes but hearkening intently to the thin swish and rustle of the silk dress sweeping on before him. Odintsova sank down into the same armchair in which she had been sitting the previous evening, and Bazarov reassumed his place of the day before.

'What was the title of that book?' she began after a brief pause.

'Pelouse et Frémy, *Notions générates*,'[1] answered Bazarov. 'Now I come to think of it you might also try Genot, *Traité élémentaire de physique expérimentale*.'[1] In that work the figures are clearer, and generally speaking that textbook—'

Odintsova stretched out a hand towards him.

'Yevgeny Vasil'evich, forgive me, but I did not invite you up here to speak of textbooks. I wanted to go on with our conversation of yesterday. You left so suddenly. It won't bore you?'

'I am at your disposal, Anna Sergeyevna. But what was it that we were discussing last night?'

Odintsova shot a sidelong glance at Bazarov.

'We were talking of happiness, I believe. I was telling you about myself. By the way, since I mentioned the word happiness ... Tell me, why is it that when we are enjoying something, music for instance, a fine evening, conversation with people who are sympathetic to us; why is it that all this seems to be a foretaste of some joy without measure which exists somewhere apart and beyond, rather than real happiness, that is a happiness which is actually within our grasp? Why should this be? Or are you, perhaps, not visited by such feelings?'

'You know the saying, "Happiness is always just round the next corner",' retorted Bazarov. 'And then you said yourself yesterday that you were unfulfilled. However, you're quite right – thoughts like that never come into my head.'

'Perhaps they strike you as ludicrous?'

1 In French in the original.

'No, they just don't come into my head.'

'Really? You know I should very much like to know what it is you *do* think about.'

'What do you mean? I don't follow you.'

'Listen, I have been wanting to talk things over with you for a long time. It is quite unnecessary to tell you – for you are perfectly well aware of it yourself – that you are not an ordinary man. For what are you preparing yourself? What future awaits you? I mean to say – what goal do you seek to attain, where are you going, what is in your heart? In a word, who and what are you?'

'You astonish me, Anna Sergeyevna. You know that I study natural sciences, and as to who I am—'

'Yes, who are you?'

'I have already informed you that I am a future provincial doctor.'

Anna Sergeyevna made a gesture of impatience.

'Why do you say that? You don't believe it yourself. Arkady might answer me like that, but not you.'

'But in what way does Arkady—'

'Do stop! How is it possible that you should remain satisfied with so modest an activity, and do you not always say yourself that medicine does not exist for you? You – with your opinion of yourself – a provincial doctor! You answer me just to fob me off because you have no confidence in me. But do you know, Yevgeny Vasil'evich, that I could understand you: I myself have been poor and proud like you; perhaps I have suffered the same trials as yourself.'

'All that is very well, Anna Sergeyevna, but you must hold me excused. I am not in the habit of pouring my heart out, and there is such a distance between you and me—'

'What distance? Are you going to tell me that I am an aristocrat again? Enough, Yevgeny Vasil'evich; surely I have proved to you—'

'Yes, and besides,' Bazarov broke in, 'why should we talk about the future, which doesn't depend on us at all for the most part? If the opportunity to do something worth while presents itself, well and good; if it doesn't, then at least there'll be the satisfaction of knowing that one hasn't wasted one's breath on empty talk.'

'You call a friendly discussion empty talk? Or possibly you don't consider me, as a woman, worthy of your confidence? Of course, you hold us all in contempt.'

'I don't hold you in contempt, Anna Sergeyevna, and you know it.'

'No, I know nothing of the sort – but let us assume that that is so. I understand that you don't wish to talk about what you are going to do in the future, but what is taking place within you now.'

'Taking place!' mimicked Bazarov. 'Just as though I were a state or a society! In my case it's of no interest whatsoever. And besides, can a man always say out loud what is "taking place" within him?'

'I see no reason why one should not say everything one has on one's mind.'

'Can *you*?' asked Bazarov.

'Yes,' answered Odintsova after a moment's hesitation.

Bazarov bowed his head.

'You are luckier than I am.'

Anna Sergeyevna looked at him questioningly.

'As you wish,' she went on, 'but still something tells me that we have not been brought together for nothing, that we shall become good friends. I am convinced that that – how can I put it? – that constraint, that reserve of yours, will eventually disappear.'

'And you have noticed this reserve in me, this – what was the word you used? – constraint?'

'Yes.'

Bazarov stood up and went over to the window.

'And you want to know the reason for this reserve, you want to know what's taking place inside me?'

'Yes,' repeated Odintsova with a trepidation which she herself did not yet understand.

'And you won't be angry?'

'No.'

'No?' Bazarov was standing with his back to her. 'Well you

might as well know, then, that I love you – stupidly, beyond all reason. There, now you have what you have been angling for.'

Odintsova held out both her hands to him, but Bazarov pressed his forehead against the window-pane. He was fighting for breath; his whole body was shaking visibly. But it was no trembling of youthful shyness, no sweet awe of a first declaration, which had taken possession of him: it was passion that throbbed in him, heavy and potent – a passion not unlike anger, and perhaps akin to it. Odintsova felt a mounting fear of him – and pity.

'Yevgeny Vasil'evich,' she said, and her voice vibrated on an involuntary note of tenderness.

He turned quickly, devoured her with one eager look and seizing both her hands suddenly pulled her against his chest.

She did not at once free herself from his embrace but a moment later she was standing well away in a corner regarding Bazarov from across the room. He lunged towards her.

'You misunderstood me,' she whispered with hasty fear. Another step from him, it seemed, and she must have cried out. Bazarov bit his lip and left the room.

Half an hour later the maid brought Anna Sergeyevna a note from Bazarov; it consisted of one line only: 'Must I leave today or may I stay till tomorrow?'

'Why leave? I misunderstood you – you misunderstood me,' replied Anna Sergeyevna, and thought: 'I didn't even understand myself.'

She did not appear until luncheon but paced up and down in her room, her hands behind her, pausing sometimes before the window, sometimes before the mirror, and slowly passing a kerchief over her neck where she still fancied she could feel a burning patch. She asked herself what had compelled her to 'angle for', to use Bazarov's own expression, this open declaration, and whether she had not suspected something. 'It's my fault,' she said aloud, 'but I could not have foreseen it.' She fell into a reverie and felt herself blushing at the memory of Bazarov's almost bestial face when he had sprung towards her.

'Or?' she suddenly said aloud, and stopped dead and shook

her curls. She caught sight of herself in the glass; the backward tilt of her head with the secretive smile playing about her half-closed, half-open eyes and lips seemed at that moment to be telling her something which put her quite out of countenance.

'No,' she decided at last, 'God knows where that would lead, and it's not a thing to enter upon lightly; peace of mind is the best thing on earth in spite of everything.'

Her peace of mind had not been shaken; but she felt sad and once even began to cry a little: without knowing the reason herself, only that it was not because of any insult she had suffered. She did not feel herself insulted; rather she felt guilty. Under the influence of various ill-defined feelings, the realization that life was passing her by, the desire for novelty, she had forced herself to go on to a certain boundary line, forced herself to look beyond it; and beyond it she had seen not the abyss even, but emptiness – or formless outrage.

XIX

HOWEVER great Odintsova's self-control, however far above all forms of prejudice she might be, even she felt some embarrassment when she appeared in the dining-room for luncheon. Nevertheless all passed off fairly well. Porfiry Platonovich was there and had various anecdotes to recount; he had just returned from town. Among other things he told them that the governor, Bourdalou, had ordered his secretaries to wear spurs, just in case the occasion should arise for him to dispatch them somewhere on horseback for greater speed. Arkady chatted in a low voice with Katya and lent a diplomatic ear to the princess. Bazarov preserved a stubborn and gloomy silence. Once or twice Odintsova – openly and without concealment – looked across at his face, set in stern, bitter lines, the eyes lowered and the impress of contemptuous decision in every feature, and thought: 'No – no – no....' After luncheon she led the whole company out into the garden and, seeing that Bazarov wished to speak to her, went a few paces to one side and halted. He approached her but even now would not raise his eyes, and said in an expressionless voice:

'I have to beg your pardon, Anna Sergeyevna. You must be very angry with me.'

'No, I am not angry with you, Yevgeny Vasil'evich,' answered Odintsova, 'but I am distressed.'

'So much the worse. In any case my punishment is sufficiently hard. My position, as you will probably agree, could not be more ridiculous. You wrote: "why leave?" I can't and I won't stay on here. Tomorrow I shall be gone.'

'Yevgeny Vasil'evich, why—'

'Why am I leaving?'

'No, that is not what I was going to say.'

'You can't bring back the past, Anna Sergeyevna – and sooner or later this was bound to happen. Consequently it is for me to go away. There is only one condition on which I could remain here; and that will never be. You see – forgive my audacity – you don't love me and will never come to love me.'

For a moment Bazarov's eyes glinted from beneath his dark eyebrows.

Anna Sergeyevna made no reply. 'I am afraid of that man,' was the thought which flashed through her mind.

'Goodbye, ma'am,' enunciated Bazarov as though he had guessed her thought, and set off back for the house.

Anna Sergeyevna followed him slowly and, calling Katya to her, went on arm in arm. She kept her sister by her side until the evening. She refused to play cards and began to laugh more and more, which was quite out of keeping with her pale face and confused expression. Arkady could not make it out, and set himself to observe her behaviour in the way that young men do, that is, he asked himself continually: 'What does this mean?' Bazarov shut himself up in his room. He did, however, come down for tea. Anna Sergeyevna wanted to say something nice to him, but she did not know how to begin.

An unexpected turn of events extricated her from the difficulty. The butler announced the arrival of Sitnikov.

It is almost beyond the power of words to describe what a sorry figure the young radical presented as he fluttered into the room. Having, in his usual encroaching fashion, formed the decision of travelling into the country to visit a woman with whom he was barely acquainted, who had never invited him, but with whom, as he had discovered, two such clever and such intimate friends of his happened to be staying, he was nevertheless overcome with timidity and, instead of trotting out his well-rehearsed excuses and greetings, burbled some utter rubbish to the effect that Yevdoksiya, so he said, Kukshina had sent him to inquire after the health of Anna Sergeyevna and that Arkady Nikolayevich had also always spoken to him in the highest terms of ... Here he hesitated and so lost all presence of mind as to sit down upon his own hat. However, as no one offered to turn him out and Anna Sergeyevna even introduced him to her aunt and her sister, he soon came to himself and began to chatter away for all he was worth. In this life, manifestations of the commonplace are frequently salutary; they serve to ease strings which have been tuned too high, to sober sentiments too self-assured or self-annihilating by bringing to mind the close relationship between the sublime and the ridiculous. With the arrival of Sitnikov everything became somehow less acute – and simpler; everybody even managed to eat a better supper and parted company to seek their beds half an hour earlier than usual.

'I can now repeat to you what you once said to me,' Arkady remarked from his bed to Bazarov, who was also in his night things. ' "Why are you so sad? Can it be that you have just accomplished some sacred duty?" '

For some time now the young men had fallen into a falsely familiar, mocking way of talking to one another which is always a sign of suppressed dissatisfaction and unspoken suspicions.

'I'm off to my father tomorrow,' announced Bazarov.

Arkady raised himself on one elbow. He was both surprised and for some reason pleased.

'Ah!' he said. 'And is that why you're sad?'

Bazarov yawned.

'If you learn too much you'll be old before your time.'

'But how has Anna Sergeyevna taken it?'

'What has Anna Sergeyevna to say to it?'

'I mean, will she really let you go?'

'I haven't hired myself out to her.'

Arkady relapsed into thought and Bazarov got into bed and lay down with his face to the wall.

A few minutes went by in silence.

'Yevgeny!' Arkady exclaimed suddenly.

'Well?'

'I shall leave with you tomorrow.'

Bazarov did not answer.

'Only I shall go home', Arkady continued. 'We'll go together as far as the Khokhlov settlements and there you can hire horses from Fyedot. I should have liked to meet your people, but I'm afraid I'll only be a nuisance to them and to you. You're coming back to us afterwards, aren't you?'

'I've left my things with you,' responded Bazarov without turning round.

'Why doesn't he ask me why I am leaving just as suddenly as he is?' thought Arkady. 'In fact why am I leaving, and why is he?' he pursued his train of thought. He could find no satisfactory answer to his own question and something caustically painful welled up in his heart. He felt that it would be difficult for him to leave behind this life to which he had grown so accustomed, but it seemed somehow strange to stay on alone. 'Something's happened between them,' he reasoned with himself. 'Why should I stay to dangle after her after he's gone? I shall only bore her to death, and then everything will be lost.' He began to picture Anna Sergeyevna to himself, then other features gradually superimposed themselves on the lovely image of the young widow.

'I'll miss Katya too!' whispered Arkady to his pillow, on which a tear had already fallen. Suddenly he shook back his hair and said aloud:

'Why the devil did that ass Sitnikov have to come here?'

Bazarov first shifted on his bed and then delivered himself of the following:

'I can see, brother, that you're still a fool. Sitnikovs are essential to us. I need them, understand that, I need dolts like that. It's not for the gods to fire pots, after all!'

'Oho – ho!' thought Arkady to himself, and for the first time he caught a momentary glimpse of the bottomless depths of Bazarov's pride.

'So you and I are gods, are we? Or rather you're a god, and I suppose I must be a dolt?'

'Yes,' confirmed Bazarov sullenly, 'you're still a fool!'

Odintsova expressed no particular surprise when on the following morning Arkady informed her that he would be leaving with Bazarov; she appeared absent-minded and weary. Katya gave him a serious look but said nothing; the princess even made the sign of the cross[1] – under her shawl, yet in such a way that he could not help but notice; Sitnikov, on the other hand, worked himself up into a terrible flurry. He had just come down to breakfast in a new and dandified outfit, not in the Slavophile tradition this time; the evening before he had amazed the servant appointed to attend on him by the quantity of linen which he had brought, and now his friends were deserting him! He made little mincing movements with his feet, darted hither and thither like a hunted hare uncertain whether to break covert, and suddenly, almost with terror, almost with defiance, announced that he too had formed the intention of leaving. Odintsova made no effort to dissuade him.

'I have a very comfortable barouche,' added the unhappy young man, turning to Arkady. 'I could give you a lift and Yevgeny Vasil'evich could have your tarantass. It would even be more convenient that way.'

'But for heaven's sake, it's right out of your way, and it's a good distance to my home.'

'That's quite all right, quite all right; I have plenty of time, and also I've business in that direction.'

'Farming business?' asked Arkady, unable to conceal his contempt.[2]

But Sitnikov was in such despair that for once he did not even laugh.

1 Here a gesture of profound relief.
2 See footnote, p. 71.

'I assure you that the barouche is very comfortable,' he murmured, 'and there'll be room for us all.'

'Don't distress Monsieur Sitnikov by refusing,' intervened Anna Sergeyevna.

Arkady looked at her and inclined his head significantly. The guests left after breakfast. On taking leave of Bazarov, Odintsova gave him her hand and said:

'We shall see each other again, shall we not?'

'As you wish,' answered Bazarov.

'In that case we shall see each other.'

Arkady was the first to step out into the porch: he climbed up into Sitnikov's barouche. The butler respectfully saw him comfortably installed, and Arkady would have liked to hit him – or to burst into tears. Bazarov took his place in the tarantass. Arrived at the Khokhlov settlements, Arkady waited while Fyedot, the landlord of the posting-house, changed the horses, then walking over to the tarantass he looked up at Bazarov with his old smile and said:

'Yevgeny, take me with you! I want to go home with you.'

'Get in,' acceded Bazarov grudgingly between his teeth.

Sitnikov, who was strolling round the wheels of his equipage whistling jauntily, merely gaped at these words, and Arkady calmly took his things out of the barouche, seated himself beside Bazarov and, with a polite bow to his erstwhile travelling companion, called out: 'Let them go!' The tarantass rolled off and was soon lost to view. Sitnikov, now finally put out of countenance, looked at his coachman, but this worthy was absorbed in flicking his whip over the tail of the trace-horse. Then Sitnikov leapt into the barouche and having thundered at two peasants who happened to be passing, 'Put your hats on, you fools!' took himself off back to the town, where he arrived very late and where, on the following day at Kukshina's house, he had much to say to the detriment of those two 'revolting stuck-up ignoramuses'.

Having taken his seat in the tarantass with Bazarov, Arkady gripped his hand tightly and said nothing for a long time. It seemed as though Bazarov understood and appreciated both the handshake and the silence. The night before he had not slept and had refrained from smoking, and he had eaten practically nothing for several days. His wasted profile showed dark and sharp under the cap which he had pulled down over his eyes.

'Well, brother,' he said in the end, 'give me a cigar. And look and see, is my tongue yellow?'

'Yellow,' confirmed Arkady.

'Yes, of course – and the cigar's tasteless. The machine's come unstuck.'

'You really have changed these last few weeks,' remarked Arkady.

'Never mind, I'll recover. The only bother is my mother's so soft-hearted: if you haven't developed a paunch and don't eat ten times a day she's miserable. Now my father – he's all right, he's been around the world himself and seen all sorts. No, I mustn't smoke,' he added, and hurled the cigar into the dust of the road.

'It'll be about sixteen miles to your place, won't it?' asked Arkady.

'Yes. But you can ask this sage.'

He indicated the peasant sitting on the box, one of Fyedot's hired hands.

However, the sage answered merely: 'Who can say for sure? The miles thisaways bain't never been measured,' and continued to curse the shaft-horse in his beard because she would 'kick with her headpiece' – that is to say, toss her head.

'Yes, yes,' Bazarov began again. 'There's a lesson for you, my young friend, an edifying example of some sort. Why such nonsensical things happen the devil alone knows! Every man's life hangs on a thread, the ground may give way beneath his feet at any moment, and what must he do but think up all sorts of unpleasant complications and ruin his own life!'

'What are you hinting at?' asked Arkady.

'I'm not hinting at anything, I'm saying straight out that you and I have behaved very stupidly. Talking won't mend matters! But I've already noticed in the clinic that the patient who is angry with his pain always overcomes it.'

'I don't altogether understand you,' said Arkady. 'It seems to me that you had nothing to complain of.'

'Well, if you don't altogether understand me I'll tell you this: in my opinion it's better to break stones on the highway than to give a woman power over so much as the last joint of your little finger. All that's . . .' Bazarov almost pronounced his favourite word romanticism, but refrained and said: 'Rubbish. You won't believe me now but I can tell you that you and I got into female company – and we liked it; but that to get out of such company is as good as a bucketful of cold water on a hot day. A real man has no time to spend on such fribbles. There's an excellent Spanish proverb which says a man should be fierce. Hey, you there,' he added, addressing the peasant on the box, 'you, wise man, have you got a wife?'

The peasant turned so that the friends could see his flat face and weak eyes.

'A wife? I 'ave that. What 'ud I be doing without a wife?'

'Do you beat her?'

'Beat me wife? Could be. Doan't beat 'er without reason.'

'All very proper. And does she beat you?'

The peasant jerked at the reins.

'That's a funny thing to say, sir. But you will be 'aving your joke.' He had obviously taken offence.

'Do you hear that, Arkady Nikolayevich! And you and I have taken a good hiding – that's what comes of being educated people!'

Arkady forced a laugh but Bazarov turned away and did not open his mouth again for the rest of the journey.

The sixteen miles seemed more like sixty to Arkady. But at last, on the slope of a gentle hill, there came into view the little village where Bazarov's parents lived. Near by, in a grove of young birches, they could see a small manor-house with a thatched roof. In front of the first cottage two peasants wearing caps were standing cursing one another. 'You're a great swine,' said one to the other, 'and worse than a little piglet.' 'And your wife's a witch,' retorted the other.

'By their uninhibited manners,' remarked Bazarov to Arkady, 'and by their pleasant terms of speech you may see

that my father's peasants are not too repressed. And here he
is himself coming out on to the porch of the ancestral home.
He must have heard our harness-bells. It's him all right – I
recognize the figure. Oho-ho! How grey he's grown, though,
poor old fellow!'

XX

BAZAROV leant out of the tarantass and Arkady craned his
neck from behind his friend and saw on the porch of the
manor-house a tall, lean man with ruffled hair and a fine aqui-
line nose, dressed in an old military coat with the buttons all
undone. He stood with his legs astraddle smoking a long pipe
and wrinkling up his eyes against the sun.

The horses came to a halt.

'Well, here you are at last,' Bazarov's father greeted them,
continuing to smoke although the pipe appeared to be positively jumping about between his fingers. 'Come on, hop out,
hop out, give us a kiss.'

He began to embrace his son. 'Yevgeny, Yevgeny, my little
one,' came a trembling woman's voice. The door was flung
open and on the threshold there appeared a plump little
woman in a white cap and a short many-coloured jacket. She
gasped, staggered and would probably have fallen had not
Bazarov been there to support her. Her dimpled arms were
round his neck in a moment, her head pressed against his
breast, and there was a sudden silence. The only sound was
the sharp, uneven intake of her breathing.

Old man Bazarov breathed deeply and screwed up his eyes
still tighter than before.

'There, there now, Arina! That's enough,' he began,
exchanging glances with Arkady, who was standing rooted by
the tarantass, while the peasant on the box had even turned
away. 'What is all this now! That'll do, please.'

'Eh, Vasily Ivanovich,' stammered the old woman, 'it's
such an age since my dearie, my honey, my little Yevgeny
love . . .' And without untwining her arms she raised her face,
all crumpled and wet with tears and soft with emotion, from

Bazarov's shoulder and looked at him with droll and blissful eyes, and once again fell upon his chest.

'Well, yes, that's all in the nature of things,' pronounced Vasily Ivanovich, 'only we'd better go indoors. Yevgeny's brought a guest with him.'

'You must excuse us,' he added, turning to Arkady and clicking his heels. 'You will understand a woman's weakness and – er – the heart of a mother. . . .'

His own mouth was working, his eyebrows twitching and his chin quivering, but he evidently wished to control himself and to appear almost indifferent. Arkady bowed.

'Come, Mother, indeed we must go in,' said Bazarov, and led the tottering old woman into the house. Having sat her down in a comfortable armchair he briefly embraced his father again and presented Arkady to him.

'Very happy to make your acquaintance,' said Vasily Ivanovich, 'only pray don't be too exacting: we live very simply here, like old campaigners. Arina Vlas'evna, calm yourself, come now; how can you be so poor-spirited? Our guest must think it very strange.'

'Good sir,' said the old woman through her tears, 'I haven't the honour to know your name. . . .'

'Arkady Nikolayevich,' Vasily Ivanovich prompted her in a low voice with some self-importance.

'Forgive me, a foolish old woman.' Arina Vlas'evna blew her nose and, tilting her head first to the right and then to the left, carefully wiped one eye after the other. 'Forgive me, you see I thought I might die and not be spared to see my d–d–dearie.'

'Well, you have been spared, madam,' broke in Vasily Ivanovich.

'Tanyushka.' He turned to a barefooted girl of thirteen in a bright cotton dress who was peering nervously from behind the door. 'Bring the mistress a glass of water – on a tray, do you hear? And you, sirs,' he added with a kind of old-fashioned playfulness, 'permit me to invite you into the den of a retired veteran.'

'Just one more hug, Yevgeny love,' moaned Arina

Vlas'evna. Bazarov bent down to her. 'Eh, but how handsome you've grown!'

'Huh! Handsome is as handsome does,' remarked Vasily Ivanovich. 'But he's a man now, an *om fay*[1] as they say, and now, Arina Vlas'evna, I hope that having satiated your motherly heart you'll make ready to satiate our dear guests, for as you know fine words do not make full stomachs.'

The old lady half rose from her chair.

'I'll have the table laid this very minute, Vasily Ivanovich, and I'll run into the kitchen myself and tell them to put on the kettle. Everything will be as it should, everything. Just to think, it's three years now since I last saw him, or got him aught to eat or drink: is it so easy?'

'Well, well, do your best, little hostess, bustle about, don't let your reputation down. And you, sirs, you'll be very welcome to come with me, I'm sure. Here's Timofeyich come to make his bow to you, Yevgeny. Even he's pleased, the old tyke. What? You are pleased, aren't you, old tyke? Now follow me, if you please.'

And Vasily Ivanovich bustled on ahead of them, shuffling and dragging his much-mended slippers.

His entire house consisted of six tiny rooms. One of these, into which he now conducted our friends, was known as the study. A thick-legged table piled with papers so blackened with ancient dust that they looked as though they had been smoked took up all the space between the two windows; the walls were hung with Turkish rifles, whips, sables, two maps, some anatomical charts, a portrait of Hufeland, a monogram made from hair in a black frame and a framed diploma. A sofa, with the leather upholstery torn in places and some broken springs, was wedged between two enormous cupboards of Karelian birch. On the shelves were disorderly piles of books, boxes, stuffed birds, tins and phials; in one corner lay a broken electric battery.

'I warned you, my dear guest,' began Vasily Ivanovich, 'that we live here as you might say in bivouac style.'

---

1 French written in Russian characters in the original (= '*homme fait*').

'Enough of that! Why should you apologize?' interrupted Bazarov. 'Kirsanov knows perfectly well that you and I aren't Croesuses and that you don't own a palace. Where shall we put him to sleep, that's the question?'

'Why, that needn't trouble you, Yevgeny. I have a splendid room out there in the annexe: Arkady Nikolayevich will be quite comfortable there.'

'So you've built an annexe too, have you?'

'Ay, that we have, down in the bath-house,'¹ Timofeyich broke in.

'Next to the bath, that is,' Vasily Ivanovich interposed hastily. 'It's summertime now – I'll run down there straight away and have everything shipshape; and you, Timofeyich, might bring their things in in the meantime. And as for you, Yevgeny, I'll put my study at your disposal, of course. *Suum cuique.*'²

'There you are then! The funniest old fossil – and the kindest,' added Bazarov as soon as Vasily Ivanovich had gone. 'An eccentric, like yours, only in another way. He does talk a lot though.'

'And your mother seems to be a very good kind of woman,' remarked Arkady.

'Yes, she's a very genuine person. And you'll see what a dinner she'll give us!'

'They didn't expect you today, master, and the beef's not come,' announced Timofeyich, who had just brought in Bazarov's trunk.

'We'll manage without the beef, if it's not there it's not. Poverty, so they say, is no vice.'

'How many serfs has your father?' Arkady asked suddenly.

'The estate's my mother's, not his; there's fifteen serfs, as far as I can remember.'

'Twenty-two altogether,' corrected Timofeyich reprovingly.

The sound of shuffling slippers came to their ears and Vasily Ivanovich came back into the room.

1 In the country most Russian houses have an outside steam-bath, much like the Finnish sauna.
2 'To each his own' (Lat.).

'In a few minutes your room will be ready to receive you,' he announced formally. 'Arkady – Nikolayevich? That is how you are called, is it not? And here is the servant who will attend to you,' he added, indicating a boy with short-cropped hair, a long blue belted tunic torn at the elbows and someone else's boots, who had followed him into the room. 'He's called Fed'ka. I repeat once more, although my son forbids it, you mustn't be too exacting. Not but that he knows how to fill a pipe. You do smoke, do you not?'

'I smoke cigars mostly,' answered Arkady.

'And very wise of you to do so. I myself have a preference for cigars, but in our wild part of the world they are very difficult to come by.'

'Now that's enough playing the beggar,' Bazarov cut him short again. 'Sit down on the sofa instead and let's have a look at you.'

Vasily Ivanovich burst out laughing and sat down. He was very like his son in face, only his forehead was lower and narrower, his mouth a little wider and he could never be still, shrugging his shoulders as though his jacket cut him under the arms, coughing and fidgeting with his fingers; whereas his son was distinguished by a kind of careless immobility.

'Playing the beggar!' repeated Vasily Ivanovich. 'Don't you take it into your head that I want to make our guest sorry for us by telling him what a backwater it is we live in. On the contrary, I am of the opinion that for a thinking man there is no such thing as a backwater. At least I do my best not to grow moss, as they say, not to fall behind the times.'

Vasily Ivanovich pulled from his pocket a new yellow kerchief; which he had managed to lay hands on when hurrying over to Arkady's room, and went on, waving it about in the air:

'I am not speaking of the fact that, for instance – not without depriving myself in a way which I could ill afford – I've introduced the *obrok* system and given my peasants their land in return for half the produce as rent. I considered that to be my duty. Reason itself was the moving factor in the case, although other landlords are not yet dreaming of it: I am speaking of the sciences, of education.'

'Yes; I see you have the *Friend of Health* for 1855,' remarked Bazarov.

'I've a friend who sends it to me for old time's sake,' said Vasily Ivanovich hurriedly; 'but for instance we have some knowledge of phrenology,' he added, addressing himself, however, more to Arkady and pointing out a small plaster head marked off into numbered triangles which stood on top of the cupboard. 'Shönlein is not unknown to us – and Rademacher.'

'And do they still believe in Rademacher in the province of X?' asked Bazarov.

Vasily Ivanovich was taken with a fit of coughing.

'In the province. . . . Of course you, sirs, are in a position to know better; how can we expect to keep up with you? After all, you have come to carry on our task for us. In my time there was a certain *humoralist*, Hoffmann, and a certain Brown with a theory of *vitalism*, who seemed very ridiculous but they must have been famous once. Someone new has replaced Rademacher for you; he is now your idol and in twenty years' time, perhaps, people will be laughing at him in his turn.'

'For your comfort,' said Bazarov, 'I may tell you that now we laugh at the whole concept of medicine and have no idols.'

'How is this? Surely you want to be a doctor?'

'I do, but the one doesn't hinder the other.'

Vasily Ivanovich jabbed his third finger into the bowl of his pipe, which still contained a little hot ash.

'Well, perhaps, perhaps – I won't argue. What am I, after all? A retired regimental doctor, *vollatoo*;[1] and now I've blundered into farming. I served in your grandfather's brigade.' He turned again to Arkady. 'Yes, yes; I have seen many things in my time. And in what unexpected society I moved, and what people I came up against. I, this same I who sits here before you, have felt the pulse of Prince Wittgenstein and of Zhukovsky the poet! Those ones, the ones that were in the southern command in the fourteenth,[2] you understand' (and

1 French written in Russian characters in the original (= '*voilà tout*').
2 Vasily Ivanovich is here referring to a revolutionary nucleus of officers

here Vasily Ivanovich compressed his lips significantly). 'I knew every one of them. Well, but then of course my business never took me into the limelight; keep to your lancet, and *basta*!¹ But your grandfather was a very respected man, a real soldier.'

'You might as well admit he was a frightful blockhead,' remarked Bazarov lazily.

'Oh, Yevgeny, what an expression! For pity's sake! Of course General Kirsanov was not of the number of—'

'Well, let him be,' Bazarov cut in. 'As I came up to the house I was admiring your great grove of birch-trees. They've come on splendidly.'

Vasily Ivanovich revived.

'You must come and see what a fine little garden I have now! I planted every tree in it myself. And there's fruit, and berries, and all sorts of medicinal herbs. Whatever you may think up next, you gentlemen of the younger generation, what old man Paracelsus said still holds good: *in herbis, verbis et lapidibus*.² You see, as you know I've retired from my practice, but two or three times a week I still have to rake up the old skills. People come for advice – you can't very well throw them out on their necks. Sometimes it's the very poor who come for help. But in fact there are no doctors round here anyway. One of my neighbours here, a retired major if you please, also deals in cures. I asked whether he had studied medicine. Do you know what they told me? No! He hadn't studied, he did it more from philanthropy. Ha ha! Ha ha! From philanthropy! Eh? How do you like that! Ha ha!'

'Fed'ka! Fill my pipe for me!' Bazarov spoke grimly.

'And then there's another doctor here who came to visit a patient,' continued Vasily Ivanovich with a sort of desperation, 'and the patient had already been gathered *ad patres*:³ the servant wouldn't let the doctor in, and told him that he

who rose against Nicholas I in 1825, the southern Society of Decembrists led by P. I. Pestel.
1 In Italian in the original.
2 'In herbs, words and stones' (Lat.).
3 'To his fathers' (Lat.).

wouldn't be needed any more. The doctor hadn't expected this, didn't know what to say and asked: "And did the master hiccough before he died?" "Yes, sir." "Did he hiccough much?" "Yes, a lot." "Ah, well – that's a good sign." And off he went. Ha ha ha!'

Only the old man was laughing; Arkady managed an expression resembling a smile. Bazarov merely inhaled. The talk went on in this way for nearly an hour; Arkady found time to go and see his room, which was simply the changing-room of the bath-shed, but very clean and homely.

At last Tanyushka appeared and announced that dinner was ready.

Vasily Ivanovich was the first to rise.

'Let us go in, gentlemen! Be generous and forgive me if I have bored you. With luck my wife's housekeeping will prove more to your taste.'

The meal, although improvised in something of a hurry, turned out to be very good and even abundant; only the wine did not quite come up to standard: the almost black sherry which Timofeyich had bought from a merchant acquaintance in town had a taste of copper about it, or possibly of turpentine; and the flies were a nuisance. Usually the boy servant fended them off with a big green fan; but on this occasion Vasily Ivanovich had sent him off for fear of the disapproval of the younger generation. Arina Vlas'evna had found time to dress up for the occasion; she had put on a high cap with silk ribbons and a pale blue shawl with an all-over pattern. Tears came to her eyes as soon as she set eyes on her Yevgeny again, but it did not prove necessary for her husband to call her to order: she herself hastened to wipe away the tears so that they should not mark her shawl. Only the young people ate; their hosts had dined some time ago. Fed'ka waited at table, obviously worried by the unfamiliar boots, and he was helped by a woman called Anfisushka, with a manlike face and a twisted body, who fulfilled the functions of housekeeper, poultry-woman and laundress.

Vasily Ivanovich paced up and down the room all the time they were eating and held forth with an utterly happy and even beatific air on the grave fears induced in him by the policy of Napoleon III and the intricacies of the Italian question. Arina Vlas'evna had no eyes for Arkady, not even to see that he was well provided with food. She sat with her fist supporting her round face, to which the childishly pouting cherry-red lips and the moles on the cheeks and above the eyebrows lent an expression of extreme good nature, and she never took her eyes from her son's face, sighing constantly; she was desperately anxious to know how long he was going to stay with them but was afraid to ask him.

'What if he says "for a day or two"?' she thought, and her heart failed her. After the joint Vasily Ivanovich disappeared for a moment and came back with a ready-opened half-bottle of champagne.

'There,' he exclaimed, 'we may live at the back of beyond, but we still have something to brighten a festive occasion!' He filled three champagne glasses and a liqueur glass, proposed the health of the 'inestimable guests' and tossed off his glass at one gulp in true military fashion, and then saw to it that Arina Vlas'evna drank hers down to the last drop. When they came to the preserves, Arkady, who detested anything sweet, nevertheless considered it his duty to try four different sorts of home-made jam, all the more since Bazarov flatly refused them and immediately lit one of his cigars. The preserves were succeeded by tea with cream and *croissants* and butter; then Vasily Ivanovich led them all out into the garden to admire the beauty of the evening. As they passed the bench he whispered to Arkady:

'In this place I love to sit and meditate as I watch the rising of the sun, as becomes a hermit. And over there, a little further on, I have planted some of the trees beloved of Horace.'

'What trees are those?' inquired Bazarov, who had been listening.

'Why, acacias, of course.'

Bazarov began to yawn.

'I assume it is time our travellers were in the arms of Morpheus,' remarked Vasily Ivanovich.

'Which means it's time we were in bed!' Bazarov took him up. 'The assumption is correct. It is indeed – high time.'

Taking leave of his mother he kissed her forehead, but she embraced him and as soon as his back was turned made the sign of the cross over him surreptitiously three times.

Vasily Ivanovich saw Arkady to his room and wished him 'such sweet slumber as I myself knew at your happy age'. And Arkady really did sleep very soundly in his changing-room: there was a smell of mint and two crickets kept up an alternate soporific chirruping behind the stove. Vasily Ivanovich went straight from Arkady to the study and, settling down on the sofa at his son's feet, prepared to have a comfortable chat with him; but Bazarov sent him away at once, saying that he wanted to go to sleep, though in fact he did not doze off until the morning. His eyes wide open he stared resentfully into the darkness. Childhood memories held no charm for him, and in addition he had not yet had time to shake off the bitter impressions of the last few days.

Arina Vlas'evna first prayed to her heart's content, then enjoyed a long, long chat with Anfisushka, who, standing in front of her mistress as though she had taken root there and fixing her with her single eye, confided to her in a mysterious whisper all that she had noticed and imagined about Yevgeny Vasil'evich. The old woman's head was spinning from happiness, from wine and from cigar smoke; her husband made an attempt to speak to her and gave it up as a bad job.

Arina Vlas'evna was a genuine product of the lesser Russian nobility of a previous age; she should have lived about two hundred years earlier in ancient Muscovy. She was very devout and emotional and believed in all kinds of portents, divinations, spells and dreams; she believed in the power of the fools in Christ,[1] in house-spirits, in wood-spirits, in ill-omened meetings, in ill-wishing, in popular medicines, in the wisdom of eating specially prepared salt on Holy Thursday and in the

1 Men who wandered in the guise of half-witted beggars amongst the people, renouncing even sanity in the name of Christ. Sometimes people of great spiritual power, these 'saints' enjoyed great freedom of speech and were often regarded as prophets.

imminence of the end of the world; she believed that if, on
Easter Day, the candles were not blown out during the midnight service there would be a good crop of buck-wheat and
that mushrooms stop growing after human beings have set
eyes on them; she believed that the Devil likes to be where
there is water to hand and that every Jew has a bloody mark on
his chest; she was afraid of mice, grass-snakes, frogs, sparrows,
leeches, thunder, cold water, draughts, horses, goats, red-
haired people and black cats. Dogs and crickets she considered
unclean creatures; she would eat neither veal nor pigeon nor
shellfish, cheese, asparagus, Jerusalem artichokes, nor red
water-melons, because when cut they looked like the head of
John the Baptist. As for oysters, she could not speak of them
without a shudder; she enjoyed her food but observed the fasts
strictly; she slept ten hours a day and would not go to bed at
all if Vasily Ivanovich had so much as a headache; she had
never read a single book other than *Aleksis, or Huts in the
Forest*,[1] wrote one or at most two letters a year and knew all
there was to know about housekeeping and the drying and
preserving of fruit, although she did nothing with her own
hands and generally disliked any form of physical activity.
Arina Vlas'evna was very kind and, in her own way, far from
stupid. She knew that the world was made up of the gentry,
whose business it was to give orders, and of the common
people, whose lot it was to obey, and for this reason saw nothing
repugnant in servility of manner or in the ancient usage of
bowing the forehead to the ground before a superior; yet she
was mild and kindly in her dealings with her dependants, never
refused a beggar and never set herself up in judgment on
anyone, although not altogether averse to gossip. In her youth
she had been very sweet-looking, had played the clavichord
and had spoken a little French; but in the course of long years
of wandering by the side of her husband, to whom she had
been married against her will, she had grown stout and had
forgotten her music and her French. Her son she both loved
and feared beyond telling. The administration of the estate she

---

1 A sentimental novel by the French author Dueré-Dumesnil.

left to Vasily Ivanovich and now she took no further part in it: she would sigh gustily, fan herself with her handkerchief and raise her eyebrows higher and higher from horror as soon as the old man began to discuss the impending land reforms and his own plans. She was over-anxious, lived in constant expectation of some major catastrophe and was always ready to weep the moment she remembered anything sad.

Today women of this sort are already beginning to die out. God knows whether or not we ought to be glad of it.

XXI

HAVING risen from his bed, Arkady opened wide the window – and the first object to meet his gaze was Vasily Ivanovich. Clad in a Bokharan dressing-gown belted round the waist with a large pocket handkerchief, the old man was busily digging his vegetable garden. He noticed his young guest and, leaning on his spade, called out:

'Good health to you! Did you have a good night?'

'Splendid,' answered Arkady.

'And here am I, as you can see, preparing a bed for late turnips like one Cincinnatus. Now the times are such – and thank God for it! – that every man must get his nourishment with his own hands and can no longer depend on others: he must labour himself. And it turns out that Jean-Jacques Rousseau was right. Half an hour ago, my good sir, you would have seen me in quite another position. I was – how should I say? – pouring opium into a woman who said she had the cramps: that's what they call it, but we would say dysentery; and I've pulled a tooth for another. I offered that one a whiff of ether – only she wouldn't have it. I do all that sort of thing gratis – *anamatter.*[1] Still, that's nothing strange for me: I'm a plebeian, *homo novus.*[2] Not one of the old stock like my good wife. But wouldn't you like to come out here into the shade, to breathe the freshness of the morning before breakfast?'

1 French in Russian characters in the original (= '*en amateur*').
2 'A new man' (Lat.).

Arkady joined him outside.

'Good morning to you once again!' pronounced Vasily Ivanovich, raising his hand to his greasy skull-cap in a military salute. 'You, I know, are used to luxury, to pleasure, but even the great of this world do not scorn to spend a short time under a humble roof.'

'For goodness' sake,' protested Arkady, 'how do I qualify as one of the great of this world? And I'm not used to luxury.'

'Come, come,' argued Vasily Ivanovich, twisting his face into an expression of self-conscious amiability, 'I may be on the shelf now, but I've rubbed about the world a bit myself – I can tell a bird by its flight. Also I'm a psychologist in my own way, and a physiognomist. If I hadn't had that – that gift, I think I may be permitted to call it – I should have come to grief long ago; a little man like me would have been trampled underfoot. Compliments aside, I will tell you that the friendship which I have noticed between you and my son gives me sincere pleasure. I have just seen him; he jumped out of bed very early, according to his habit, with which you are doubtless familiar, and went off round the countryside. Permit me to be a little curious – have you known my Yevgeny for long?'

'Since last winter.'

'I see. And might I also ask you – but shouldn't we sit down? – might I also ask you, as a father, in all frankness: what is your opinion of my Yevgeny?'

'Your son is one of the most remarkable people I have ever met,' answered Arkady with animation.

Vasily Ivanovich's eyes flew open and a faint colour rose in his cheeks. The spade fell from his hands.

'And so you think . . .' he began.

'I am certain,' Arkady took him up, 'that your son has a great future before him, that he will make your name famous. I've been convinced of that from our first meeting.'

'How – how did that happen?' Vasily Ivanovich could barely speak. An ecstatic smile had parted his wide lips and appeared to be permanently fixed there.

'You wish to know how we met?'

'Yes – and in general. . . .'

Arkady began to talk about Bazarov with still more warmth, with still more enthusiasm, than when he had danced the mazurka with Odintsova.

Vasily Ivanovich listened and listened, blew his nose, mangled his handkerchief in both hands, coughed, ruffled up his hair – and finally could control himself no longer: he bent down to Arkady and planted a kiss on his shoulder.[1]

'You have made me completely happy,' he said, smiling all the time. 'I must tell you that I idolize my son; I don't need to say anything about my old lady: everyone knows – a mother! But I never dare to express my feelings when he's there, because he doesn't like it. He hates all effusions; many people even condemn him for such strength of character and think it a sign of pride or want of proper feeling; but people like him can't be judged by ordinary standards, can they? There's one thing, for instance: another in his place would have gone on getting what he could out of his parents; but would you believe it, he's never taken a penny more than was absolutely needful from us since the day he was born.'

'He's a disinterested, honourable man,' remarked Arkady.

'That's it exactly – disinterested. And as for me, Arkady Nikolayevich, I don't only idolize him, I am proud of him, and all my ambition consists in this: that in time these words may appear in his biography: "The son of a simple regimental doctor who, however, recognized his true nature at an early age and willingly made every sacrifice for his education."' The old man's voice broke.

Arkady pressed his hand.

'What do you think,' asked Vasily Ivanovich after a brief silence, 'will he achieve the fame which you prophesy for him in the field of medicine?'

'Of course not in medicine, though there too he will be among the leading scholars.'

'In what then, Arkady Nikolayevich?'

'That is hard to say now, but he will be famous.'

---

1 A sign of respect and humility. Favoured household serfs would salute their masters in this fashion.

'He will be famous!' repeated the old man, and became lost in thought.

'Arina Vlas'evna ordered me to ask you to come in to breakfast,' announced Anfisushka, walking past them with a great dish of fresh raspberries.

Vasily Ivanovich started.

'And will there be chilled cream with the raspberries?'

'There will, sir.'

'See that it's really cold then! Don't stand on ceremony, Arkady Nikolayevich, take a good helping. Why doesn't Yevgeny come?'

'I'm here,' came Bazarov's voice from Arkady's room.

Vasily Ivanovich swung round sharply.

'Aha! You wanted to call in on your friend, but you came too late, *amice*,[1] and he and I have already had a nice long chat. Now we must go and have breakfast: your mother has sent for us. By the way, I want a word with you.'

'What about?'

'There's a peasant here. He's suffering from icterus.'

'You mean jaundice?'

'Yes, a chronic and very stubborn case of icterus. I have prescribed centaury and St John's wort for him, made him eat turnips, given him soda; but all those are merely palliative measures; the case calls for something more drastic. Although you laugh at medicine I am sure you will be able to give me some good advice. But we'll talk about that later. Now let's go and have breakfast.'

Vasily Ivanovich jumped nimbly up from the bench and burst into song from *Robert the Devil*:

> 'A law, a law, a law we have unto ourselves,
>   To li-i-, to li-i, to live in pleasure!'

'But what animation!!' remarked Bazarov, turning away from the window.

Came midday. The sun beat down from behind a flimsy curtain of whitish cloud which covered the whole sky.

1 'Friend' (Lat.).

Everything was still. Only the cocks crowed challengingly to one another in the village, exciting a strange feeling of lethargy and boredom in all who heard them; and somewhere high up in the treetops there sounded, like a whining entreaty, the incessant squeaking of a young hawk. Arkady and Bazarov lay in the shade of a small haystack, having made a bed from a few armfuls of the rustling, dry but still green and fragrant grass.

'That aspen-tree,' said Bazarov, 'reminds me of my childhood; it grows on the edge of a pit, all that's left of a brick barn, and at that time I was certain that that pit and that aspen had some kind of magic power: I was never unhappy when I was near them. I didn't understand then that I wasn't unhappy because I was a child. Well, now that I'm grown up the magic doesn't work.'

'How long did you live here altogether?' asked Arkady.

'About two years without a break. Then we used to come here when we could. We led a roving life, trailing about from town to town.'

'And has the house been there a long time?'

'Yes. My grandfather built it, my mother's father.'

'Who was he, your grandfather?'

'The devil alone knows. Some kind of major. He served under Suvorov and was full of tales about the crossing of the Alps. Made it all up, most probably.'

'So that's why there's a portrait of Suvorov hanging in your drawing-room. But I like little houses like yours, old and cosy; and they have a special sort of smell.'

'Lamp oil and herbs,' pronounced Bazarov, yawning. 'And the flies in those dear little houses – faugh!'

'Tell me,' began Arkady, after a short pause, 'were you strictly brought up as a child?'

'You've seen what my parents are like. Not what you'd call stern folk.'

'Do you love them, Yevgeny?'

'I do, Arkady!'

'They love you so much!'

Bazarov was silent for a while.

'Do you know what I'm thinking about?' he asked finally, clasping his hands behind his head.

'No. What?'

'I'm thinking what an easy time my parents have of it! Father has been bustling about for sixty years talking of "palliative" measures, healing people, making generous gestures with the peasants – been having a high old time, in fact; and my mother has an easy life, her days so crammed with all kinds of things to do and with "oh"s and with "ah"s that she never has time to stop and think; but—'

'But you?'

'But I think. Here I lie under a haystack. The narrow little place that I occupy is so minute compared to the rest of space where I am not and where I am of no importance; and the part of time during which I shall manage to keep alive is so insignificant in the face of eternity, where I was not and will not be. Yet in this atom, in this mathematical point, the blood circulates, the brain works, and even forms desires. It's scandalous! Absurd!'

'Let me remind you that what you are saying has a general application to all human beings.'

'You're right,' Bazarov took him up. 'I just wanted to say that they, my parents I mean, are busy and aren't worried by their own insignificance: it doesn't stink in their nostrils; but I – I feel only boredom and anger.'

'Anger? Why anger?'

'Why? How can you ask that? Surely you haven't forgotten?'

'I remember everything, but still I don't consider you have the right to be angry. You're unfortunate, I agree, but—'

'Ugh! I can see that you, Arkady Nikolayevich, have the same idea of love as all modern young men: chuck, chuck, chuck, chucky-hen – and the moment the hen begins to come towards you, you take to your heels! I'm not like that. But that's enough. It's ignominious to go on talking of what can't be mended.' He turned on his side. 'Oho! There's a fine young ant dragging a half-dead fly along! Pull away, brother, pull away! Don't mind if she struggles! Just take advantage of the fact that you, as an animal, have the right not to admit the sentiment of compassion, unlike our brother man, the self-destructive creature.'

'You have no right to say that, Yevgeny! When did you ever practise self-destruction?'

Bazarov raised his head.

'That's the one thing I'm proud of. I haven't destroyed myself, and no woman's going to do it for me. Amen! Finished! You'll never hear another word from me on that subject.'

Both friends lay for a time in silence.

'Yes,' began Bazarov, 'man is a strange creature. When you look from the side and from a distance at the quiet life the "fathers" live here, you think: what could be better? Eat, drink and rest assured that you're acting in the soundest, the most reasonable manner. But no; you're eaten up with tedium. You want to do something for people, even if it's only to swear at them, but to do something for them.'

'One ought to organize one's life so that each moment should be significant,' Arkady pronounced reflectively.

'You don't say so! The significant, although it may sometimes be illusion, is always sweet; still, it's quite possible to come to terms with the insignificant; but all the petty unpleasantnesses – that's the trouble.'

'Petty unpleasantnesses don't exist for the man who refuses to acknowledge their existence.'

'Hm. What you've just said is an *antipodal truism.*'

'A what? What do you understand by that expression?'

'This is what: to say, for instance, that education is useful is a truism; but to say that education is harmful is an antipodal truism. It sounds smarter, but essentially it's all one and the same.'

'But where is the truth then, on which side?'

'Where indeed? I answer you like an echo: where?'

'You are in a melancholy mood today, Yevgeny.'

'Really? I must have had too much sun, and I shouldn't have eaten so many raspberries.'

'In that case it wouldn't be a bad thing to doze for a bit,' remarked Arkady.

'Perhaps; only don't watch me: everybody's face looks silly when they're asleep.'

'But do you mind what people think of you?'

'I don't know how to answer that. A real man shouldn't mind; a real man is one of whom there's nothing to think, but who has to be obeyed or hated.'

'Strange! I don't hate anyone,' announced Arkady after a moment's thought.

'And I so many. You're a tender soul, a softie, what have you to do with hate! You're timid, you've got no self-confidence—'

'And you,' interrupted Arkady, 'you have self-confidence? You have a high opinion of yourself?'

Bazarov did not answer at once.

'When I meet the man who can hold his own beside me,' he said deliberately, 'then I shall revise my opinion of myself. Hatred! Now you said today for instance, as we were passing the *izba* of our bailiff Fillip – it's that nice white one – you said Russia will attain perfection when every last peasant has quarters like that and each of us should do his best to bring this about. And I conceived a hatred for that last peasant, Fillip or Sidor, for whom I'm supposed to work myself to the bone and who won't even thank me for it; and what good would his thanks do me, anyway? Well, there he'll be in his white *izba* and I'll be under the wild flowers; well, and then what?'

'Stop it, Yevgeny; to listen to you today one can hardly help but agree with the people who reproach you for having no principles.'

'You're talking like your uncle. There are no such things as principles – you haven't got that far yet! – but there are sensations. Everything depends on them.'

'In what way?'

'Well, it just does. I, for instance: I always take the line of negation – thanks to the sensation it affords me. I enjoy negation, my brain's constructed that way – and *basta*![1] Why do

1 In Italian in the original.

I like chemistry? Why do you like apples? All thanks to sensation. It's all the same thing. People will never get beyond that. Not everyone would admit it, in fact I might not admit it myself on another occasion.'

'What of honesty then? Is that a sensation?'

'I should rather think it was!'

'Yevgeny,' began Arkady in a miserable voice.

'So you don't like it, eh?' interrupted Bazarov. 'No, brother! If you've made up your mind to put the scythe to everything then you must start with your own legs! However, that's enough philosophy. "Nature invokes the quietude of sleep", as Pushkin said.'

'He never said anything of the sort,' retorted Arkady.

'Well, if he didn't he might have, in fact as a poet he ought to have. By the way, I suppose he was in military service?'

'Pushkin was never a soldier!'

'Good gracious, on every page he's written something about: To arms, to arms! For the glory of Russia!'

'What nonsense you do talk! Why, that's pure libel!'

'Libel? How pompous! A pretty word to frighten me with! Whatever libel you may choose to put on a man, you may be sure that in fact he deserves something twenty times worse.'

'Oh, let's go to sleep!' snapped Arkady.

'With the greatest pleasure,' answered Bazarov.

But neither of them could sleep. A feeling almost of hostility had taken possession of the hearts of both young men. Five minutes later they opened their eyes and surveyed one another in silence.

'Look,' said Arkady suddenly, 'a dead maple leaf detaches itself from the tree and falls to the ground; its movements are exactly like those of a butterfly in flight. Isn't that strange? The saddest and deadest things resemble those that are the most joyful and alive.'

'Oh my friend, Arkady Nikolayevich!' exclaimed Bazarov. 'I only ask one thing of you: don't talk in fine phrases.'

'I talk as I can. And what's more that's sheer despotism. The thought came into my head; why shouldn't I express it?'

'All right; but then why shouldn't I express my thought?
I consider that to use fine phrases is indecent.'

'What's decent, then? to swear?'

'Oho! I see you really do mean to follow in your uncle's
footsteps. How that idiot would rejoice if he could hear you
now!'

'What did you call Pavel Petrovich?'

'I called him what he is – an idiot.'

'But this is intolerable!' cried Arkady.

'Aha! Family feeling raising its voice,' pronounced Bazarov
calmly. 'I have noticed how deep-rooted it is in people. A man
will give up anything, will renounce any prejudice; but to
admit, for instance, that his brother, who steals other people's
handkerchiefs, is a thief – that's beyond his powers. And,
when you come to think of it: *my* brother, *mine* – yet not a
genius: is this possible?'

'It was a straightforward feeling for justice which raised its
voice in me and not in the least family feeling,' retorted
Arkady with quick anger. 'But since you don't understand
that feeling, and you don't happen to experience that *sensation*, you're no judge of the matter.'

'In other words, Arkady Kirsanov is too elevated for my
understanding. I bow before him and will say no more.'

'Enough, please, Yevgeny; we'll end up by quarrelling.'

'Ah, Arkady! Do me a favour and let's have one real, good
quarrel – till one of us throws in the sponge, till the death.'

'But if we go on like that we might end—'

'By fighting?' Bazarov took him up. 'And why not? Here, in
the hay, in such an idyllic spot, far from the world and curious
eyes, it wouldn't matter. But you'd be no match for me. I'd
take you by the throat at once.'

Bazarov spread out his long, sinewy fingers. Arkady rolled
over and prepared, as if in sport, to fight back. But his friend's
face appeared so threatening, the crooked sneering lips and
burning eyes held a menace which seemed so far from jest,
that he felt an involuntary touch of fear.

'Ah! So this is where you've got to!' Vasily Ivanovich's voice
broke in upon them at that moment, and the old doctor

materialized before the young people bedight in a home-made
cloth jacket and with a straw hat, also home made, on his
head. 'I've been searching for you all over the place. But
you've chosen an excellent spot and a splendid occupation.
To lie on the "earth", to gaze into the "heavens". You know,
there's some deep significance in that.'

'I only gaze into the heavens when I want to make myself
sneeze,' growled Bazarov and, turning to Arkady, added in an
undertone: 'Pity he interrupted.'

'Come, let's forget it,' whispered Arkady, and squeezed his
friend's hand surreptitiously. But no friendship on earth will
hold out long against such clashes.

'I look at you, my youthful companions,' Vasily Ivanovich
was saying meanwhile, shaking his head and leaning with
folded hands on a cunningly wrought walking-stick of his own
making with the figure of a Turk for a handle, 'I look at you
and I can't look my fill. How much strength there is in you,
how much of the very bloom of youth, what abilities, talents!
Clearly, Castor and Pollux.'

'Now look where he's gone soaring off to – mythology!' said
Bazarov. 'You can see at once that he must have been a good
classics man in his time. I seem to remember you once won a
silver medal for Latin composition, didn't you?'

'The Dioscuri, the Dioscuri,' repeated Vasily Ivanovich.

'Yes, but that'll do, Father. Don't gush over us.'

'Just once in a while surely it's permissible,' muttered the
old man. 'However, gentlemen, I did not seek you out to pay
you compliments, but in the first place to tell you that we're
soon going to have dinner, and in the second I wanted to warn
you, Yevgeny – you're an intelligent man, you know people
and you know women and so you will excuse.... Your dear
mother wanted to hold a thanksgiving service in the house in
gratitude for your safe arrival. Don't imagine that I am inviting you to attend this service: it is already over; but Father
Aleksey—'

'The parson?'

'Well, yes, the priest; he's going to have dinner with us.
I wasn't expecting it and even advised against it, but it just

happened – he misunderstood me. Well, and Anna Vlas'evna
... And then he's a very good, enlightened sort of man.'

'But he won't eat my share of the dinner, will he?' asked
Bazarov.

Vasily Ivanovich burst out laughing.

'Good gracious, the things you say!'

'That's all I ask. I'm prepared to sit down to table with
anybody.'

Vasily Ivanovich adjusted his hat.

'I was sure in advance,' he declared, 'that you were above
prejudices of any sort. I'm an old man and have lived sixty-
two years, and in all that time I too have learnt not to have
them.' (Vasily Ivanovich dared not admit that he had wanted
the thanksgiving service himself – he was no less devout than
his wife.) 'And Father Aleksey wanted so much to make your
acquaintance. You will like him, you'll see. He's not above
having a game of cards, and even – but that's between ourselves – smokes a pipe.'

'Fine. After dinner we'll sit down to a game of cards and
I'll fleece him.'

'Ha ha ha, we shall see! It might be a case of the biter bit.'

'What's that? Not recalling the days of your youth, are
you?' inquired Bazarov with peculiar emphasis.

Vasily Ivanovich's bronzed cheeks coloured faintly.

'Yevgeny, you ought to be ashamed of yourself. Let
bygones be bygones. Oh well, I'm prepared to admit to
Arkady Nikolayevich that I did suffer from that passion in my
youth – it's quite true; yes, and I paid for it! How hot it is,
though. May I sit down with you? I'm not disturbing you?'

'Not at all,' answered Arkady.

Vasily Ivanovich lowered himself wheezing on to the hay.

'Your present couch, gentlemen,' he began, 'reminds me of
my bivouacking days in the army, of the field dressing
stations, any old where, sometimes under a haystack just like
this, and lucky if we were.' He sighed. 'I have been through a
deal, a great deal, in my life. For instance, if you'll permit
me, I'll tell you about a curious episode during the plague in
Bessarabia.'

'For which you were awarded the Vladimir cross?' broke in Bazarov. 'You've told us about that. By the way, why aren't you wearing it?'

'But I told you I didn't have any prejudices,'[1] muttered Vasily Ivanovich – only the day before he had given orders for the red ribbon to be ripped off his jacket – and settled down to tell the story of the plague. 'Why, he's gone to sleep,' he whispered suddenly to Arkady, pointing at Bazarov and winking good-naturedly. 'Yevgeny! Get up!' he added aloud. 'Let's go in to dinner.'

Father Aleksey, an impressive, stout figure of a man with thick carefully combed hair and an embroidered belt girding his cassock of lilac silk, proved to be a very adroit and ready-witted person. He was quick to make the first move to shake hands with Arkady and Bazarov, as though he had understood in advance that they did not require his blessing, and, in general, he behaved without embarrassment. He neither laid himself open to criticism nor provoked others; he made an appropriate joke about seminary Latin and stood up for the bishop of his diocese; drank two glasses of wine and refused a third; accepted a cigar from Arkady but refrained from smoking, saying that he would take it home with him. The only objectionable thing about him was that now and again he would raise his hand slowly and cautiously to catch flies on his face and in doing this would occasionally squash one. He took his place at the green table with a moderate show of pleasure and ended by winning two roubles fifty copecks in notes from Bazarov: in Arina Vlas'evna's household nobody had the least notion of how to reckon in silver. She sat close beside her son as before (she did not play cards) and, as before, she propped her cheek on her fist and only rose from her place to see that her guests were well supplied with refreshment.

1 So great was the contempt of the radical Russian intelligentsia for the society in which they lived that no recognition of service to this society – such as a medal – could pretend to their respect. Bazarov's father instinctively takes the simpler view that success and the awards which go with it are something to be proud of, but discards this 'prejudice' in deference to the convictions of his son.

She was afraid to be demonstrative in her tenderness for Bazarov and he gave her no encouragement, never inviting her
caresses; also Vasily Ivanovich advised her not to 'bother' him.
'Young men don't like that sort of thing,' he was always
informing her. (As to the dinner served that day, there is no
need to describe it: Timofeyich in person had gone galloping
off at daybreak to fetch some special Cherkassian beef; the
bailiff had driven in the opposite direction for freshwater eels,
ruff and crayfish; for mushrooms alone the peasant-women
received forty-two copecks in copper.) Yet Arina Vlas'evna's
eyes, as they rested fixedly on Bazarov, held something more
than tenderness and devotion; there was a sadness in them
too, mingled with curiosity and fear, and a kind of humble
reproach.

Not that Bazarov was in the mood to try to make out what
exactly the expression in his mother's eyes might signify; he
seldom spoke to her, and then only to ask some brief question.
Once he asked her to give him her hand 'for luck'; she gently
placed her soft hand in his hard broad palm.

'Well,' she asked, after waiting a little while, 'didn't it help?'

'It's going worse than ever,' he answered with a careless,
sardonic smile.

'They play a very rash game,' pronounced Father Aleksey
as though he were sorry for it, and stroked his handsome
beard.

'Napoleon's maxim, Father, Napoleon's,' Vasily Ivanovich
retorted, and led with an ace.

'Which led him to the island of St Helena,' retorted Father
Aleksey, and covered his ace with a trump.

'Wouldn't you like some black-currant cordial, Yevgeny
love?' asked Arina Vlas'evna.

Bazarov merely shrugged his shoulders.

'No!' he said to Arkady the following day. 'I shall leave here
tomorrow. I'm bored; I want to work, and there's no doing
that here. I'll go back with you to your home; I left all my
apparatus there. At least you can lock yourself in at your place.
But here my father keeps saying "My study is at your service
– no one will disturb you," and then never leaves me alone for

a minute himself. And anyway it gives me a guilty conscience somehow to lock myself away from him. And then there's Mother too. I hear her sighing away in the next room, and when I do go through to her I don't know what to say.'

'She'll be very upset,' said Arkady, 'and he will be too.'

'I'll come back and see them again.'

'When?'

'When I go back to Petersburg.'

'I'm especially sorry for your mother.'

'Why so? Has she got round you with all those raspberries?'

Arkady dropped his eyes.

'You don't know your mother, Yevgeny. She's not only an excellent woman, she's very shrewd, honestly. Today she and I talked for more than half an hour, and all that she said was so interesting and to the point.'

'I suppose she was going on about me all the time?'

'We didn't only talk about you!'

'Possibly! The onlooker sees more of the game. If a woman can keep a conversation going for half an hour, then that at least is a good sign. But I shall still leave.'

'You're not going to find it easy to break it to them. They are always discussing what we are going to do in two weeks' time.'

'No, it won't be easy. The Devil got into me today to annoy Father: he ordered one of his peasants to be flogged the other day – and quite right too; yes, yes, and you needn't look at me with such horror – he did quite right, because the fellow's a thief and a frightful drunkard. But Father hadn't expected me "to have received information on this head" as they say. He was quite overcome, and now I shall have to disappoint him into the bargain. Never mind! He'll get over it.'

Bazarov had said 'never mind!' but the whole day passed before he plucked up courage to tell Vasily Ivanovich of his intention. In the end it was not until he was actually bidding him good night in the study that he said with a strained yawn:

'Ah yes, I almost forgot to ask you. Would you give orders for Fyedot to be ready with a change of horses for us tomorrow?'

Vasily Ivanovich was dumbfounded.

'Surely Mr Kirsanov isn't leaving us?'

'Yes, he is, and I'm going with him.'

Vasily Ivanovich spun round where he stood.

'You're leaving?'

'Yes, I must. You will make arrangements about the horses, won't you?'

'Very well,' stammered the old man, 'a change of horses – very well – only – only . . . How is this?'

'I shall have to stay with him for a little while. Then I'll return here.'

'Yes! for a little while. . . . Very well.' Vasily Ivanovich drew out his handkerchief and almost bent double over the business of blowing his nose. 'Ah well! Everything will come all right. I thought that you would be with us a bit longer. Three days. . . . That's, that's rather short after three years; rather short, Yevgeny!'

'But I'm telling you I shall be back soon. I'm obliged to go.'

'Obliged – oh well! Duty must always be our first consideration. Send about the horses, then? Very well. Of course Arina and I were not expecting this. She's begged some flowers from the woman down the way, wanted to put them in your room.' (Vasily Ivanovich did not mention how every morning at crack of dawn, standing bare-legged in his slippers, he would confer with Timofeyich and, producing one bank-note after another with shaking fingers, would send him off to make various purchases, setting particular store by eatables and red wine, which, in so far as he had been able to tell, the young people had particularly enjoyed.) 'The main thing is freedom; that is my maxim – no use interfering – no. . . .'

He suddenly broke off and made for the door.

'We'll see each other again soon, Father, honestly.'

But Vasily Ivanovich just made a gesture with his hand without turning round and went out. Back in his bedroom he found his wife in bed and began to say his prayers in a whisper so as not to waken her. However, she did wake up.

'Is that you, Vasily Ivanovich?' she asked.

'Yes, Mother.'

'Have you just come from Yevgeny? You know, I'm worried; do you think he sleeps well on the sofa? I told Anfisushka
to give him your camp mattress and the new pillows; I would
have given him our feather mattress only I seem to remember
that he doesn't like a soft bed.'

'Never mind, Mother, don't worry. He's all right. God,
have mercy upon us sinners,' he went on with his prayers
under his breath. Vasily Ivanovich wished to spare his old
lady; he could not bring himself to tell her what sorrow
awaited her before she slept.

Bazarov and Arkady left the following day. From early
morning all was dejection in the house; Anfisushka kept on
dropping things; even Fed'ka couldn't make out what was
going on and ended by taking off his boots. Vasily Ivanovich
bustled around more than ever before. He was evidently
determined to put a good face on things, spoke loudly and
stamped his feet, but his face was drawn and he avoided looking directly at his son. Arina Vlas'evna was quietly weeping;
she would have succumbed completely and lost all self-control
had not her husband devoted two whole hours to talking her
round earlier that morning. When Bazarov, after repeated
promises to return in not more than a month's time, had
finally torn himself from their reluctant arms and had taken
his place in the tarantass; when the horses started off and the
bells on their harness began to tinkle and the wheels were set
in motion; when there was already nothing left to look after
and the dust was laid and Timofeyich, all bent and tottering
on his feet, had wandered aimlessly back into his little room;
when the two old people found themselves alone in the house,
which also seemed to have suddenly shrunk and grown
decrepit: Vasily Ivanovich, who but a few moments earlier
had still been waving his handkerchief bravely from the porch,
sank on to a chair and dropped his head on his breast. 'He's
deserted us, left us,' he muttered, 'gone; he feels bored with
us now. I'm alone now, all alone!' he repeated several times
and each time stretched his hand in front of him, the index
finger sticking out pathetically as though to illustrate his own
isolation.

Then Arina Vlas'evna came up to him, and laying her grey head against his grey head she said: 'What can we do, Vasya! Our son's his own master now. He's like a free bird of the skies: he wanted to come – came flying down to us; wanted to go – and flew away. And you and I, the mushrooms in a hollow, sit here side by side and can't fly after him. Only I'll stay by you and be the same for ever, as you will do for me.'

Vasily Ivanovich took his hands from his face and embraced his wife, his love, more fiercely than ever he had embraced her in their youth: she comforted him in his sorrow.

XXII

IN silence, only now and again exchanging some insignificant words, our friends travelled as far as Fyedot's. Bazarov was not altogether pleased with himself. Arkady was not pleased with him. In addition he felt in his heart that unaccountable sadness known only to the very young. The coachman changed the horses and, having clambered up on to the box, inquired: 'Right or left?'

Arkady started. The way to the right led to the town and from there to his home; the way to the left to Odintsova's.

He looked at Bazarov.

'Yevgeny,' he asked, 'to the left?'

Bazarov turned away.

'What's this foolishness?' he muttered.

'I know it's foolishness,' answered Arkady. 'But what does it matter? It's not as if it was the first time.'

Bazarov pulled his cap down over his eyes.

'Do as you like,' he said finally.

'To the left!' cried Arkady.

The tarantass moved off in the direction of Nikol'skoye. But, having made up their minds to this 'foolishness', the friends preserved their silence more stubbornly than before and even appeared to be angry about something.

If only by the demeanour of the butler when he met them on the porch of Odintsova's house the friends might have realized that they had acted unwisely in yielding to their sudden whim. They were clearly not expected, and were left sitting for some time in the drawing-room. At last Odintsova came down to them.

She welcomed them with her customary good manners, but expressed surprise at their early return and, so far as might be judged from the languor of her speech and gestures, was not too pleased at it. They made haste to explain that they had only called in on their way to town and that they would resume their journey in about four hours. She contented herself with a mild exclamation, asked Arkady to convey her respects to his father and sent for her aunt.

The princess appeared, obviously just awakened from her afternoon nap, which lent her wrinkled old face still greater malevolence of expression. Katya was indisposed and could not leave her room. Arkady suddenly felt that he had wanted to see Katya at least as much as he had wanted to see Anna Sergeyevna. The four hours passed in trifling talk of this and that; Anna Sergeyevna both listened to them and spoke herself without a smile. Only as they were actually taking their leave did a spark of her former friendliness appear to reanimate her.

'I am feeling depressed just now,' she said, 'but pay no attention to that and come to see me again a little later on. I say this to both of you.'

Both Bazarov and Arkady responded with a silent bow, installed themselves in their carriage and, making no further halts on the way, set off home for Marino, where they arrived safely on the evening of the next day.

Throughout the journey neither the one nor the other made any mention of Odintsova; Bazarov in particular scarcely opened his mouth, but gazed out to the side away from the road with a kind of desperate concentration.

At Marino everyone was extremely glad to see them. Nikolay Petrovich had begun to worry over his son's prolonged absence; he cried out with delight and began to swing his legs and to bounce up and down on the sofa when Fenechka came running in to him with shining eyes and announced the arrival of 'the young masters'; even Pavel Petrovich felt a certain agreeable excitement and smiled affably as he shook hands with the returning wanderers.

There was much chatter and many questions. Arkady did most of the talking, especially over supper which went on till well after midnight. Nikolay Petrovich gave orders to serve bottles of porter newly brought from Moscow, and grew so merry that his cheeks were flushed crimson and he kept on laughing a laugh which seemed now childish, now nervous. The general high spirits spread even to the servants. Dunyasha ran hither and thither like one possessed and kept banging the doors, and, even after two o'clock in the morning, Pyotr was still struggling to play the *Valse-Cossaque* on his guitar. The strings twanged plaintively and sweetly in the heavy air, but nothing came of the educated valet's efforts except for a brief preliminary flourish; nature had accorded him no more talent for music than for anything else.

Yet all this time things had not been going too well at Marino and poor Nikolay Petrovich was having a bad time. Anxieties about the farm multiplied daily – joyless, senseless anxieties. The hired labourers were proving more trouble than they were worth. Some demanded a rise in pay or to be released from their contract, others left immediately on receipt of their advance bonus; the horses fell sick; the harness was falling to pieces; all work about the farm was performed carelessly; one threshing-machine specially ordered from Moscow had proved useless because of its weight; another was mishandled and broke down the first time it was brought into commission; half the cow-sheds burnt down because a blind old woman (one of the servants) had taken out a smouldering torch in windy weather to perform some magic rite of fumigation on her cow – although if the old woman was to be believed the true cause of the disaster was the master's notion of introducing some unheard-of new cheeses and other dairy products. The bailiff had suddenly turned indolent and had even begun to put on weight, as any Russian will if he comes into easy money. When he caught sight of Nikolay Petrovich in the distance he would demonstrate his zeal by throwing a faggot at a passing piglet or making a threatening gesture at some half-naked little boy, but most of the time he slept. The peasants on the newly established *obrok*[1] system did not pay their rent on time and stole wood from the forest; almost every night the watchman caught some of the peasants' horses on the farm meadows and sometimes he forcibly confiscated them. Nikolay Petrovich was always meaning to exact a monetary fine for damage, but the whole business would usually end with the horses being returned to their owners after having been kept for a day or two on the landlord's fodder.

To crown all this the peasants had begun to quarrel amongst themselves: brothers demanded division of property since their wives could not live in peace under the same roof; fights would flare up and the entire community would suddenly rise to its feet, as at the word of command, and come running up to the porch before the office, thrusting themselves into the landlord's presence, often with battered faces and the worse for drink, to demand judgment and retribution; there would be much noise and shouting and the shrill whining of the women would alternate with the curses of the men. It was then necessary for the landlord to sort out the opposing sides and to shout until he was hoarse to make himself heard, knowing in advance that whatever happened it would be impossible to arrive at an equitable decision. There were not enough hands to help with the harvest; a neighbouring smallholder with the most honest and comely face offered to find reapers at two roubles to the acre, and let Nikolay Petrovich down in the most shameless manner. The peasant women belonging to the estate demanded exorbitant wages and in the meantime the corn was spoiling; here they had not yet finished mowing; there the Council of Trustees was issuing threats and demanding immediate and full payment of interest due. . . .

'It is beyond my powers!' Nikolay Petrovich had more than once exclaimed in despair. 'I can't start knocking sense into them myself, to send for the district police-officer is against

1 *See* footnote, p. 12.

my principles, and without fear of punishment we'll never get anywhere!'

'*Du calme, du calme,*'[1] Pavel Petrovich would remark in reply to these outbursts, and himself would mutter and frown and pull at his moustaches.

Bazarov kept aloof from these petty squabbles and, indeed, as a guest it would have been unbecoming in him to interfere in what was after all not his business. Within two days of his arrival at Marino he was again absorbed in his frogs, in his infusoria and in chemical compositions. Arkady, on the other hand, considered it his duty if not actually to help his father at least to make a show of being willing to do so. He would hear him out patiently, and once he even delivered himself of some advice, not so much in the hope that it would be followed as in order to show some active interest. He did not hold estate management in aversion and even enjoyed imagining what he would do in the agrarian field, but at that time other thoughts were beginning to crowd through his head.

Arkady, to his own amazement, could not stop thinking about Nikol'skoye. Had anyone told him before that he could feel bored under the same roof as Bazarov – and, what is more, not just anywhere but under his own parental roof – he would merely have shrugged his shoulders. But he was bored and he longed to be elsewhere. He tried walking until he was tired out, but even this brought him no relief. Once when he was talking to his father he learnt that in Nikolay Petrovich's possession were several rather interesting letters written to his late wife by Odintsova's mother.

Arkady gave his father no peace until he had obtained these letters. To find them Nikolay Petrovich had to turn out twenty different drawers and boxes. Having gained possession of these half-decaying papers Arkady seemed to feel calmer, as though he had perceived the goal towards which he must make. 'I say that to both of you,' he whispered again and again. 'She added that herself. I will go, damn it, I will.' But

1 In French in the original.

he kept remembering the last visit, the cool reception, the awkwardness, and he was overcome by shyness. The incurable optimism of youth, the secret wish to put his luck to the test and to try his wings alone, without help or protection from anyone, finally triumphed. Ten days had not gone by since his return to Marino when he again went galloping off to town, offering the explanation that he was going to study the organization of Sunday-schools, and from there to Nikol'skoye. Continually urging on the driver he swept down upon his objective like a young officer going into battle: he was at once afraid and elated; impatience threatened to suffocate him. 'The main thing is not to think,' he kept on repeating to himself. He had been allotted a wild driver who pulled up before every inn inquiring 'Shall we have one?' or 'What about having one?' but who, having 'had one', did not spare the horses.

There at last came into view the high roof of the familiar house. 'What am I doing?' The thought suddenly flashed through Arkady's head. 'Well, I can't go back now anyway!' The team of three galloped on merrily; the driver hiccoughed and whistled. Here the bridge was already resounding with the beat of hoofs and the thunder of wheels; here already was the alley of clipped spruce. A pink dress fluttered amidst the dark green, a youthful face peeped out from under the scant fringe of a parasol. He recognized Katya, and she him. Arkady ordered the driver to pull in the excited horses, leapt down from his place in the vehicle and went to meet her.

'It's you!' she said, and a slow blush spread up to the roots of her hair. 'Let us go to my sister, she's there in the garden; she will be happy to see you.'

Katya led Arkady into the garden. The encounter seemed to him a particularly happy omen; he was as pleased to see her as though she had been a sister. Everything was going so well: no butler, no formal announcement. At a turn in the path he saw Anna Sergeyevna. She was standing with her back to him. Hearing steps she turned round unhurriedly.

Arkady nearly lost his self-possession again, but her opening words set him at his ease at once.

'How do you do, truant!' she said in her even, caressing voice, and came forward to meet him, smiling and screwing up her eyes against the sun and the wind. 'Where did you find him, Katya?'

'Anna Sergeyevna,' he began, 'I have brought you something that will surprise you. . . .

'You have brought yourself; that is better than anything.'

XXIII

AFTER seeing Arkady off with mocking compassion, and giving him to understand that he was under no illusion as to the true object of his journey, Bazarov finally retired into himself: he was working feverishly. He no longer argued with Pavel Petrovich, all the more since in his presence the elder Kirsanov assumed an exaggeratedly aristocratic manner and gave vent to his opinions through the medium of sounds rather than of words. On one occasion only did Pavel Petrovich almost join battle with the *nihilist* on the much-discussed question of the rights of the Baltic barons,[1] but checked himself suddenly, remarking with icy courtesy:

'However, we shall never understand one another; I at least find you quite beyond my humble understanding.'

'I should rather think you do,' exclaimed Bazarov. 'The intellect of man can encompass anything – the vibrations of the ether and what is happening on the sun; but that another

---

1 'Baron' is a German rather than a Russian title, and the nobility of the Baltic provinces were largely of German origin. They occupied a unique position with regard to the question of the emancipation of the serfs, for their own serfs had been freed – without land – by Alexander I in 1819. The all-Russian emancipation contemplated at the time the action of this novel was taking place envisaged a grant of land to each peasant family, and the 'barons' feared that this reform would also be applied on their estates. They sought to establish that the right to own land was the exclusive privilege of the nobility, although this had not in fact been the case since this right had been granted to individuals of all classes except the serfs in 1801. Liberal opinion in Russia strongly condemned their point of view because liberation without land would perpetuate the complete dependence of the peasant on the landowner.

man can blow his nose differently from how he blows his own is beyond the scope of his understanding.'

'Oh, a witty remark?' pronounced Pavel Petrovich on a note of interrogation, and took himself off.

However, he did sometimes ask permission to be present at Bazarov's experiments and once even approached his face, all scented and washed with some excellent preparation, to the microscope in order to observe how a transparent protozoa swallowed a green speck at which it chewed away busily with what appeared to be exceedingly dexterous little fists lining the inside of its throat. Nikolay Petrovich would drop in on Bazarov much more frequently than his brother; he would have come every day to 'study', as he called it, had not the exigencies of his obligations as landlord distracted him. He did not disturb the young naturalist but would sit down in a corner of the room and watch attentively, occasionally permitting himself a cautious question. At meals he tried to steer the conversation towards physics, geology or chemistry, since all other subjects, even estate management, not to mention politics, were liable to lead, if not to open clashes, then at least to mutual dissatisfaction. Nikolay Petrovich suspected that his brother's hatred of Bazarov had in no way abated. One trifling incident, taken in conjunction with many others, served to confirm him in this suspicion. The cholera had begun to spread to some parts of the neighbouring countryside and had even 'taken' two people from Marino itself. One night Pavel Petrovich suffered a fairly violent attack. He remained in considerable pain until the morning but would not have recourse to Bazarov's skill.

When they met the following day Pavel Petrovich, still pale but already carefully combed and shaved, replied to Bazarov's question as to why he had not been sent for:

'But I seem to remember that you said yourself that you do not believe in medicine?'

So the days went by. Bazarov worked stubbornly and grimly. But there was one person in Nikolay Petrovich's household to whom, if he did not precisely pour out his soul, he was always pleased to talk; that person was Fenechka.

He met her most often in the early mornings, in the garden or about the farm; he did not visit her in her room and she had only once come up to his door to ask whether or not she should allow Mitya to bathe. She not only trusted him, not only had no fear of him, but with him she conducted herself more freely and with less reserve than with Nikolay Petrovich himself. It is difficult to say why this was so; possibly because she instinctively felt in Bazarov the absence of the specifically aristocratic, of all that inbred superiority which at once attracts and repels. In her eyes he was both an excellent doctor and a plain man. She would occupy herself with her child without embarrassment in his presence and once, when she had suddenly felt giddy with a sick headache, she had taken a spoonful of medicine from his hands. When Nikolay Petrovich was there she tended to avoid Bazarov: she did this not from shyness but from some feeling of what was fitting. Of Pavel Petrovich she was more afraid than ever; for some time lately he had been interesting himself in her movements and would appear at unexpected moments, just as though he had popped up behind her back from the bowels of the earth, his hand in the pocket of his suit and his face expressionless and vigilant.

'He gives you the shivers,' Fenechka complained to Dunyasha, who would only sigh in answer and think of another 'heartless' man. Bazarov, without having the least suspicion of it, had become the *cruel tyrant* of her soul.

Fenechka liked Bazarov; but he liked her too. Even his face would alter when he was talking to her and assume a serene, almost kindly, expression and his usual indifferent coolness would be enlivened by a sort of joking gallantry. Fenechka grew prettier every day. There are times in the lives of young women when they suddenly begin to open out and to come into bloom like summer roses; such a time had come for Fenechka. Everything conspired to bring this about, even the July heat-wave they were experiencing just then. Dressed in a flimsy white dress she herself appeared white and more fragile; her skin did not tan, but the heat, from which there was no protection, lightly flushed her cheeks and ears and, infusing her whole body with a gentle indolence, was reflected in the drowsy languor of her pretty little eyes. She could hardly force herself to work; her hands just slipped down into her lap. She could hardly even walk but sighed constantly and complained with a comical feebleness.

'You ought to bathe more often,' Nikolay Petrovich told her.

He had made a large swimming-pool, screened with canvas, from the only one of his ponds which had not yet quite dried up.

'Eh, Nikolay Petrovich, by the time you've got down to the pool you're dead; and by the time you've got back you're dead again! There's not a bit of shade in the garden.'

'You're quite right, there is no shade,' answered Nikolay Petrovich, and mopped his brow.

Once, on his way back from his walk at about seven o'clock in the morning, Bazarov came upon Fenechka in the arbour of lilac bushes whose flowers had long since fallen but whose foliage was still dense and green. She was seated on the bench, a white kerchief on her head as was her custom; beside her lay a great bunch of red and white roses, still wet with dew. He bade her good morning.

'Ah! Yevgeny Vasil'evich!' she exclaimed, raising the edge of her kerchief a little to look at him, so that her sleeve fell back to expose her arm to the elbow.

'What are you doing there?' asked Bazarov, sitting down beside her. 'Making up a bouquet?'

'Yes; for the breakfast table. It pleases Nikolay Petrovich.'

'But it's a long time till breakfast. What a mass of flowers!'

'I picked them now because later on it gets too hot to go outside. You can only breathe now. I've grown quite weak from this heat. I'm beginning to be afraid, perhaps I'm getting ill?'

'What's this you've taken into your head! Let me feel your pulse.' Bazarov took her wrist, found the evenly throbbing vein and did not even begin to count the beats.

'You'll live to be a hundred!' he said, releasing her hand.

'Oh, heaven forbid!' she exclaimed.

'Now why? Don't you want to live a long time then?'

'But a hundred years! My grandmother lived to be eighty-five – and what a martyr she was, to be sure! Black in the face, deaf, bent, always coughing; nothing but a trial to herself. What sort of life is that!'

'So it's better to be young?'

'Well, what do you think?'

'What are the advantages? You tell me that!'

'How can you ask? Why, look at me now. I'm young, I can do what I like – go and come and fetch and carry, and I don't have to ask help of anyone; what more would you ask?'

'Well, it's a matter of indifference to me whether I'm young or old.'

'How can you say such things – a matter of indifference! It can't be true what you are saying.'

'Well, judge for yourself, Feodos'ya Nikolayevna, what good is my youth to me? I live alone, a solitary man.'

'That always depends on you.'

'That's just the trouble, it doesn't depend on me! If only someone would take pity on me!'

Fenechka gave him a sidelong glance but said nothing.

'What book have you there?' she asked, after waiting for a moment.

'That one? It's a scholar's book, not easy to understand.'

'And you're still studying? Aren't you tired of it? You must know everything there is to be known already, I should think.'

'Not everything, it would seem. You try reading a bit.'

'But I wouldn't understand anything. Is it in Russian?' inquired Fenechka, taking the heavily bound volume in both hands. 'What a thick one!'

'Yes, it's in Russian.'

'I still wouldn't understand anything.'

'I didn't ask you to make you understand. I just want to watch you reading. The end of your nose moves so nicely when you're reading.'

Fenechka, who had begun to spell out to herself the article on creosote at which she had opened the book, burst out laughing and gave it up; she slipped from the bench on to the ground.

'I like the way you laugh too,' said Bazarov.

'Give over now.'

'I like it when you talk. It's like a little stream gurgling.'

Fenechka turned her head away.

'You are a one!' she pronounced, fingering the flowers. 'And what does listening to me mean to you? You've talked with such clever ladies.'

'Ah, Feodos'ya Nikolayevna! Believe me, all the clever ladies in the world aren't worth your little finger.'

'There now, what will you think up next, I wonder,' whispered Fenechka and folded her arms tight against her.

Bazarov picked the book up from the ground.

'That's a doctor's book, why did you throw it down?'

'A doctor's book?' repeated Fenechka, and turned towards him. 'Do you know what? Ever since you gave me those drops, do you remember, Mitya's been sleeping so well! I just don't know how I can thank you; you're so kind, you really are.'

'Well, if you want to do the thing properly you have to pay doctors,' remarked Bazarov teasingly. 'Doctors, as you know yourself, are rapacious folk.'

Fenechka raised her eyes to Bazarov. They seemed even darker because of a whitish gleam which fell on the upper half of her face. She could not make out whether he were joking or not.

'If you wish, we would gladly . . . I must ask Nikolay Petrovich—'

'So you think I want money?' Bazarov interrupted her. 'No, I don't want money from you.'

'What then?' asked Fenechka.

'What?' repeated Bazarov. 'Guess.'

'I'm not good at guessing.'

'Then I'll tell you! I want – one of those roses.'

Fenechka again burst out laughing and even threw up her hands, so funny did Bazarov's wish seem to her. She laughed and at the same time she felt flattered. Bazarov watched her narrowly.

'You're welcome, you're welcome,' she said at last, and bending over the bench began to sort out the roses. 'Which would you like, a red one or a white one?'

'A red one, and not too big.'

She stood up straight.

'Here, take this one,' she said, but suddenly snatched back her outstretched hand and, biting her lips, glanced towards the entrance to the arbour, then bent her head and listened intently.

'What's the matter?' asked Bazarov. 'Nikolay Petrovich?'

'No, Nikolay Petrovich has gone out to the fields – and I'm not afraid of him; but you see, Pavel Petrovich – I thought . . .'

'What?'

'I thought that *he* was walking by. No, there's no one there. Take it.' Fenechka handed Bazarov the rose.

'What makes you afraid of Pavel Petrovich?'

'He's always frightening me. Not that he says anything, but he just looks so queerly. And you don't like him either. Remember how you were always quarrelling with him before? I don't know what it is you argue about, but I see that you are always twisting him round your finger, this way and that.'

Fenechka demonstrated with her hands how, in her opinion, Bazarov twisted Pavel Petrovich round his finger.

Bazarov smiled.

'And if he was the one who was winning,' he asked, 'would you come to my defence?'

'*Me* come to your defence? Oh no, no one could get the better of you.'

'You think so? But I know a hand which could flick me over with one finger if it wanted.'

'Whose hand is that?'

'Can it be that you don't know? Smell what a lovely scent this rose that you gave me has.'

Fenechka stretched out her neck and approached her face to the flower; the kerchief slipped from her head on to her shoulders, showing the soft mass of black, shining, slightly dishevelled hair.

'Wait, I want to smell it with you,' said Bazarov, and bent his head and kissed her firmly on her parted lips.

She started, put up both hands to his chest to ward him off, but so weakly that he was able to renew and prolong the kiss.

A dry cough sounded from behind the lilacs. In a second Fenechka was sitting at the other end of the bench. Pavel Petrovich appeared, bowed slightly and, remarking with a kind of malevolent melancholy 'So you're here', walked on. Fenechka at once gathered up all the roses and left the arbour.

'You should be ashamed of yourself, Yevgeny Vasil'evich,' she whispered as she went. A genuine reproach sounded in her whisper.

Bazarov remembered another recent scene, and he felt both ashamed and contemptuously annoyed. But he at once shook his head, ironically congratulated himself on his 'formal entry into the order of Don Juan' and went off to his room.

But Pavel Petrovich walked out of the garden and, pacing slowly, went on into the forest. He remained there for quite a long time and when he returned to breakfast Nikolay Petrovich asked him in some concern whether he were well, so black was his expression.

'You know there are times when I suffer from liver attacks,' Pavel Petrovich answered him calmly.

XXIV

Two hours later he knocked on Bazarov's door.

'I must beg your pardon for disturbing you at your studies,' he began, sitting down on a chair by the window and folding his hands on the ivory handle of a handsome cane (he did not usually carry a cane), 'but I must ask you to spare me five minutes of your time – no more.'

'My time is entirely at your disposal,' replied Bazarov, across whose face had passed a fleeting change of expression as soon as Pavel Petrovich had appeared in the doorway.

'Five minutes will suffice me. I came to ask you a question.'

'A question? What about?'

'I will tell you if you will be so good as to hear me out.

When you first came to stay in my brother's house, before I had to deny myself the pleasure of conversing with you, I had the opportunity of hearing your opinions on a number of subjects; but, if my memory serves me aright, neither between us nor in my presence did the talk ever turn to duels, to the practice of duelling in general. May I ask you what are your opinions on this subject?'

Bazarov, who had made as if to stand up to greet Pavel Petrovich, now perched himself on the edge of the table and folded his arms.

'Here are my opinions,' he said. 'From the theoretical point of view duelling is absurd; but from the practical point of view – that's quite another matter.'

'That is to say, if I understand you correctly, that whatever your theoretical views on duelling, in practice you would not allow yourself to be insulted without demanding satisfaction?'

'You have taken my meaning exactly.'

'Very well, sir, I am delighted to hear this from you. Your words free me from uncertainty—'

'From indecision, you mean.'

'That, sir, is of no matter; I speak so that people can follow my meaning – I am no hair-splitting seminary rat. Your words relieve me of a certain regrettable necessity. I have decided to call you out.'

Bazarov opened his eyes wide.

'Me?'

'Certainly you.'

'But why, for heaven's sake?'

'I could explain the reason to you,' began Pavel Petrovich. 'However, I prefer to remain silent on that head: your presence here is not to my taste; I detest you, I despise you and, if that is not enough for you—'

Pavel Petrovich's eyes were blazing; there was a sparkle in Bazarov's also.

'Very well, sir,' he said. 'No further explanations are necessary. It is your whim to try your knightly mettle on me. I might deny you that pleasure, but what does it matter anyway!'

'I am most obliged to you,' replied Pavel Petrovich, 'and

FATHERS AND CHILDREN

now I may hope that you will accept my challenge without constraining me to resort to more forceful measures.'

'That is, speaking without allegories, to that stick?' remarked Bazarov coolly. 'That is quite correct. It is quite unnecessary for you to insult me. Also it would not be altogether safe. You may remain a gentleman. I, also, accept your challenge in a gentlemanly spirit.'

'Excellent,' pronounced Pavel Petrovich, and stood his cane in a corner. 'Now we must say a few words about the conditions of our duel; but first I should like to know whether you think it necessary to have recourse to the formality of some slight quarrel which might serve as a pretext for my challenge?'

'No, better without formalities.'

'I think so myself. I assume also that it would be out of place to go into the real reasons of our disagreement. We detest one another. What more could one ask?'

'What more indeed?' repeated Bazarov ironically.

'As to the conditions of our duel, since there will be no seconds – for where would we go to find them?'

'Precisely, where would we?'

'So I have the honour to propose the following: we will fight tomorrow morning early, say at six o'clock, behind the coppice, with pistols; the distance will be ten paces—'

'At ten paces? Very suitable; it is at that distance that we hate one another.'

'At eight, if you will,' remarked Pavel Petrovich.

'At eight then. Why not!'

'We will fire twice; and, to be prepared for all eventualities, each will put a letter in his pocket in which he will take the responsibility for his own death.'

'Now there I can't altogether agree,' said Bazarov. 'It's all beginning to sound rather like a French novel, unconvincing somehow.'

'Perhaps. But you will agree that it would be unpleasant to be suspected of murder?'

'I do agree. But there is a way to avoid this sad suspicion. Seconds we cannot have, but there could be a witness.'

'Who exactly, if I may ask?'

'Pyotr, of course.'

'Which Pyotr?'

'Your brother's valet. He's a man who has enjoyed all the benefits of a modern education and will fulfil his role with all the *komilfo*[1] necessary to such cases as these.'

'I think you must be joking, my dear sir.'

'Not in the least. If you consider my suggestion you will realize that it is full of common sense and simplicity. Murder will out, you know, but I'll undertake to prepare Pyotr in the proper fashion and to bring him to the place of slaughter.'

'You persist in joking,' pronounced Pavel Petrovich, rising from his chair. 'But after the kind readiness which you have shown I have no right to be offended with you. And so we are agreed. By the way, have you pistols?'

'Where should I get pistols from, Pavel Petrovich? I'm no warrior.'

'In that case I offer you mine. You can rest assured that it is five years now since I last fired them.'

'That is most reassuring news.'

Pavel Petrovich picked up his cane.

'For this, my dear sir, it only remains for me to thank you and to leave you to your work. I have the honour to take my leave.'

'Farewell, dear sir, till our next merry meeting,' said Bazarov as he escorted his guest to the door.

Pavel Petrovich went out; Bazarov remained standing before the door and suddenly exclaimed: 'Oh, the devil! How beautifully done – and how stupid! What a comedy we went through! Like circus dogs dancing on their hind legs! But it was impossible to refuse; why, he might easily have hit me, and then . . .' Bazarov turned white at the very thought; all his pride positively reared up. 'Then I'd have had to strangle him like a kitten.' He returned to his microscope, but his heart was thudding and the calm essential to scientific observation had deserted him. 'He saw us today,' he thought, 'but surely

1 French in Russian characters in the original (= '*comme il faut*').

he's not acting like this in defence of his brother? And what's a kiss after all? There's something else to it. Bah! Could it be that he's in love himself? Of course he is; it's as clear as daylight. What a situation! Just think! It's a bad business!' he decided finally. 'A bad business, whichever way you look at it. In the first place I'll have to stand there waiting to be shot at, and whatever happens I'll have to leave; and then there's Arkady, and that bleating innocent Nikolay Petrovich. A bad, bad business.'

The day passed somehow exceptionally slowly and uneventfully. Fenechka might not have existed; she was sitting in her room like a little mouse in its hole. Nikolay Petrovich looked preoccupied. He had been informed that his wheat, on which he had set high hopes, had begun to show signs of brand. Pavel Petrovich oppressed everybody, even Prokof'ich, with his icy civility. Bazarov began a letter to his father, but tore it up and threw it under the table. 'If I die,' he thought, 'they'll find out; anyway I won't die. No, I'll have to drag about the world for a long time yet.' He told Pyotr to come to him as soon as it was light next morning on important business; Pyotr took it into his head that Bazarov wanted to take him with him to Petersburg. Bazarov went to bed late and was tormented all night by disjointed dreams. Odintsova hovered before him: she was also his mother; behind her walked a little cat with black whiskers, and the cat was Fenechka; and Pavel Petrovich appeared to him as a great forest, with whom he had nevertheless to fight a duel. Pyotr woke him up at four o'clock and he dressed at once and went out with him.

The morning was fine, fresh; little clouds of many shades of colour were ranged like lambs against the clear, pale blue; small dewdrops were scattered over grass and leaf and sparkled silver in the spiders' webs; the damp, dark earth, it seemed, still held the ruddy afterglow of sunrise; songs of larks poured down from all over the sky. Bazarov walked as far as the coppice and sat down in the shade on the edge of the trees; only then did he reveal to Pyotr the nature of the services required of him. The educated lackey was frightened to death, but Bazarov calmed him down with the assurance that he would have nothing to do but stand at a distance and watch and that in no way would he be held responsible. 'And in the meantime,' he added, 'just think what an important part you will have to play!'

Pyotr made a helpless gesture, cast down his eyes and, green with fright, sank back against a birch-tree.

The road from Marino skirted the spinney; it was covered by a light dust, untouched since the day before by wheel or foot. Involuntarily Bazarov kept looking down this road; he plucked grasses and chewed them, and kept repeating to himself: 'What stupidity!' The early morning chill made him shiver once or twice. Pyotr gave him a dismal look, but Bazarov only grinned sardonically: he was not afraid.

The sound of horses' hoofs came from the road. A peasant appeared from behind the trees. He was driving a couple of hobbled horses before him and accorded Bazarov a curious glance as he passed him without removing his cap, which obviously troubled Pyotr, who took it for an evil omen.

'There's somebody else who got up early,' thought Bazarov, 'but at least on honest business, whereas we—'

'Seems he's coming, sir,' whispered Pyotr suddenly.

Bazarov raised his head and saw Pavel Petrovich. Clad in a light check jacket and snow-white trousers he was walking briskly up the road; under his arm he carried a box wrapped in green cloth.

'Forgive me, it seems that I have kept you waiting,' he pronounced, bowing first to Bazarov and then to Pyotr, in whose person he at that moment recognized something in the nature of a second. 'I did not wish to wake my valet.'

'It doesn't matter,' replied Bazarov, 'we've only just come ourselves.'

'Ah! So much the better!' Pavel Petrovich looked around him. 'No one to be seen, no one to interfere. May we begin?'

'Yes.'

'I presume you do not require any further explanations?'

'No.'

'Will you load?' inquired Pavel Petrovich, taking the pistols from their case.

'No; you load and I'll measure the paces. My legs are longer,' added Bazarov satirically. 'One, two, three . . .'

'Yevgeny Vasil'evich,' Pyotr murmured with difficulty (he was trembling as though with an ague), 'with your permission I'll go further away.'

'Four, five . . . Do, brother, do; you may even stand behind a tree and block your ears, only don't shut your eyes; and if anyone falls over run and pick him up. Six, seven, eight.' Bazarov halted. 'Enough?' he asked, addressing Pavel Petrovich. 'Or shall I put on another two paces?'

'As you wish,' pronounced the other, ramming home the second bullet.

'Well then, we'll put on another two.' Bazarov made a line in the ground with the toe of his boot. 'Here's the mark. Oh, by the way: how many paces should each of us walk back from our mark? That's an important point too. It wasn't brought up yesterday.'

'Ten, I believe,' replied Pavel Petrovich, offering Bazarov both pistols. 'Have the goodness to select your weapon.'

'Very well, I will have the goodness. But confess, Pavel Petrovich, our duel is so extraordinary as to be comic. Just take a look at the physiognomy of our second.'

'You will still have your joke,' replied Pavel Petrovich. 'I do not deny the peculiarity of our duel, but I consider it my duty to warn you that I intend to fight in earnest. *A bon entendeur, salut.*'[1]

'Oh! I don't doubt that we have made up our minds to exterminate one another; but why not have a laugh and combine *utile dulci*?[2] There: you address me in French, I you in Latin.'

'I shall fight in earnest,' repeated Pavel Petrovich, and went to take up his position. Bazarov, in his turn, counted ten paces from his mark and halted.

'Are you ready?' asked Pavel Petrovich.

'Perfectly.'

---

1 In French in the original (= 'He that has ears to hear, let him hear – salute!').
2 'The useful with the agreeable' (Lat.).

'We may approach one another.'

Bazarov moved slowly forward and Pavel Petrovich kept pace with him, his left hand thrust in his pocket, gradually raising the muzzle of his pistol. 'He's aiming straight at my nose,' thought Bazarov, 'and look at the conscientious way he's screwing up his eyes, the villain! Who'd have thought it'd be such an unpleasant sensation! I'll start looking at his watch-chain. . . .' Something pinged sharply just by Bazarov's ear and at the same instant a shot rang out. 'I heard it, so it must be all right,' flashed through his head. He took another step and without taking aim pressed the trigger.

Pavel Petrovich started slightly and clapped his hand to his thigh. A thin stream of blood began to run down his white trousers.

Bazarov threw down his pistol and went towards his opponent.

'You're wounded?' he said.

'You had the right to call me up to the mark,' pronounced Pavel Petrovich. 'The wound's nothing. According to the conditions we each have another shot.'

'Well, excuse me, but that'll be for another time,' answered Bazarov, and caught hold of Pavel Petrovich, who had begun to lose colour. 'Now I'm not a duellist any more but a doctor, and first of all I must have a look at your wound. Pyotr! Come here, Pyotr! Where have you hidden yourself?'

'This is nonsense – I don't need anyone's help,' pronounced Pavel Petrovich jerkily. 'And – we have – another . . .' He tried to pull at his moustache, but his hand failed him, his eyes rolled and he lost consciousness.

'Here's something new! A swoon! What could have caused that!' Bazarov exclaimed involuntarily, lowering Pavel Petrovich on to the grass. 'Let's have a look what's happened!' He drew out his handkerchief; wiped away the blood and felt around the wound. 'The bone's untouched,' he muttered between his teeth. 'The bullet's gone straight through and not deep, only the *vastus externus*[1] muscle is touched. He'll be able

---

1 In Latin in the original.

to dance in three weeks! But a swoon! Oh, these excitable people! Look how fine the skin is.'

'Dead, sir!' Pyotr's trembling voice hissed behind his back. Bazarov glanced round.

'Run and get some water as quick as you can, brother, and we'll see him through yet.'

But the model servant, it seemed, did not understand his words and did not move from where he stood. Pavel Petrovich slowly opened his eyes. 'He's going!' whispered Pyotr, and began to cross himself.

'You're quite right – such an idiotic physiognomy!' declared the wounded gentleman with a forced smile.

'Go and get some water, damn you!' cried Bazarov.

'Unnecessary. It was a momentary *vertige*.[1] Help me to sit up – that's it. This scratch only wants something wound round it and I'll walk home on foot, or if I can't they can send the trap for me. If you agree, the duel won't be renewed. You have acted chivalrously – today. Today, notice.'

'There's no point in recalling the past,' retorted Bazarov, 'and as for the future, you don't need to worry your head about that either, because I intend to make myself scarce. Let me bind up your leg now; your wound is not dangerous, but it's always better to stop the blood. But first it's essential to bring this mortal to his senses.'

Bazarov took Pyotr by the collar and shook him, then sent him for the trap.

'See you don't frighten my brother,' Pavel Petrovich admonished him. 'Don't take it into your head to report this to him.'

Pyotr went running off; and while he was fetching the trap the two opponents sat on the ground in silence. Pavel Petrovich tried not to look at Bazarov; in spite of everything he had no wish to make up the quarrel; he was ashamed of his arrogance, of his failure, was ashamed of this whole affair of his planning, although he felt that it could scarcely have ended more fortunately. 'At least he won't go on hanging around

1 In French in the original.

here,' he consoled himself, 'that's one thing to be thankful for.' The silence continued, heavy and awkward. Both were ill at ease. Each realized that the other understood him. To friends this is an agreeable feeling, but to enemies it is most disagreeable, particularly when it is impossible either to speak one's mind or to separate.

'Have I not bandaged your leg too tightly?' inquired Bazarov finally.

'No, it's all right, splendid in fact,' answered Pavel Petrovich, and added after a moment's pause: 'We'll never keep this from my brother. We'll have to tell him we had a stupid quarrel about politics.'

'Very well,' said Bazarov, 'you can tell him I started to abuse all Anglo-maniacs.'

'Excellent. What do you think that man is thinking about us now?' continued Pavel Petrovich, indicating the same peasant who had driven the hobbled horses past Bazarov a few minutes before the duel and who now, on his way back, stepped off the road and raised his cap at sight of the 'gentlefolk'.

'Goodness knows!' answered Bazarov. 'Most probably he's not thinking anything. The Russian peasant is that same mysterious stranger of whom Mrs Radcliffe once had so much to say. Who can begin to understand him? He doesn't understand himself.'

'Ah! So that's what you think!' Pavel Petrovich was beginning, but broke off to exclaim: 'Look what your idiot Pyotr has gone and done! There's my brother galloping towards us!'

Bazarov turned and saw the pale face of Nikolay Petrovich, who was sitting in the trap. He jumped down before it had come to a halt and ran to his brother.

'What does this mean?' he demanded in a shaken voice. 'Yevgeny Vasil'evich, for heaven's sake what is going on?'

'It's nothing,' answered Pavel Petrovich; 'you shouldn't have been worried about it. Mr Bazarov and I had a little disagreement and I am a little the worse for it.'

'But what was the cause of it all, in God's name?'

'I don't really know how to tell you. Mr Bazarov spoke

disrespectfully of Sir Robert Peel. I hasten to add that in all this I alone am to blame and Mr Bazarov has conducted himself admirably. I called him out.'

'But good gracious, you're bleeding!'

'And did you expect me to have water in my veins? But this blood-letting will even do me good. Will it not, doctor? Help me to get into the trap and stop moping. I shall be well again tomorrow. That's the way; splendid. Let them go, driver.'

Nikolay Petrovich set out after the trap on foot; Bazarov would have hung back.

'I shall have to ask you to take care of my brother,' Nikolay Petrovich said to him, 'until another doctor can be fetched from the town.'

Bazarov silently inclined his head.

An hour later Pavel Petrovich was already lying in bed, his leg neatly bandaged. The whole house was in an uproar; Fenechka was prostrate. Nikolay Petrovich wrung his hands surreptitiously and Pavel Petrovich laughed and joked, especially with Bazarov. He put on a fine cambric shirt, a dandified jacket and a fez, refused to allow the blinds to be drawn over the windows and complained comically of the necessity of forgoing his food.

Towards evening, however, he developed a fever; his head began to ache. The doctor from town appeared. (Nikolay Petrovich had ignored his brother's protests, and Bazarov himself had wished it so; he had sat the entire day in his room, all yellow and ill-tempered, and had only looked in on his patient for the shortest possible time; twice he had run into Fenechka, but she had whisked away from him in horror.) The new doctor advised cooling drinks and incidentally confirmed Bazarov's assurances that there was no foreseeable danger. Nikolay Petrovich told him that his brother had wounded himself by mistake, to which the doctor replied 'Hum!' But on having twenty-five roubles in silver slipped into his hand he conceded: 'Really! Such things often happen, it's true.'

No one in the house went to bed or even undressed. Nikolay Petrovich tiptoed in to his brother every now and again and tiptoed out again. Pavel Petrovich, in a state of semi-consciousness, would sigh a little, say to him in French *'Couchez-vous'* and ask for something to drink. Once Nikolay Petrovich made Fenechka take him a glass of lemonade; Pavel Petrovich gave her a searching look and drank the glass to the dregs. Towards morning the fever had increased a little and the patient was suffering from slight delirium. At first Pavel Petrovich spoke incoherent phrases; then he suddenly opened his eyes and, catching sight of his brother standing by his bed and bending over him solicitously, pronounced:

'Don't you think, Nikolay, that Fenechka has something in common with Nelly?'

'With which Nelly, Pasha?'[1]

'How can you ask such a thing! With Princess R. Especially about the upper part of the face. *C'est de la même famille.'*[2]

Nikolay Petrovich made no reply, but inwardly he wondered at the tenacity with which old sentiments live on in a man. 'And at a time like this it comes to the surface,' he thought.

'Oh, how I love that empty creature!' groaned Pavel Petrovich, wistfully linking his hands behind his head. 'I will not permit that any insolent fellow should dare to lay a finger ...' he muttered a few moments later.

Nikolay Petrovich merely sighed; he did not even suspect to whom these words might refer.

Bazarov entered his room on the following day at about eight o'clock. He had already packed his things and set free all his frogs, insects and birds.

'Have you come to take your leave of me?' asked Nikolay Petrovich, rising to meet him.

'Precisely, sir.'

'I understand you and I am quite sure that you are doing the right thing. My poor brother, of course, is at fault; still, he is suffering for it. He has told me himself that he placed you in a position which made it impossible for you to act

1 Diminutive of Pavel.
2 In French in the original.

otherwise. I believe that you could not have avoided this duel, which – which may be explained to some extent by the constant antagonism of your views.' Nikolay Petrovich began to founder in his words. 'My brother is a man of the old school, hot-tempered and wilful. Thank God that it ended no worse. I have taken all necessary steps to avoid a scandal.'

'I shall leave you my address in case there should be any fuss,' remarked Bazarov negligently.

'I hope there will not be any fuss, Yevgeny Vasil'evich. I am very sorry that your stay in my house should have come to such a – such an end. What distresses me still more is that Arkady—'

'I shall be seeing him, I expect,' rejoined Bazarov, in whom any kind of 'explanation' or 'soul-searching' always aroused a feeling of impatience. 'Otherwise I must beg you to remember me to him and to express my regrets.'

'I also beg ...' responded Nikolay Petrovich with a bow. But Bazarov did not wait for him to finish his sentence and left the room.

On hearing that Bazarov was leaving, Pavel Petrovich asked to see him and shook him by the hand. But here too Bazarov remained as cold as ice; he understood that Pavel Petrovich wished to appear generous. He had no opportunity to take his leave of Fenechka, but merely exchanged glances with her through the window. He fancied that her face was sad. 'She'll come to grief, probably!' he said to himself. 'Oh well, she'll struggle through somehow!' Pyotr, on the other hand, was so overcome that he wept on his shoulder until Bazarov sobered him by inquiring whether he kept a reservoir behind his eyes; Dunyasha had to run off into the spinney to hide her emotion. The object of all these heart-burnings swung himself up into the cart in which he was to travel, lighted a cigar, and when, three miles further on at a bend in the road, he saw stretched out before him for the last time the single line of straggling buildings which comprised the Kirsanovs' farm and new manor-house, he merely spat on to the road and, muttering 'Damned little aristocrats', wrapped himself more tightly in his greatcoat.

*

Pavel Petrovich soon began to feel better; but he had to remain in bed for nearly a week. He bore with his *captivity*, as he was pleased to call it, fairly patiently, merely taking particular care of his appearance and constantly asking for the room to be sprayed with eau-de-Cologne. Nikolay Petrovich read aloud to him from periodicals, Fenechka waited on him as before, bringing him broth, lemonade, soft-boiled eggs and tea; yet a secret horror took possession of her whenever she went into his room. The unexpected action of Pavel Petrovich had frightened everybody in the house, and her more than anyone; only Prokof'ich remained imperturbable and explained that in his time gentlemen frequently fought with one another, 'only noble gentlemen between themselves, but commoners like that they'd have had taken out to the stables and thrashed for their impertinence'.

Conscience troubled Fenechka hardly at all, but she was sometimes tormented by the thought of what the real cause of the quarrel might have been; and then Pavel Petrovich looked at her so strangely, in such a way that even when she turned her back on him she was conscious of his eyes upon her. She grew thinner from this constant inner anxiety and, as might have been expected, began to look even prettier.

Once – it was in the morning – Pavel Petrovich was feeling better and had moved from his bed to the divan. Nikolay Petrovich, having inquired after his health, had gone out to superintend the threshing. Fenechka brought in a cup of tea and, having put it down on a little table, was about to leave the room. Pavel Petrovich called her back.

'Where are you going to in such a hurry, Feodos'ya Niko-layevna?' he began. 'Are you really so busy?'

'No, sir – yes, sir – I must go and pour out the tea.'

'Dunyasha will do that without you; stay and sit for a little while with a sick man. Which reminds me. I have been wanting to talk to you.'

Fenechka sat down on the edge of an armchair without a word.

'Listen,' said Pavel Petrovich, and pulled at his moustache,

'I have been wanting to ask you for a long time; you seem to be afraid of me.'

'Me, sir?'

'Yes, you. You never look straight at me, almost as though you had a guilty conscience.'

Fenechka blushed but looked up at Pavel Petrovich. He seemed somehow strange to her, and her heart began to flutter softly.

'After all, your conscience is clear, isn't it?' he asked her.

'Why shouldn't it be clear?' she whispered.

'There might be any number of reasons! But when you come to think of it, towards whom could you feel guilty? Towards me? That seems improbable. Towards other people in this house? That also seems scarcely feasible. Could it be towards my brother? But then you love him, do you not?'

'I love him.'

'With all your heart and with all your soul?'

'I love Nikolay Petrovich with all my heart.'

'Really? Look at me, Fenechka.' (It was the first time he had called her this.) 'You know, it's a black sin to lie!'

'I am not lying, Pavel Petrovich. If I didn't love Nikolay Petrovich – why, if that were so I wouldn't want to go on living.'

'And you wouldn't exchange him for anyone?'

'Who could I exchange him for?'

'There might be any number of people! That gentleman who has just left here for one.'

Fenechka rose to her feet.

'Lord God in heaven, Pavel Petrovich, why must you torture me so? What have I done to you? How can you say things like that?'

'Fenechka,' pronounced Pavel Petrovich in a sorrowful voice. 'You see, I saw—'

'What did you see, sir?'

'Why, there – in the arbour.'

Fenechka grew all red up to her ears and the roots of her hair.

'And how was that my fault?' she uttered with difficulty.

Pavel Petrovich half rose.

'Was it not your fault? Was it not? Not the least little bit?'

'Nikolay Petrovich is the only one I love in the whole world and I shall love him all my life!' declared Fenechka with sudden fervour, even while the sobs were rising in her throat. 'And as to what you saw, I'll answer for it at the Last Judgment that there is no fault of mine there, no, nor never has been, and it would be better for me to die this minute than to be suspected of a thing like that, that I could do such to my benefactor, to Nikolay Petrovich....'

But here her voice betrayed her and at the same time she felt that Pavel Petrovich had caught hold of her hand and was pressing it. She looked at him and froze where she stood. He was even paler than before; his eyes glittered and, most astonishing of all, a single heavy tear was rolling down his cheek.

'Fenechka!' he said in a kind of uncanny whisper. 'Love my brother, love him! He's such a kind, good man! Don't betray him for anyone in the world, don't listen to anyone's sweet speeches! Just think, what could be worse than to love and not to be loved! Don't ever abandon my poor Nikolay!'

Fenechka's eyes were dry and her fear was gone, so great was her astonishment. But what could she do when Pavel Petrovich, Pavel Petrovich himself, pressed her hand to his lips and held it there, not kissing it but from time to time sighing convulsively.

'Oh Lord!' she thought. 'Could he be going to have a fit?'

But at that moment a whole wasted life was quivering within him.

The staircase creaked under swift steps; he thrust her away from him and threw his head back on the pillow. The door burst open and in came Nikolay Petrovich, ruddy-cheeked, fresh-faced and cheerful. Mitya, as fresh and ruddy as his father, was jumping up and down against his chest in nothing but a shirt, gripping the big buttons of his country coat with his bare toes.

Fenechka positively hurled herself to meet him and, flinging her arms about both him and their son, snuggled her head against his shoulder. Nikolay Petrovich was surprised; Fenechka, usually so shy and modest, never caressed him in the presence of a third person.

'What has come over you?' he asked and, glancing at his brother, handed over Mitya to her. 'You're not feeling worse?' he asked, going up to Pavel Petrovich.

His brother buried his face in a cambric handkerchief.

'No – so–so – all right.... On the contrary, I feel much better.'

'You shouldn't have been in such a hurry to move on to the sofa. Where are you going?' added Nikolay Petrovich, turning to Fenechka; but the door had already slammed to behind her. 'I wanted to bring my young Hercules in to see you, he was pining for his uncle. Why did she go and take him away? What is the matter with you though? Has something happened between you?'

'Brother!' pronounced Pavel Petrovich solemnly.

Nikolay Petrovich started. He could not tell why, but he began to feel acutely uneasy.

'Brother,' repeated Pavel Petrovich, 'give me your word to grant me one request.'

'What request? Tell me.'

'It is very important; in my opinion the whole happiness of your life hangs on it. I have been thinking all this time about what I now wish to say to you. Brother, fulfil your obligation, the obligation of an honest and honourable man; put an end to the temptation and the bad example which is being set by you, the best of men!'

'What do you mean, Pavel?'

'Marry Fenechka. She loves you, she is the mother of your son.'

Nikolay Petrovich took a step backwards and threw up his hands.

'You say that, Pavel? You, whom I always thought most inflexibly opposed to such marriages! You say that! But can it be that you don't know that it is only out of consideration for you that I have not yet fulfilled what you have rightly called my duty!'

'In that case you certainly should not have considered me,' retorted Pavel Petrovich with a melancholy smile. 'I begin to think that Bazarov was right when he reproached me with being too much the aristocrat. No, dear brother, enough of putting on airs and worrying what the world may think; we are already old people, and humble; it's time we laid aside all kind of vanity. Just as you say, we will begin to do our duty; and, who knows, we may get happiness added unto us.'

Nikolay Petrovich cast himself on his brother's neck.

'You have finally opened my eyes!' he cried. 'I was quite right when I always said you were the kindest and cleverest man on earth; and now I see that you are as reasonable as you are generous.'

'Gently, gently,' Pavel Petrovich interrupted him. 'Mind the leg of your reasonable brother, who's been fighting duels like a young ensign when he's nearly fifty. Well, so that's decided: Fenechka will be my – *belle-sœur*?'[1]

'My dear, dear Pavel! What will Arkady say?'

'Arkady? It will be a triumph for him, of course! Marriage is against his principles but to make up for it his feeling for equality will be flattered. And really, what kind of caste system can exist *au dix-neuvième siècle*?'[1]

'Ah, Pavel, Pavel! Let me hug you once more. Don't be afraid, I'll be careful.'

The brothers embraced.

'What do you think would be best, do you think you should tell her of your intention at once?' asked Pavel Petrovich.

'What's the hurry?' objected Nikolay Petrovich. 'You weren't discussing it with her, were you?'

'We discussing that? *Quelle idée!*'[1]

'Well, that's fine, then. First of all you must get better, and meanwhile it won't run away from us, it requires careful thought, planning.'

'But you have made up your mind?'

'Of course I've made up my mind and I thank you with all my heart. Now I'll leave you, you need rest, all excitement is

1 In French in the original.

bad for you. But we'll talk about this again. Go to sleep, my dear, and God send you better health!'

'Why does he thank me so?' thought Pavel Petrovich when he found himself alone. 'As though it didn't depend on him! As for me, as soon as he's married I'll go away somewhere, as far as possible, to Dresden or Florence, and there I'll live till I lie down and die.'

Pavel Petrovich refreshed his forehead with eau-de-Cologne and closed his eyes. In the bright light of day his handsome, wasted head lay on the white pillow like the head of a corpse. But then he was a corpse. . . .

XXV

IN the garden at Nikol'skoye, in the shade of a tall ash-tree, Katya was sitting with Arkady on a turf seat; Fifi was lying on the ground beside them, having laid out her long body in that elegant curve known to sportsmen as the 'hare bend'. Both Arkady and Katya were silent; he had a half-open book on his knees and she was picking out the crumbs of white bread left at the bottom of her basket and throwing them to a small family of sparrows who, with the nervous cheekiness of their species, were hopping and chirruping at her very feet. A faint breeze stirred in the branches of the ash-tree, and set the dapples of pale golden light gently swaying backwards and forwards along the dark pathway and over Fifi's yellow back; unbroken shadow enveloped Arkady and Katya; only every now and again a bright streak in her hair would catch the light. Neither of them spoke, but in the very manner of their silence, in the way they sat side by side, there was an assumption of trustful intimacy; neither of them appeared to be giving their neighbour any thought, yet each was privately glad of the other's presence. And their faces had changed since we last saw them: Arkady seemed calmer, Katya more animated, self-assured.

'Don't you think,' began Arkady, 'that the ash-tree is very well named in Russian: the word for it sounds like "the bright one", and no other trees let through the light and air so generously or so *brightly*.'

Katya gazed up into the tree and answered 'Yes' and Arkady thought: 'Well, *she* doesn't blame me for talking like a book anyway.'

'I don't like Heine,' Katya began in her turn, glancing at the book which Arkady was holding, 'neither when he laughs nor when he cries; I only like him when he's sad and thoughtful.'

'And I like him when he laughs,' remarked Arkady. 'Those are just the old traces of your satirical tendencies. . . .' ('Old traces!' thought Arkady. 'What would Bazarov say if he heard that!') 'Just wait, we'll change you.'

'Who will change me? You?'

'Who? My sister; Porfiry Platonovich, with whom you don't quarrel any longer; Auntie, whom you escorted to church the other day.'

'I couldn't very well refuse! And as to Anna Sergeyevna, she herself agreed with Yevgeny on a lot of things, remember.'

'My sister was under his influence then, like you.'

'Like me! Have you noticed that I'm no longer under his influence then?'

Katya said nothing.

'I know you never liked him,' Arkady continued.

'I cannot judge him.'

'You know what, Katerina Sergeyevna? Every time I hear that answer I disbelieve it. There is no such person whom any one of us *cannot* judge. It's just an excuse!'

'Well then I'll tell you that he's – that I don't precisely dislike him, but he's alien to me and I to him. Yes, and you're alien to him.'

'Why?'

'How can I explain – he's a beast of prey and you and I are domestic animals.'

'I'm a domestic animal?'

Katya nodded her head.

Arkady scratched behind his ear.

'Now listen, Katerina Sergeyevna: what you say there is rather insulting.'

'Surely you don't want to be predatory?'

'Predatory, no; but strong, vital.'

'That's something you can't have by wishing. Your friend, for instance, he doesn't want to be like that, he just is.'

'Hmm! So you think that he had a great influence over Anna Sergeyevna?'

'Yes. But no one can get the better of her for long,' added Katya quietly.

'Why do you think that?'

'She is very proud – that's not quite what I wanted to say – she sets a great value on her independence.'

'Who doesn't?' asked Arkady, but at the same moment the thought flashed through his mind: 'What good is it? What good is it?' The same thought passed through Katya's mind. Young people who spend much time amicably in each other's company are often visited by identical thoughts.

Arkady smiled and, moving a little closer to Katya, whispered: 'Confess, you are a little afraid of her.'

'Of whom?'

'*Her*,' Arkady repeated significantly.

'And you?' Katya asked in her turn.

'I also; notice, I said I *also*.'

Katya shook her finger at him.

'That surprises me,' she began. 'My sister has never liked you so well as she does now; much more than the first time you came.'

'I see!'

'But haven't you noticed it? Aren't you glad?'

Arkady considered.

'What have I done to be in Anna Sergeyevna's good graces? Surely it wasn't that I brought her your mother's letters?'

'That is one reason, and there are others that I shan't tell you.'

'Why?'

'I won't say.'

'Oh, I know: you're very stubborn.'

'Very stubborn.'

'And observant.'

Katya stole a sideways glance at Arkady.

'Perhaps you don't quite like that? What are you thinking about?'

'I am trying to think how you came to be so observant, because you are, you know. You're so shy, mistrustful; you avoid everybody.'

'I have lived much alone; that makes you thoughtful. But do I really avoid everybody?'

Arkady gave Katya a grateful look.

'All that is very fine,' he continued, 'but people in your position, of your means, that is, are seldom gifted in that way; like kings they are protected from truth.'

'But I'm not rich.'

Arkady was amazed and did not at once understand Katya. 'But in actual fact the estate does all belong to her sister,' he realized; this thought was not unwelcome to him.

'How nicely you said that,' he commented.

'What do you mean?'

'You said it nicely; simply, as though you were neither ashamed of it nor wanting to dramatize yourself. And that makes me think: I imagine that anyone who knows himself to be poor, and says so, must experience some particular kind of feeling, a sort of pride.'

'I have never felt anything like that, thanks to my sister; I only mentioned my fortune because it happened to come up.'

'Yes, but confess that there is an element of that pride which I mentioned, even in you.'

'For instance?'

'For instance, you wouldn't – forgive my asking you – you wouldn't marry a rich man?'

'If I loved him very much ... No, I don't think I would marry him even so.'

'Ah, there you are, you see!' exclaimed Arkady, and added after waiting for a moment: 'But why wouldn't you marry him?'

'For the same reason given in the song about the poor girl who married above her station.'

'Perhaps you want to be the one who calls the tune or—'

'Oh no! What's the point of that? On the contrary I am prepared to be submissive, it is only inequality which is hard to bear. But to keep one's self-respect and to submit, now that I understand; that is happiness. But existence as an inferior – no, I've had enough of that as it is.'

'Enough of that as it is,' Arkady repeated after Katya. 'Yes, yes,' he continued, 'it is not for nothing that you and Anna Sergeyevna are of one family: you are as independent as she is; but you are more secretive. You, I am sure, would never be the first to declare your sentiments, however intense and sacred they might be.'

'But how could that be otherwise?' asked Katya.

'You are both equally clever; you have just as much character as she, if not more—'

'Do not compare me with my sister, please,' Katya broke in hurriedly, 'it must be too much to my disadvantage. You seem to have forgotten that my sister is a beauty, and very clever and – you especially, Arkady Nikolayevich, should not be saying such things, and with such a serious face into the bargain.'

'What does that mean: you especially – and what makes you think that I am joking?'

'Of course you're joking.'

'You think so? And what if I'm convinced that what I say is true? What if I am beginning to think that I didn't express myself strongly enough?'

'I don't understand you.'

'Truly? Well, now I see that I did indeed exaggerate your powers of observation.'

'How?'

Arkady made no reply and turned away, and Katya discovered a few more crumbs at the bottom of the basket and began throwing them to the sparrows; but the sweep of her arm was too vigorous and they flew away without taking anything.

'Katerina Sergeyevna,' said Arkady abruptly, 'I don't expect it matters to you; but I would like you to know that I wouldn't exchange you, not only for your sister, but for anyone else in the world.'

He got up and walked quickly away, as though frightened by the words which had burst from his lips.

But Katya let both her hands fall into her lap, together with the basket and, tilting her head, remained gazing after Arkady for a long time. Very slowly a scarlet flush suffused her cheeks; but there was no smile on her lips and the dark eyes expressed amazement and some other feeling, as yet ill-defined.

'All alone?' Anna Sergeyevna's voice sounded close beside her. 'I thought Arkady was with you when you went into the garden?'

Katya unhurriedly turned her eyes to her sister (elegantly, even exquisitely, dressed, she was standing on the path tickling Fifi's ears with the end of her open parasol) and answered unhurriedly:

'Yes, I'm alone.'

'So I see,' answered the other, laughing. 'I suppose he's gone back to his room?'

'Yes.'

'Were you reading together?'

'Yes.'

Anna Sergeyevna took Katya by the chin and raised her face.

'You haven't quarrelled, I hope?'

'No,' said Katya, and gently put aside her sister's hand.

'How solemnly you answer! I thought to find him here and to ask him to go for a walk with me. He himself is always begging me to do so. Some boots have just been sent from town for you. Go and try them on; I noticed yesterday that your old ones were quite worn out. In general you don't pay enough attention to such things, and you have such pretty little feet. Your hands are good too, only rather big; so you must make up for it by showing off your feet. But my little sister is not flirtatious.'

Anna Sergeyevna continued her way along the path, her beautiful dress rustling lightly as she went; Katya rose from her seat and, taking Heine with her, also walked away – but not to try on boots.

'Pretty little feet,' she thought to herself, leisurely and

easily mounting the stone steps to the terrace. 'Pretty little feet, you say – well, he will be at my feet.'

But she immediately felt ashamed of herself and went running lightly to the top of the steps.

Arkady was walking along the corridor to his room when he was overtaken by the butler, who informed him that Bazarov was sitting there waiting for him.

'Yevgeny,' muttered Arkady almost fearfully, 'has he been there long?'

'He has just arrived this minute and he gave orders not to announce him to Anna Sergeyevna but to be shown straight to your room.'

'Could something dreadful have happened at home?' thought Arkady and, running quickly up the stairs, opened the door without further hesitation.

Bazarov's appearance set his mind at rest immediately, although a more experienced eye would probably have at once perceived signs of suppressed emotion in the figure of the unexpected guest which, full of vitality as before, was yet distinctly emaciated. He was sitting on the window-sill, his dusty greatcoat over his shoulders and his cap on his head; he made no attempt to rise even when Arkady, clamorous and exclamatory, flung himself on his neck.

'Here's a surprise! How do you come to be here?' he kept on repeating, bustling about the room like one who is himself convinced and who certainly wishes to show that he is overjoyed. 'Everything all right at home? Everyone's well, aren't they?'

'Everything's all right, but not everyone is well,' pronounced Bazarov. 'Now stop jabbering, order me some *kvass*[1] and sit down and listen to what I have to tell in a few but, I hope, reasonably well-chosen words.'

Arkady quieted down and Bazarov told him the story of his duel with Pavel Petrovich. Arkady was very surprised and even distressed, but he did not consider it necessary to say so; he only asked whether his uncle's wound were really not

[1] A cooling summer drink with low alcoholic content.

dangerous and, receiving the answer that it was excessively interesting, only not from the medical point of view, forced himself to smile, although in his heart he felt anxious and somehow ashamed. Bazarov seemed to understand him.

'Yes, brother,' he said, 'that's what happens when you live with relics of the feudal system. You go all feudal yourself and start to take part in knightly tournaments. Well, I'm going back to my ancestors,' concluded Bazarov, 'and on the way I turned in here – to inform you of all this, as I might say if I didn't happen to consider that to tell a lie which is bound to be disbelieved anyway is a mark of sheer stupidity. No, I turned in here – the devil alone knows why. You see, sometimes it does a man good to take himself by the scruff of the neck and throw himself out, like pulling a turnip out of a vegetable patch; I did that the other day. But I took a fancy to have another look at what I have left behind me, at that patch of ground where I was growing.'

'I hope those words don't apply to me,' rejoined Arkady excitedly. 'I hope that you're not thinking of leaving *me* behind you.'

Bazarov looked at him fixedly, almost piercingly.

'Would that distress you so much then? It occurs to me that *you* have already left *me* behind. You look so nice and fresh and clean. I have to suppose that your dealings with Anna Sergeyevna are going extremely well.'

'What dealings with Anna Sergeyevna?'

'Wasn't it for her sake that you came here from town, fledgling? By the way, how are the Sunday-schools progressing there? Aren't you in love with her? Or have you already reached the stage where you have to be bashful about it?'

'Yevgeny, you know I've always been frank with you; I can assure you, I can swear by God to you, that you are mistaken.'

'Hmm! A new word,' remarked Bazarov half to himself. 'But there's no reason for you to get worked up, it's a matter of indifference to me after all. A romantic would say I feel that our paths are beginning to diverge; but I simply say that we're getting fed up with one another.'

'Yevgeny—'

'My dear, it's not a tragedy; if that were all one got fed up with in this world! But now, I think, isn't it time for us to say goodbye? Ever since I came here I've been feeling as sick as a dog, just as though I had been reading Gogol's letter to the wife of the governor of Kaluga.[1] By the way, I gave orders not to unharness the horses.'

'For goodness' sake, that's impossible!'

'And why?'

'I won't say anything more about myself, but it would be extremely discourteous to Anna Sergeyevna, who is certain to want to see you.'

'Now there you are wrong.'

'But I, on the contrary, am quite certain that I am right,' retorted Arkady. 'And what's the point of shamming? Now we're on the subject, didn't you yourself come here for her sake?'

'That may be true, but even so you are mistaken.'

But Arkady was right. Anna Sergeyevna did want to see Bazarov and she summoned him to her side through the butler. Bazarov changed his clothes before presenting himself to her: it happened that he had packed his new suit so that it was easily available.

Odintsova did not receive him in the room where he had so unexpectedly declared his love for her but in the drawing-room. She courteously extended the tips of her fingers to him, but her face expressed an involuntary constraint.

'Anna Sergeyevna,' Bazarov hastened to say, 'first I must set your mind at ease. You see before you a being who has long since regained control of himself and who hopes that others have forgotten his follies. I am going away for a long time and you'll agree that, although I'm not precisely a gentle

1 The reference is to a letter written in 1846 by N. V. Gogol to the wife of a provincial governor. The letter, brimming over with pious, conservative sentiment, was in the spirit of Gogol's *Correspondence with Friends*, a book which the great satirist's radical admirers regarded as a betrayal of the common cause and as a classic example of canting hypocrisy, but was only published in 1860 in a radical periodical and would, therefore, have only recently come into Bazarov's orbit.

soul, it would still be unpleasant for me to go off with the thought that you remember me with repulsion.'

Anna Sergeyevna took a deep breath like someone who has just reached the top of a high mountain and her face lit up with a vivid smile. For the second time she gave Bazarov her hand and returned the pressure of his.

'We'll let bygones be bygones then,' she said, 'all the more because, to be quite honest, I was to blame as well, if not for deliberate flirtatiousness then for something else. In a word, let us be friends as we were before. All that was just a dream, wasn't it? And who remembers dreams?'

'Who indeed? And anyway, love – it's an artificial feeling.'

'Really? I am very happy to hear you say so.'

So spoke Anna Sergeyevna, and so spoke Bazarov; they both thought that they were speaking the truth. But did their words really contain the truth, the whole truth? They did not know themselves, the author of this tale still less. Be that as it may, they began to converse in a way which seemed to show that they had believed one another implicitly.

Among other things, Anna Sergeyevna asked Bazarov what he had been doing at the Kirsanovs'. He almost told her about his duel with Pavel Petrovich but restrained himself at the thought that she might think he was putting on airs to be interesting, and he answered that he had been working the whole time.

'And I,' declared Anna Sergeyevna, 'was so depressed to begin with, heaven knows why, and I even thought of going abroad, if you will credit it! Then that passed; your friend Arkady Nikolayevich came and he has got back into his rut, into his true part.'

'What part is that, if I may ask?'

'The part of a dear aunt, a governess, a mother – call it what you will. By the way, you know I used never to understand your close friendship with Arkady Nikolayevich; I always found him rather insignificant. But now I've got to know him better and have discovered that he is intelligent; and the main thing is that he's young, so young – not like you and I, Yevgeny Vasil'evich.'

'Is he still so shy when you're about?' inquired Bazarov.

'But surely...' Anna Sergeyevna began, and continued after a moment's thought: 'Now he has become more confiding, he talks to me. Before he used to avoid me. Not that I sought his company either. He's great friends with Katya.'

Bazarov began to feel annoyed. 'Why can't women ever give you a straight answer!' he thought.

'You say that he used to avoid you,' he pronounced with cold sarcasm, 'but possibly it has not escaped your notice that he was in love with you?'

'What? He too?' The words were out before Anna Sergeyevna could check them.

'He too,' repeated Bazarov with a humble bow. 'Can it be that you were not aware of this and that what I have just told you is news to you?'

Anna Sergeyevna lowered her eyes.

'You are mistaken, Yevgeny Vasil'evich.'

'I don't think so. However, perhaps I should not have mentioned it. And don't try to play off any more of your airs on me,' he added to himself.

'Why should you not have mentioned it? But I believe that there also you have ascribed too much significance to a fleeting impression. I begin to think that you have a tendency to exaggerate.'

'It would be better if we were to drop the subject, Anna Sergeyevna.'

'Why should we?' she retorted. Nevertheless it was she who introduced a new topic of conversation. In spite of everything she was not at her ease with Bazarov, although she had said to him and assured herself that all was forgotten. Exchanging the most innocuous remarks, even joking with him, she felt a slight constriction of fear. So people at sea in a steamer will talk and laugh in a carefree manner, precisely as though they were safe on dry land; but the slightest hitch, the least sign of anything exceptional, and immediately all faces reflect an expression of peculiar anxiety which bears witness to the unremitting consciousness of constant danger.

Anna Sergeyevna's talk with Bazarov did not last long. Her

mind began to wander, she answered him at random and finally she suggested that they should go through into the hall. There they found the princess and Katya.

'But where is Arkady Nikolayevich?' demanded their hostess and, on learning that he had not been seen for over an hour, she sent for him. He was not soon found; he had penetrated the wildest part of the garden and was sitting lost in thought, his chin resting on his clasped hands. His thoughts were profound and important, but not sad. He knew that Anna Sergeyevna was sitting alone with Bazarov, but he felt none of his old jealousy; on the contrary his face looked quietly radiant; it seemed as though he were amazed at something, and glad, and was feeling his way towards some decision.

XXVI

THE late Odintsov had disliked innovations, but he was ready to tolerate 'a certain latitude of enlightened taste', and in accordance with this principle had erected a building of Russian brick in the style of a Greek portico in his garden between the conservatory and the pond. In the windowless back wall of this portico or gallery there were six niches for statues which Odintsov had intended to order from abroad. These statues were intended to represent Solitude, Silence, Meditation, Melancholy, Modesty and Tenderness. One of these, the Goddess of Silence with a finger to her lips, had actually been brought to her destination and would have been set in her niche had not the house-boys broken off her nose on the day of her arrival. Although a neighbouring plasterer had undertaken to give her a new nose 'twice as good as the old one', Odintsov had ordered her to be removed and she was put in a corner of the threshing barn, where she remained lying for many years filling the peasant women with superstitious horror. The façade of the portico had long since been overgrown by a dense shrubbery; only the cornices of the pillars showed above the solid wall of greenery. In the portico itself it was always cool, even at midday. Anna Sergeyevna had avoided visiting the place ever since she had once seen a grass-snake there; but Katya often came to sit on the great stone bench built under one of the niches. Surrounded by freshness and shadow she would read, sew or abandon herself to that feeling of absolute quiet which is probably familiar to every one of us and the charm of which consists in a scarcely conscious, mute, yet wholly concentrated contemplation of the wide wave of life as it rolls on ceaselessly within and around us.

The day after Bazarov's arrival Katya was sitting on this favourite seat and beside her once more sat Arkady. He had asked her to go with him to the 'portico'.

There was about one hour to go till lunch time; the dewy morning had turned into a hot day. Arkady's face still wore the same expression as on the previous day, Katya was looking worried. Her sister had called her into her study immediately after breakfast and, having first shown herself particularly affectionate, which always put Katya on her guard, had advised her to be more careful in her dealings with Arkady and particularly to avoid tête-à-têtes with him in lonely places which, she said, were remarked by their aunt and by the whole household. Apart from this, Anna Sergeyevna had not been in her usual spirits the evening before either, and Katya herself felt uneasy, as though this were somehow her fault. Agreeing to Arkady's request, she had told herself that it was for the last time.

'Katerina Sergeyevna,' he began with a kind of bashful intimacy, 'since I have had the happiness of living in the same house with you we have talked of many things, but there is still one question, a very important one for me, on which I have not yet touched. You said yesterday that I had been changed while I was here,' he added, at once seeking to meet and avoiding the questioning gaze with which Katya was regarding him. 'It's true that I have changed in a lot of things, and *that* you know better than anyone else – you, to whom in fact I owe this change.'

'I? Me?' repeated Katya.

'I'm no longer the same arrogant boy I was when I came here,' Arkady continued. 'I haven't reached the age of twenty-four for nothing. I still want to be useful, want to dedicate my life to the service of truth; but now I don't look for my ideals where I sought them before, they seem to me much more immediate. Until now I didn't understand myself, I set myself tasks which were beyond my strength. My eyes were opened just lately, thanks to a sentiment . . . I am not expressing myself very clearly, but I hope that you will understand me.'

Katya made no reply, but she no longer looked at Arkady.

'I think,' he went on, his voice reflecting his increasing agitation while a finch in the leaves of a birch-tree above him sang its carefree song, 'I think that it is the duty of every honest man to be completely frank with those – with those people whom – in a word, with people who are near to him, and that is why I – I intend . . .'

But here Arkady's eloquence deserted him; he lost the thread, faltered and had to keep silent for a few moments; Katya never raised her eyes. It seemed as though she did not understand what he was leading up to all this time and was waiting for something.

'I foresee that I am going to surprise you,' Arkady began, having once more nerved himself to continue. 'All the more that this sentiment has to do to some extent – to some extent, mind you – with you. Yesterday, I seem to remember, you accused me of a lack of seriousness,' went on Arkady with all the air of a man who has wandered into a bog, feels that he is sinking deeper and deeper with every step and yet still lunges forward in the hope of coming more quickly to the other side. 'That reproach is often directed to – often falls on – young men, even after they have ceased to merit it; and if I only had a little more self-assurance . . .' ('Help me, can't you, help me out of this!' thought Arkady in despair, but Katya never turned her head.) 'If only I could hope . . .'

'If only I could be certain that what you say is true,' Anna Sergeyevna's clear voice sounded at that very moment.

Arkady immediately stopped talking and Katya turned pale. Right past the bushes which screened the portico there was a path. Anna Sergeyevna was walking along it accompanied by Bazarov. Katya and Arkady could not see them, but they could hear every word, the rustle of Anna Sergeyevna's dress, their very breathing. They walked on another few paces and, as if on purpose, came to a halt directly opposite the portico.

'So you see,' Anna Sergeyevna continued, 'you and I were both mistaken; neither of us is in our first youth, I particularly; we have seen something of life, we are weary; we are both – why should we stand on ceremony? – intelligent; at first we intrigued one another, our curiosity was awakened – and then—'

'And then I fizzled out,' interjected Bazarov.

'You know that that was not the cause of our falling out. But however it may have been, we found we had no need of one another, that is the main thing; we – how can I put it? – we had too much in common. We didn't understand that to begin with. Arkady, on the other hand—'

'You have need of him?' asked Bazarov.

'Enough, Yevgeny Vasil'evich. You say that he's not indifferent to me, and it did always seem to me as though he was attracted to me. I know that I might well be his aunt, but I will not conceal from you that I have begun to think about him more often. In so young and fresh a sentiment there is a kind of charm—'

'The word *fascination* is more often used in such cases,' interrupted Bazarov; there was an undertone of seething bitterness in his calm but hollow voice. 'Arkady was being somewhat secretive with me yesterday and said nothing to me either about you or about your sister. It's a significant symptom.'

'He's just like a brother to Katya,' declared Anna Sergeyevna, 'and that is something I like in him, although perhaps I ought not to allow such a close friendship between them.'

'Are you speaking as a sister?' drawled Bazarov.

'Naturally. But what are we standing here for? Let us walk on. And how could I have expected that I should ever speak to you like this? You know, I am afraid of you – and at the same time I trust you, because basically you are very kind.'

'In the first place I am not kind in the least; and in the second I no longer mean anything to you, and then you tell

me that I am kind. It's just the same as crowning the head of
a corpse with a wreath of flowers.'

'Yevgeny Vasil'evich, it is not in our power . . .' began Anna
Sergeyevna; but there was a sudden gust of wind which set
the leaves rustling and carried away her words.

'You know you are free,' came Bazarov's voice a little later.

After that the listeners could distinguish nothing more; the
footsteps went further and further away, everything fell silent.

Arkady turned to Katya. She was sitting in the same position, only her head had sunk a little lower.

'Katerina Sergeyevna,' he declared in a trembling voice,
twisting his hands, 'I love you for ever and irrevocably, and
I love no one but you. I wanted to tell you that, to see your
reaction and to ask your hand in marriage, because I am not
rich and I feel ready for any sacrifice. You don't answer? You
don't believe me? You think that I'm speaking without due
consideration? But remember these last days! Surely you must
long since have convinced yourself that everything else – do,
please, understand me – that absolutely everything else has
vanished without a trace? Look at me, answer me one word.
I'm in love – I love you. Please believe me!'

Katya looked up at Arkady with solemn, radiant eyes and
after a long moment of hesitation, pronounced with the suggestion of a smile:

'Yes.'

Arkady jumped up from the seat.

'Yes! You said yes, Katerina Sergeyevna! What do you
mean by that word? Do you mean that I love you, that you
believe me – or – or – I daren't finish. . . .'

'Yes,' repeated Katya, and this time he understood her. He
caught up her large, beautiful hands and, catching his breath
with ecstasy, pressed them to his heart. He could hardly stand
on his feet and only kept repeating 'Katya, Katya,' and she
began to cry in a way which was somehow very innocent, and
herself laughed softly at her own tears. Who has never seen
such tears in the eyes of the being he loves has never known
to what degree, stricken powerless with thankfulness and
unworthiness, a man can be happy on this earth.

*

On the following day, early in the morning, Anna Sergeyevna summoned Bazarov to her study and, with a conscious
laugh, handed him a folded sheet of writing-paper. It was a
letter from Arkady: in it he asked for the hand of her sister.

Bazarov glanced swiftly through the letter and made a cred-
itable effort not to show the malicious satisfaction which
instantly flared up in his heart.

'So that's how it is,' he remarked, 'and you, it seems,
thought only yesterday that he loved Katerina Sergeyevna
with a purely brotherly emotion. What are you going to do
now?'

'What do *you* advise?' asked Anna Sergeyevna, still
laughing.

'Well, I suppose,' replied Bazarov, also with laughter,
although he was not in the least amused and had no more real
inclination to laugh than she had, 'I suppose that the right
thing to do is to give the young people your blessing. It's a
good match from every point of view: Kirsanov has quite a
tidy fortune; he is the only son of his father and what's
more his father is a kindly fellow; he'll have nothing to say
against it.'

Odintsova took a turn about the room. Her face grew red
and then pale alternately.

'Do you think so?' she said. 'Well then I see no objection.
I am pleased for Katya's sake – and for Arkady Nikolayevich.
Of course I shall wait for his father's reply. I shall send Arkady
to break the news himself. But it seems as though I was right
yesterday when I told you that we had both grown old. How
is it that I never noticed anything? It astonishes me!'

Anna Sergeyevna again broke into laughter and instantly
turned away.

'The youth of today has become distressingly cunning,'
remarked Bazarov, and also burst out laughing. 'Goodbye,' he
began again after a brief silence. 'I hope that you may finish
off this business in the pleasantest possible way; and I shall be
glad from a distance.'

Odintsova turned swiftly towards him.

'Are you really going? Why shouldn't you stay *now*? Do stay – it's amusing to talk to you, like walking along the edge of a precipice. To begin with one is frightened, and then from somewhere or other one draws courage. Do stay.'

'Thank you for the invitation, Anna Sergeyevna, and for your flattering opinion of my conversational talents. But I find that I've already moved for too long in a sphere which is alien to me. Flying-fish can stay in the air for a time, but soon they have to splash back into the water; allow me also to plop back into my element.'

Odintsova looked at Bazarov. A bitter, ironic smile contracted her pale face. 'That one did love me!' she thought, and she felt sorry for him and held out her hand with compassion.

But he too understood her.

'No!' he said, and took a pace backward. 'I am a poor man, but I've never yet accepted charity. Goodbye, madam, and good health to you.'

'I am certain that this is not the last time we shall meet,' uttered Anna Sergeyevna with an involuntary gesture.

'Stranger things than that can happen!' answered Bazarov, bowed and went out.

'So you're planning to build yourself a nest?' he remarked that same day to Arkady, squatting down on his haunches to pack his trunk. 'Well, there's nothing wrong with that. Only you didn't need to sham it so. I thought your intentions lay in quite another direction. Or perhaps it took you aback yourself?'

'I must say I didn't expect it when I parted from you last,' answered Arkady. 'But why are *you* shamming and saying that "there's nothing wrong with that" as though I didn't know your views on marriage?'

'Oh, good my friend!' pronounced Bazarov. 'What expressions you use! Do you see what I'm doing? There's an empty space in my trunk and I'm packing hay into it. It's just the same with the trunk of our life; the main thing is to pack it tight, to avoid empty spaces. Don't be offended, please: you probably remember what my opinion of Katerina Sergeyevna has been from the beginning. Some young ladies only have a reputation for being clever because they know how to breathe a sigh at the right moment, but yours will stand up for herself, yes, and she'll stand up for herself so well that she'll take you in hand too – well, and that's as it should be.' He slammed down the lid of his trunk and rose from the floor. 'And now I repeat to you at parting – because there's no sense in deceiving ourselves: we're parting for ever and you feel that yourself – you're doing the right thing; you weren't made for our bitter bachelor life. You have neither boldness nor anger in you, but you have the courage of youth and a youthful dash; for our job that's not the right qualification. You and your brother aristocrats will never go beyond noble humility or noble fury, and that's just moon-shine. For example, you don't fight – and yet you imagine that you're game for anything – but *we* want to fight. And what of it! The dust we raise will eat your eyes away, the mud we stir up will blot you out, you can't help standing back and contemplating yourselves admiringly, you wallow in self-reproach; but that bores us – we want others to work on! We need to break in other people! You're a good fellow; but you're still just a soft, liberal little aristocrat – *ay vollatoo*[1] as my father would say.'

'You are saying goodbye to me for ever, Yevgeny,' responded Arkady sadly, 'and you have no other words for me?'

Bazarov scratched the back of his head.

'Yes, Arkady, there are other words I could say, only I'm not going to, because that would be romanticism – it would mean going all syrupy. But you go on and get married as soon as possible; and build your nest up round you and get a lot of children. They'll be clever little chaps even if only because they'll be born at a good time, unlike you and I. Aha! I see the horses are ready. It's time! I've said goodbye to everybody. Well, what about it? Is this where we embrace?'

Arkady flung himself on the neck of his former friend and mentor, and the tears fairly poured from his eyes.

---

1 In French in Russian letters in the original (= '*et voilà tout*').

'What it is to be young!' remarked Bazarov calmly. 'However, all my hope is in Katerina Sergeyevna. You'll see how well she'll comfort you!'

'Goodbye, brother!' he said to Arkady when he had already climbed on to the cart and, pointing to a pair of jackdaws on the roof of the stable, he added: 'There you are! Take a lesson from them!'

'What does that mean?' asked Arkady.

'What? Are you so weak in natural history, or have you forgotten that the jackdaw is a most respectable family bird? An example to you! Farewell, *signor*!'

The cart shuddered and rolled away.

Bazarov had spoken the truth. Talking with Katya that evening Arkady completely forgot his mentor. He had already come very much under her influence, and Katya felt this and was not surprised. It was arranged that he should go to Marino to see Nikolay Petrovich on the following day. Anna Sergeyevna had no wish to lay any restraint on the young people, and it was only for appearance's sake that she did not leave them long alone. She had kindly relieved them of the presence of the princess, whom the news of the forthcoming marriage had reduced to tearful fury. To begin with Anna Sergeyevna had been afraid that the spectacle of their happiness might be somewhat painful to herself; but in practice it had quite the opposite effect: the spectacle was not only not painful to her, but it amused her and, in the end, it touched her. Anna Sergeyevna was at once glad of this and distressed by it. 'Evidently Bazarov was right,' she thought. 'Curiosity, nothing but curiosity, and love of ease and comfort, and selfishness. . . .'

'Children!' she said aloud. 'Tell me, is love an artificial feeling?'

But neither Katya nor Arkady understood her. They felt on the defensive with her; the conversation which they had involuntarily overheard never left their minds. However, Anna Sergeyevna soon set their minds at rest; and it was not difficult for her: her mind, also, was at rest.

XXVII

THE old Bazarovs were all the more delighted by the sudden arrival of their son because it was so unexpected. Arina Vlas'evna became so flustered and scurried about the house in such agitation that Vasily Ivanovich compared her to a hen partridge; the perky tail of her brief jacket really did lend her a somewhat birdlike appearance. Vasily Ivanovich himself merely spluttered and chewed the side of the amber mouthpiece of his pipe, seized his neck with his fingers, twisting his head this way and that as though he were trying out whether or not it were firmly screwed on, and suddenly opened his wide mouth to its full extent and laughed noiselessly.

'I've come to you for six whole weeks, old man,' Bazarov informed him. 'I want to work so please don't disturb me.'

'You'll forget the look of my physiognomy, that's how much I'll disturb you!' answered Vasily Ivanovich.

He was as good as his word. Having installed his son in the study as before, he did everything short of actually hiding from him and restrained his wife from all superfluous demonstrations of tenderness. 'Little Mother,' he said to her, 'we got on Yevgeny's nerves the first time he came: now we must be more clever.' Arina Vlas'evna agreed with her husband but profited little from following his advice because she saw her son only at table and finally became afraid to speak to him.

'Yevgeny,' she would say, but before he had had time to look up she would already be fiddling with the strings of her reticule and would murmur: 'Nothing, nothing, it just slipped out.' Then she would run to Vasily Ivanovich and propping her chin on her hand she would say:

'How can we find out, dearie: what would Yevgeny like for his lunch today, cabbage soup or borstch?'

'Well, why haven't you asked him?'

'I'll get on his nerves!'

However, Bazarov soon stopped shutting himself away of his own accord: the fever of work had worn itself out and was succeeded by a state of yearning boredom and dull uneasiness. He no longer went for walks by himself but sought the society of others: drank tea in the drawing-room, wandered about the kitchen garden with Vasily Ivanovich and smoked with him in silence; once he even asked after Father Aleksey. To begin with Vasily Ivanovich was delighted with this change, but his contentment was not long-lived.

'Our Yevgeny is breaking my heart,' he complained to his wife when they were alone. 'It's not that he's discontented or irritable, that wouldn't matter so much; he's grieved, he's unhappy – that's what is so terrible. He's so silent, I'd rather he abused us; he's losing weight, his face is such a bad colour.'

'Oh Lord, oh Lord!' whispered the old woman. 'I would give him an amulet to wear round his neck, but he would never allow it.'

Vasily Ivanovich made several extremely cautious attempts to ask Bazarov about his work, about his health, about Arkady. But Bazarov replied grudgingly and indifferently and once, noticing that his father was gradually leading up to something as they talked, he said to him with some irritation:

'Why do you go on as though you were walking round me on tiptoe? It's even worse than the way you acted when I first came.'

'Come, come now, I didn't mean any harm!' replied poor Vasily Ivanovich hurriedly. Equally fruitless was it when he touched on politics. Once he hoped to win his son's sympathy by introducing the subject of progress in connection with the imminent reforms which were to lead to the emancipation of the serfs; but Bazarov merely remarked indifferently:

'Yesterday I was walking along by the fence and I heard the peasant lads bawling out a cheap popular romance instead of one of the old songs: there's progress for you.'

Sometimes Bazarov would go down into the village and start up a conversation with one of the peasants in his usual bantering style.

'Well now,' he would say to the peasant, 'expound me your views on life, brother; after all, they say that in your hands lie all the strength and all the future of Russia, that you are to lay the foundations of a new era in history, that you are to give us a real language of our own and a legal system.' The peasant would either answer nothing at all or deliver himself of a few words somewhat after the following manner:

'And we might at that – likewise, because, if you know what I mean – there is some sort of a limit to what folk can do, like.'

'Will you explain the principles of your *mir*¹ to me?' Bazarov would break in. 'And whether it's the same *mir* that stands on three fishes?'²

'No, no, master, that's the earth that stands on three fishes,' explained the peasant soothingly, his sing-song voice redolent of patriarchal good nature. 'But over against ours – our *mir*, that is – there's set the will of the gentry, as everyone knows: that's why you're as fathers to us. And the stricter the master the better it is for the peasant.'

Once, having listened to a speech of this sort, Bazarov shrugged his shoulders contemptuously and turned away and the peasant went off about his business.

'What were you talking about?' asked another peasant, a middle-aged man of morose aspect, who had been standing on the steps of his cottage observing the discussion which had arisen between the other and Bazarov from a distance. 'Arrears, was it?'

'Arrears my foot, brother!' answered the first peasant, and in his voice there was now not a trace of patriarchal softness but on the contrary a note of rough severity. 'He was just blathering on to pass the time; felt like letting his tongue wag a little. What d'you expect – he's a gentleman; don't think they understand anything, do you?'

'How should they understand!' answered the other peasant and, pushing back their caps and hauling up their belts, they settled down to discuss their own affairs and needs.

Alas! Bazarov, contemptuously shrugging his shoulders

1 Bazarov is punning: the Russian word 'mir' signifies both 'the world' and 'the village commune'. One section of the Russian intelligentsia set great hopes by the village commune, which they considered a proof of the Russian people's natural tendency to socialism and to democratic administration, and a possible model for future legislation. *See also* note on p. 60.

2 This is a reference to the medieval legend still current at that time among the peasantry that the world was flat and was supported by three enormous fishes.

and confident of his ability to talk with peasants (as he had boasted in his quarrel with Pavel Petrovich), that same self-assured Bazarov had no suspicion that in their eyes even he was something in the nature of a buffoon. However, he finally found himself something to do. Once it happened that Vasily Ivanovich was bandaging up a peasant's injured leg in his presence, but the old man's hands were shaking and he could not tie the bandage; his son helped him and after that began to take an active part in his practice: never ceasing, at the same time, to laugh at the remedies which he himself advised and at his father, who immediately put them into general circulation. But Bazarov's sarcasm did not upset Vasily Ivanovich at all, in fact it even amused him. Holding his greasy dressing-gown together across his stomach with two fingers and puffing at his pipe, he would listen to Bazarov with delight; the more malice there was in his sallies, the more good-humouredly would his proud father roar with laughter, exhibiting every single one of his blackened teeth. He would even repeat these sallies, obtuse and meaningless as some of them were. For instance, for several days on end he kept on repeating at utterly inappropriate moments 'Well, that's no very great matter!' simply because his son had used the expression on hearing that he attended matins.

'Thank God! He's come out of his melancholy,' he whispered to his wife; 'you should have seen how he put me in my place this morning! Wonderful!' To make up for all this, the thought that he had acquired such an assistant profoundly delighted him and filled him with pride.

'Yes, yes,' he would say to some peasant woman in a man's jacket and a double-pointed hood, as he handed her a bottle of Goulard's extract or a jar of henbane ointment, 'you should be thanking God every day, my good woman, that my son is staying with me; you're benefiting by the most modern and scientific methods of healing now: do you realize that? The Emperor Napoleon himself hasn't a better doctor.'

But the woman, who had come to complain that she 'had a stabbing pain that fair made her jump' (although she herself was unable to explain the precise meaning of these words), merely bowed and slid her hand into the bodice of her dress where she had concealed four eggs wrapped up in the corner of a towel.

Once Bazarov even extracted a tooth for an itinerant pedlar of fine goods, and although there was nothing exceptional about this particular tooth Vasily Ivanovich treasured it as a curiosity and, exhibiting it to Father Aleksey, repeated again and again:

'Just look what roots! The strength Yevgeny has! That pedlar was simply lifted up into the air. It seems to me that even had it been an oak-tree out it must have come!'

'Admirable!' pronounced Father Aleksey at length, not knowing how to respond or how to escape from the ecstatic old man.

Once a peasant from a neighbouring village brought his brother, who was ill with typhus, to see Vasily Ivanovich. Stretched out flat on a truss of straw the unfortunate man was dying; his body was covered with dark patches and he had long since lost consciousness. Vasily Ivanovich expressed his regret that no one had thought to have recourse to the aid of medicine any sooner and declared that there was no hope. And, in fact, the peasant never got his brother home again: he died in the cart on the way.

Three days later Bazarov entered his father's room and asked if he had any silver nitrate.

'Yes; what do you want it for?'

'I just need it to cauterize a cut.'

'Whose?'

'Mine.'

'How yours! Why must you? What sort of cut? Where is it?'

'Here, on my finger. I went to the village today, you know, the one where they brought that peasant with typhus from. For some reason or other they'd decided to open him up and I haven't had any practice at that for a long time.'

'Well?'

'Well, I wished myself on to the provincial doctor; then I went and cut myself.'

Vasily Ivanovich turned suddenly quite white and without

a word rushed into his study and returned at once with a piece of silver nitrate in his hand. Bazarov made as if to take it and go away.

'For God's sake,' pleaded Vasily Ivanovich, 'let me do that for you.'

Bazarov grinned. 'What a one you are for putting in a bit of practice!'

'Don't joke, please. Show me your finger. It's not a deep cut. Does that hurt?'

'Press harder, don't be afraid.'

Vasily Ivanovich stopped.

'What do you think, Yevgeny, wouldn't it be better to burn it out with a hot iron?'

'That ought to have been done earlier; but now, really, the nitrate won't be of much use either. If I took the infection it's too late already.'

'How, too late?' breathed Vasily Ivanovich.

'I should rather think so! It's four hours or more since I did it.'

Vasily Ivanovich burnt the cut a little more.

'Do you mean to say the provincial doctor didn't have any silver nitrate?'

'There wasn't any.'

'How could that be, dear God! A doctor, and not to have such an essential thing!'

'You should have seen his lancets,' retorted Bazarov, and walked out of the room.

Until late in the evening and throughout the following day Vasily Ivanovich seized upon every possible pretext for entering his son's room, and although he not only refrained from mentioning the cut but even attempted to talk of quite extrinsic matters, he nevertheless stared so persistently into his son's eyes and kept him under such agitated observation that Bazarov lost patience and threatened to leave. Vasily Ivanovich promised not to worry, all the more readily since Arina Vlas'evna, from whom of course he had concealed everything, was beginning to importune him with questions as to why he was not sleeping and what was happening to him.

For two whole days he remained firm, although he did not at all like the look of his son, whom he continued to observe on the sly. But on the third day at lunch he could contain himself no longer. Bazarov was sitting slumped in his chair and would not touch a single dish.

'Why aren't you eating, Yevgeny?' he asked, assuming an expression of supreme unconcern. 'The food seems well cooked.'

'I'm not hungry so I'm not eating.'

'You've no appetite? What about your head,' he added in a timid voice, 'does it ache?'

'Yes. Why shouldn't it ache?'

Arina Vlas'evna sat up straight and pricked up her ears.

'Don't be annoyed, Yevgeny, please,' continued Vasily Ivanovich, 'but won't you let me take your pulse?'

Bazarov half rose.

'I can tell you I've a fever without that.'

'And you have been shivering?'

'Yes, I've been shivering too. I'll go and lie down and you can bring me some lime-flower tea. I must have caught a cold.'

'I thought I heard you coughing last night,' contributed Arina Vlas'evna.

'I've caught a cold,' repeated Bazarov, and left the room.

Arina Vlas'evna set about the preparation of the tea from lime flowers, but Vasily Ivanovich went into the next room and silently clutched his hair.

Bazarov did not get up again that day and spent the whole of the night in a heavy, half-conscious doze. At about one o'clock in the morning he opened his eyes with an effort, saw before him in the light of the lampada the pale face of his father and ordered him out of the room. Vasily Ivanovich did as he was told but returned at once on tiptoe and, half hidden behind the doors of the cupboard, kept an unremitting watch over his son. Arina Vlas'evna did not go to bed either and, setting the study door ajar, peered in every now and again 'to hear how Yevgeny is breathing', and to steal a glance at Vasily Ivanovich. She could only see his motionless bent back, but even this reassured her somewhat.

In the morning Bazarov tried to get up; his head spun round and his nose began to bleed; he lay down again. Vasily Ivanovich waited on him in silence; Arina Vlas'evna came in and asked how he was feeling. He replied 'Better' and turned his face to the wall. Vasily Ivanovich pushed his wife away with both hands; she bit her lip so as not to burst out sobbing and went out of the room. The whole house seemed suddenly to be plunged into gloom; everyone went about with long faces and a strange hush fell. A particularly raucous cock was removed from the backyard down to the village and long remained mystified as to why he should have been thus dealt with.

Bazarov continued to lie there, huddled against the wall. Vasily Ivanovich tried addressing various questions to him, but they tired Bazarov and the old man sat stock-still in his armchair, merely cracking his fingers at long intervals. He went out into the garden for a few moments and stood there like a graven image, as though stricken by unspeakable amazement (the expression of amazement never left his face), and then he returned to his son, doing his best to avoid his wife's questions. Finally she seized him by the arm and convulsively, almost threateningly, demanded:

'What's the matter with him?' Then Vasily Ivanovich pulled himself together and forced himself to smile in reply, but to his own horror he began to laugh instead. He had sent for the doctor early that morning. He thought it necessary to inform his son about this beforehand in case he should be annoyed.

Bazarov suddenly turned over on the sofa, looked steadily and dully at his father and asked for something to drink. Vasily Ivanovich gave him some water, managing to touch his forehead at the same time. It was burning.

'Old man,' began Bazarov in a hoarse, slow voice, 'I'm in a bad way. I've taken the infection and in a few days you'll be burying me.'

Vasily Ivanovich staggered as though someone had knocked him across the legs.

'Yevgeny!' he whispered. 'You mustn't talk like that. The Lord be with you! You've taken a chill—'

'Leave that,' interrupted Bazarov deliberately. 'As a doctor you have no right to talk like that. All the symptoms of infection are present, you know it yourself.'

'What symptoms of infection, Yevgeny? For heaven's sake—'

'Well, what's this?' asked Bazarov, and rolling back the sleeve of his shirt showed his father the ominous red patches coming out on his arm.

Vasily Ivanovich shuddered and felt suddenly cold with fear.

'Assuming that you are right,' he said finally, 'assuming that – that there may be something in the nature of an infection—'

'Of pyaemia.'

'All right then – in the nature of an epidemic.'

'Of *pyaemia*,' Bazarov corrected sombrely and distinctly. 'Or have you forgotten your textbooks?'

'All right then, all right, have it your own way. But even so we'll cure you of that!'

'Not if I know it! But that's not the point. I wasn't expecting to die so soon; it's a most disagreeable trick of fate, to tell you the truth. You and my mother will have to take advantage of the fact that you're both great ones for religion; here's a chance for you to put it to the test.' He sipped a little more water. 'But I wanted to ask you one thing, while I'm still in control of my thoughts. Tomorrow, or the day after, my brain will go into retirement, you know. I'm not quite sure even now whether I'm expressing myself clearly. While I was lying here I kept on imagining there were red dogs running round me and that you were pointing at me, as though you were a setter and I a black-cock. Just as if I was drunk. Can you understand me all right?'

'Good gracious, Yevgeny, you're speaking absolutely normally.'

'All the better; you told me you'd sent for the doctor – that was to console yourself. Console me too; send an express messenger—'

'To Arkady Nikolayevich,' interjected the old man.

'Who's Arkady Nikolayevich?' Bazarov asked as though

deep in thought. 'Oh yes! that fledgling! No, don't bother him, he's turned jackdaw now. Don't be surprised, I'm not raving yet. But send the messenger to Odintsova, Anna Sergeyevna, there's – there's a landowner of that name, you know?' Vasily Ivanovich nodded his head. 'Say that Yevgeny Bazarov sends his greetings and sends to say that he's dying. Will you do that?'

'I will. Only how is it possible that you should die, Yevgeny – judge for yourself! Where's the justice of it?'

'That I can't tell you; but don't forget to send the messenger.'

'I'll send at once, and I'll write the letter myself.'

'No, why should you? Say he sends his greeting, no more is needed. And now I'll go back to my dogs. Strange, I want to concentrate on death and nothing comes of it. I see a sort of splodge – and nothing more.'

He turned back heavily towards the wall; and Vasily Ivanovich went out of the study and, dragging himself as far as his wife's bedroom, collapsed on his knees before the icons.

'Pray, Arina, pray!' he groaned. 'Our son is dying.'

The doctor, the same provincial doctor who had had no silver nitrate, came and, having examined the patient, advised them that there was nothing to be done but to wait, and immediately added a few words as to the possibility of a cure.

'Have you ever known a case when someone in my position has *not* taken off for the fields of Elysium?' asked Bazarov and, suddenly seizing hold of the leg of a heavy table standing by the sofa, he shook it and shifted its position.

'The strength's there,' he muttered, 'I've still got the strength, but I've got to die! An old man, he at least has had time to get out of the way of living, but I ... Still, just try denying the validity of death. She denies your validity, and *basta*![1] Who's that crying?' he added a little later. 'Mother? Poor Mother. Who'll she have to feed now with her wonderful borstch? And you, Vasily Ivanovich, you're sniffling too. Well, if Christianity doesn't help, be a philosopher,

1 In Italian in the original.

a stoic, why not! You always said you were a philosopher, didn't you?'

'What's philosophy to me,' sobbed Vasily Ivanovich, and the tears ran down his cheeks.

Bazarov was sinking from hour to hour; the disease progressed rapidly, as is usual in cases of surgical poisoning. He had not yet lost his memory and still understood what was being said to him; he was still making a fight for it. 'I will not rave,' he whispered, clenching his fists, 'it is too stupid!' and added immediately: 'Well, if you take ten from eight what does that come to?'

Vasily Ivanovich paced up and down like one possessed, suggesting first one remedy and then another, but did nothing but keep his son's legs covered. 'Wrap him in a cold sheet – emetic – a mustard plaster to the stomach – bleeding,' he enunciated with an effort. The doctor, whom he had implored to stay, agreed with everything he said, gave his patient lemonade to drink and for himself begged now a pipe of tobacco, now something 'warming and stimulating', or in other words vodka. Arina Vlas'evna remained seated on a low bench by the door and only left the room from time to time to pray; a few days ago a mirror had slipped from her hand and broken and that she had always considered an evil omen; even Anfisushka had no words for her. Timofeyich had set off to Odintsova.

Bazarov passed a bad night. A cruel fever tormented him. In the morning he was easier. He asked Arina Vlas'evna to comb his hair, kissed her hand and drank a sip or two of tea. Vasily Ivanovich revived a little.

'Thank God!' he kept repeating. 'The crisis has come, the crisis is over.'

'Eh, think of that!' said Bazarov. 'Just how much can one word mean! He's found it, he's said "the crisis" – and now he's comforted. Extraordinary thing, how a man will hide behind a word. If you call him a fool, for instance, he'll be miserable even though you spare him a beating; if you call him a clever fellow and don't give him his money, he'll be thoroughly pleased.'

This little speech of Bazarov's, reminiscent of his former sallies, touched Vasily Ivanovich to the heart.

'Bravo! Well said, well said!' he exclaimed, pretending to clap his hands.

Bazarov smiled sadly. 'Well, what do you think, then,' he said, 'has the crisis come or gone?'

'You feel better, that's what I see, and that's what makes me so happy,' answered Vasily Ivanovich.

'Well, that's fine then; it's never a bad thing to be happy. But to her, do you remember? Did you send to her?'

'Of course.'

The change for the better did not last long. The onsets of the disease were renewed. Vasily Ivanovich remained sitting by Bazarov. It seemed that some particular trouble was tormenting the old man. He tried to speak once or twice, but could not.

'Yevgeny,' he said at last, 'my son, my dearest, my dear son!'

This extraordinary appeal had its effect on Bazarov; he turned his head a little and, making patent efforts to struggle free of the weight of unconsciousness bearing down upon him, enunciated:

'What, my father?'

'Yevgeny,' continued Vasily Ivanovich, and went down on his knees to Bazarov, although his son did not open his eyes and could not see him. 'Yevgeny, you're a little better now; with God's help you'll get well again; but make use of this time, grant me and your mother this comfort, fulfil your duty as a Christian! It's not for me to say this to you, it's terrible; but even more terrible – it's for ever, you see. Yevgeny, just think, what . . .'

The old man's voice broke and over the face of his son, although he continued to lie with closed eyes, there crept a strange expression.

'I don't refuse, if it will comfort you,' he said at last, 'but it seems to me there's no reason to hurry yet awhile. You said yourself that I was better.'

'Better, Yevgeny, better; but who knows, it's all as God wins after all, and when you've done your duty—'

'No, I'll wait,' interrupted Bazarov. 'I agree with you that the crisis has come. And if we're wrong, what of it! Even the unconscious can receive communion.'

'Yevgeny, please—'

'I'll wait. But now I want to sleep. Don't disturb me.' And he rolled his head back to where it had rested before.

The old man rose, sat down in the armchair and, cupping his chin in his hands, began to bite his fingers.

The sound of a sprung carriage, that sound which is so particularly distinctive in the wilds of the country, suddenly smote his ears. Nearer and nearer came the light wheels; now he could already hear the snorting of the horses. Vasily Ivanovich jumped up and rushed over to the window. Into the courtyard of his house rolled a two-seater coach drawn by four horses. Not stopping to think what this might signify, in a transport of some kind of senseless joy he ran out on to the steps. A liveried footman opened the doors of the coach; a lady in a black veil and a black lace shawl stepped down from it.

'I am Odintsova,' she said, 'is Yevgeny Vasil'evich alive? Are you his father? I've brought a doctor.'

'Benefactress!' cried Vasily Ivanovich, and seizing her hand he pressed it convulsively to his lips, while the doctor brought by Anna Sergeyevna, a little man in glasses with a Teutonic cast of countenance, climbed down unhurriedly from the coach.

'He is alive still, my Yevgeny is still alive, and now he will be saved! Wife! Wife! An angel from heaven . . .'

'Oh Lord God, what is this!' murmured the old woman as she came running out of the drawing-room and, understanding nothing of what was going on, fell at Anna Sergeyevna's feet there and then in the hall and began to kiss the hem of her dress like one demented.

'Oh, do not! Do not!' repeated Anna Sergeyevna; but Arina Vlas'evna did not heed her and Vasily Ivanovich only kept repeating: 'An angel, an angel!'

'*Wo ist der Kranke?*[1] And where is ze patient?' the doctor demanded finally, not without some degree of indignation.

---

1 In German in the original (= 'Where is the patient?').

Vasily Ivanovich pulled himself together. 'Here, here, please follow me, *vertester Herr Kollega*,'[1] he added for old time's sake.

'Eh!' exclaimed the German, and bared his teeth in a sour smile.

Vasily Ivanovich led him into the study.

'A doctor from Anna Sergeyevna Odintsova,' he said, bending over to speak right into his son's ear, 'and she is here herself.'

Bazarov suddenly opened his eyes. 'What did you say?'

'I said that Anna Sergeyevna Odintsova is here and has brought this worthy doctor to you.'

Bazarov rolled his eyes round the room.

'She here, I want to see her.'

'You shall see her, Yevgeny; but first we must have a word with the worthy doctor. I'll tell him the whole story of your illness, as Sidor Sidorovich has gone away' (this was the name of the provincial doctor), 'and we will have a little consultation.'

Bazarov glanced at the German. 'Well, have your consultation as quickly as possible, only don't talk Latin; I know what *iam moritus*[2] means.'

'*Der Herr scheint des Deutschen mächtig zu sein*,'[3] began this latest disciple of Aesculapius, addressing Vasily Ivanovich.

'*Ich – gabe. . . .*[4] It would be better if you spoke Russian,' said the old man.

'Ah, ahem! Vell it iss, as you say, like dees. I vood suppose . . .'

And the consultation began.

Half an hour later Vasily Ivanovich ushered Anna Sergeyevna into the study: the doctor had had time to whisper to her that there was no hope for the sick man.

---

1 In German in Russian letters in the original (= '*wertester Herr Kollege*', 'most worthy colleague').
2 'He is already dying' (Lat.).
3 In German in the original (= 'The gentleman appears to have a command of the German tongue').
4 In German in Russian letters in the original (= '*Ich habe*', 'I have').

She looked across at Bazarov – and stopped dead in the doorway, so shocked was she by that inflamed and at the same time moribund face, with the cloudy eyes turned towards her. She was quite simply afraid with a kind of cold, oppressive fear; the thought that she would not have felt like this had she really loved him passed instantly through her head.

'Thank you.' He began to speak with an effort. 'I did not expect this. It was kind of you. Now we have seen each other once again, as you promised.'

'Anna Sergeyevna has been so kind,' began Vasily Ivanovich.

'Father, leave us alone. Anna Sergeyevna, do you permit? It seems as though now . . .' He jerked his head to indicate his prostrate helpless body.

Vasily Ivanovich went out.

'Well, thank you,' repeated Bazarov. 'This is royally done. They say queens also visit the dying.'

'Yevgeny Vasil'evich, I hope—'

'Eh, Anna Sergeyevna, let's start speaking the truth. It's all up with me. I've come under the wheel. And as it turns out there was never any point in thinking of the future. Death's an old joke, but it comes to everyone like something new. I'm not afraid yet – and then I'll lose consciousness, and then – phut!' He waved his hand feebly. 'Well, what can I say to you? . . . I loved you! That didn't make sense before, and much less so now. Love is something that must have a form, and my own form is rotting already. I'd do better to tell you what a darling you are! And now you're standing there, so beautiful . . .'

Anna Sergeyevna shivered involuntarily.

'Never mind, don't be upset – sit down there. Don't come too close to me: my disease is infectious, you see.'

Anna Sergeyevna crossed the room quickly and sat down in the armchair by the sofa on which Bazarov was lying.

'Courageous!' he whispered. 'Oh, how near and how young and fresh and pure in this filthy room! Well, goodbye! Live a long time, that's the best thing of all, and make use of the time that is given to you. Just look what a revolting exhibition: a worm that's half crushed and still wriggling. But you see I also

thought: "I'll round off a lot of jobs, I won't die, not me!
There's a task before me, and I'm a giant!" But now the giant's
whole task is to manage to die decently, although no one's
concerned about that. It makes no odds: I won't sue for mercy.'

Bazarov fell silent and began to feel for his glass: Anna
Sergeyevna helped him to drink, not taking off her glove,
breathing cautiously.

'You'll forget me,' he began again; 'the dead are no companions for the living. My father will tell you what a man
Russia is losing – that's nonsense; but don't disillusion the old
man. Anything to make it easier for him – you know. And be
gentle with my mother. You'll not find people like them in all
your high society if you look for them with a torch by daylight.
Russia has need of me.... No, evidently she hasn't. And
who's needed anyway? A cobbler is needed, a tailor is needed,
a butcher – sells meat – a butcher – wait, I'm getting confused
– there's a wood there....'

Bazarov put a hand to his brow.

Anna Sergeyevna bent over him.

'Yevgeny Vasil'evich, I'm here....'

He took his hand away and raised himself up in one gesture.

'Goodbye,' he said with sudden force, and a last flicker
lighted his eyes. 'Goodbye – goodbye – I didn't kiss you then
– blow on the dying light and let it go out....'

Anna Sergeyevna put her lips reverently to his forehead.

'And that's all,' he murmured and sank back on his pillows.
'Now – darkness....'

Anna Sergeyevna went softly out.

'How is he?' Vasily Ivanovich asked her in a whisper.

'He has fallen asleep,' she answered scarcely audibly.

Bazarov was not fated to wake again. Towards evening he
sank into complete unconsciousness and the following day he
died. Father Aleksey performed the last rites of the Church
over him. When he was being given the last unction, when
the holy oil touched his chest, one of his eyes opened and it
seemed as though, at the sight of the priest in his robes, the
smoking incense, the candles before the icons, something like
a shudder of awe was momentarily reflected in his moribund

features. When at the end he had breathed his last and the whole household was given over to lamentation, Vasily Ivano-vich was possessed by a sudden fury.

'I said that I would rebel,' he cried hoarsely, his face flam-ing and distorted, shaking his fist in the air as though he were threatening someone, 'and I do rebel, I rebel!'

But Arina Vlas'evna, the tears streaming down her face, hung on his neck and both fell to the ground.

'Just like that,' Anfisushka recounted afterwards in the servants' hall, 'both together, bless them, and they drooped their poor heads like little lambs at midday.'

But the fierce heat of midday passes, and there follows the evening and the night, and then the returning to the quiet haven where there is sweet sleep for the weary and the heavy laden. . . .

XXVIII

SIX months had gone by. White winter reigned with the cruel silence of cloudless frosts; with packed, creaking snow; rosy hoar-frost on the trees; pale emerald skies; caps of smoke above the chimneys; billowing clouds of steam from momentarily opened doors; fresh, cold-nipped human faces and the busy running of chilled horses. The January day was drawing to a close; the evening cold was compressing the motionless air still more mercilessly and the blood-red sunset was fading swiftly. Lights had been lit in the windows of the house at Marino; Prokofich, in a black tailcoat and white gloves, was laying the table for seven with more than his usual solemnity. A week earlier, in the little parish church, quietly and almost without witnesses, two weddings had been celebrated: Arkady to Katya and Nikolay Petrovich to Fenechka. On this particular day Nikolay Petrovich was giving a farewell dinner in honour of his brother, who was setting out for Moscow on business. Anna Sergeyevna, having generously endowed the young couple, had left for the same destination immediately after the wedding.

At three o'clock precisely they all foregathered round the table. Mitya was given his place with the others; he had already acquired a nanny in a silk brocade headdress. Pavel Petrovich sat at the head of the table between Katya and Fenechka; 'the husbands' took their places beside their wives. Our old acquaintances had changed over the last few months. They all seemed to be in better looks and appeared more mature; only Pavel Petrovich had grown thinner, which, however, lent his expressive features an added elegance and a still greater air of the *grand seigneur*. And Fenechka had changed. Clad in a clean silk dress with a wide velvet cap on her hair and a gold chain clasped round her neck, she sat deferentially still, deferential at once to herself and to all around her, and smiled as one who would say: 'You must forgive me, it is not my fault.' And not she alone; but the others too were all smiles and somehow apologetic; all felt a little ill at ease, a little sad and, fundamentally, profoundly contented. They all helped one another with a comical attentiveness, almost as if they had all agreed beforehand to play some simple comedy. Katya was the calmest amongst them; she looked trustingly round about her and it was noticeable that Nikolay Petrovich already adored her. Towards the end of the meal he rose and, taking his glass in his hand, turned to Pavel Petrovich.

'You are leaving us – you are leaving us, dear brother,' he began, 'though not of course for long; but I still don't know how to express to you that – that – how much I – how much we . . . The trouble is, we don't know how to make speeches! Arkady, you say it for me.'

'No, Papa dear, I haven't prepared anything.'

'And I prepared everything so beautifully! Simply, brother, permit me to embrace you, to wish you every success and happiness, and come back to us soon!'

Pavel Petrovich exchanged kisses with everybody, not excluding Mitya of course. In addition he kissed Fenechka's hand, which she did not yet know how to extend as becomes a lady of quality, and, drinking off the glass which had been refilled for him, said with a deep sigh: 'Be happy, my friends! Farewell!'[1]

1 In English in the original.

This little English appendage passed unnoticed, but all were deeply touched.

'In memory of Bazarov,' whispered Katya into her husband's ear, and clinked her glass with his. In reply Arkady squeezed her hand eloquently, but could not bring himself to propose this toast aloud.

The end, it would seem? But perhaps one of our readers may wish to know what each of the characters who figure in this story is doing now, at this moment. We are ready to satisfy his curiosity.

Anna Sergeyevna married not long since, not for love but from conviction, one of the future builders of Russia, a very intelligent man, a firm believer in law and order with a firm grasp of practical issues, great will-power and a wonderful gift of eloquence – a man who was still young, kind and as cold as ice. They live together in the utmost harmony and will perhaps live on to happiness – perhaps to love. Princess Kh ... is dead, forgotten on the very day she died. The Kirsanovs, father and son, are living at Marino. Their affairs are beginning to look up. Arkady has become a zealous landlord and the 'farm' is already bringing in quite considerable returns. Nikolay Petrovich has become an arbitrator in the implementation of the land reforms following on the emancipation of the serfs, and devotes all his energies to this work; he travels continually about his district and delivers himself of lengthy speeches. (He belongs to the school of thought which considers that the peasants must be 'made to understand', that is, slowly worn down by the repetition of the same words.) To tell the truth, in spite of all his efforts he succeeds in completely satisfying neither the educated noblemen, who speak with modish flippancy or whimsical melancholy of the 'emancipation' (pronouncing the 'an' through the nose as in French), nor yet the ill-educated, who unceremoniously consign 'that 'mancipation' to perdition. He is too soft-hearted for either set. Katerina Sergeyevna has given birth to a son, Kolya,[2] and Mitya is running about sturdily and chattering

2 Diminutive of Nikolay after Nikolay Petrovich.

loquaciously. Fenechka, Feodos'ya Nikolayevna, after her husband and Mitya, dotes on no one so much as on her daughter-in-law and when Katya sits down at the pianoforte she is happy to remain at her side all day long. While we are about it, some mention should be made of Pyotr. He has become positively rigid with stupidity and self-importance, lards his speech with curious, would-be-genteel mispronunciations, but has also married and received a sizeable dowry from his wife, the daughter of a market gardener from the town, who had previously refused two worthy suitors for the sole reason that neither of them possessed a watch; whereas Pyotr not only did possess a watch, but patent-leather shoes as well.

In Dresden, on the Brühl terrace, between two and four o'clock, at the most fashionable hour of the promenade, you may meet a gentleman in his fifties, apparently suffering from a gouty leg, his hair already quite grey, but still handsome, elegantly dressed and distinguished by that particular stamp which can only be acquired by long years of moving in the first circles of society. This is Pavel Petrovich. He went abroad from Moscow for the sake of his health and remained to take up residence in Dresden, where his acquaintance is recruited mainly from amongst the English and visiting Russians. With the English his manner is simple, almost unassuming, but not without dignity; they find him a little dull but respect him as 'a perfect gentleman'.[1] With Russians he is more casual, makes no attempt to subdue his spleen and has a mocking way of quizzing both himself and them; but all this he does with great charm and nonchalance and good taste. He holds Slavophile views; this is known to be regarded in the best circles as *très distingué*.[2] He never reads anything Russian, but on his writing-table there is a silver ash-tray in the shape of a peasant's plaited shoe. He is much courted by our tourists. Matvey Il'ich Kolyazin, finding himself *in temporary opposition*, paid him a gracious visit on his way to drink the waters in

1 In English in the original.
2 In French in the original.

Bohemia; and the natives of Dresden, with whom incidentally he has but little to do, regard him with something approaching veneration. No one can obtain a ticket for the concerts of the court choir, for the theatre, etc., so easily or so quickly as der *Herr Baron von Kirsanoff.*[1] He tries always to do what good he can; he still cuts something of a figure in society: not for nothing was he once a lion; yet his life is a burden to him – a heavier burden than he himself suspects. It is enough to see him in the Russian church when, leaning up against a wall in a quiet corner, he falls into a reverie and makes no movement for a long while, his lips bitterly compressed, and then suddenly comes to himself and begins to cross himself almost imperceptibly.[2]

Kukshina, too, has gone to live abroad. She is now in Heidelberg, where she is no longer studying natural sciences but architecture, in which, if she is to be believed, she has discovered certain new laws. As before she cultivates the company of students, particularly young Russian physicists and chemists, who abound in Heidelberg and who, having first astonished the naïve German professors by their clear-sighted and sober views, later proceed to astonish these same professors by their complete inertia and absolute idleness. In Petersburg Sitnikov rubs elbows with two or three chemists of the same ilk, unable to distinguish nitrogen from oxygen but filled with negation and self-respect, and with the great Elisevich, whose greatness he proposes to emulate, and according to his own assurances is there continuing 'the task' of Bazarov. Rumour has it that someone recently gave him a beating, but that he was not slow to take his revenge: in an obscure little article squeezed into an obscure little journal he actually hinted that the man who beat him was a coward. This he calls irony. His father orders him about as before, and his wife considers him an imbecile – and a man of letters.

1 In German in the original.
2 The finishing touch to the portrait of 'the perfect gentleman'. The Russian peasant makes the sign of the cross broadly, touching his forehead, his chest and either shoulder. The aristocrat, on the other hand, scarcely moves his hand.

In one of the far corners of Russia there is a small village graveyard. Like almost all our graveyards it presents a melancholy appearance: the ditches which mark its borders have long since become overgrown; the grey wooden crosses have fallen askew and are rotting under their once painted roofs; the stone slabs are all out of alignment, just as though someone were pushing them up from below; two or three scanty-leaved trees cast a parsimonious shadow; sheep roam shepherdless among the graves. But amongst them there is one which is never touched by man nor trampled by beast: only the birds come to perch there and to sing at dawn. An iron railing surrounds it; two young fir-trees are planted at either end: Yevgeny Bazarov lies buried in that grave. Thither, from a neighbouring hamlet, two already senile old people – a husband and wife – often come walking. Supporting one another, they walk with a step grown heavy; they approach the railing, drop to their knees and weep long and bitterly, and look long and attentively at the dumb stone beneath which lies their son; they exchange some brief word, brush the dust from the stone, put to rights some errant branch of the fir-trees and fall again to praying, and cannot leave this place, from which it somehow seems a lesser distance to their son, to memories of him. Surely their prayers, their tears, are not in vain? Can it be that love, sacred, devoted love, is not all-powerful? Ah no! However passionate, sinful and rebellious a heart may lie hidden in this grave, the flowers which bloom upon it look up at us serenely with their innocent eyes: not only of eternal peace do they speak to us, of that immense peace of 'indifferent' nature; they tell also of eternal reconciliation and of life without end.

This book is set in EHRHARDT. The precise origin
of the typeface is unclear. Most of the founts were
probably cut by the Hungarian punch-cutter
Nicholas Kis for the Ehrhardt foundry
in Leipzig, where they were left
for sale in 1689. In 1938 the
Monotype foundry pro-
duced the modern
version.